continued . . .

"Snappy first-person narrative." —*Kirkus Reviews*

"A well-crafted plot and an engaging cast of characters. A chilling conclusion will catch many readers by surprise."
—*Publishers Weekly*

Murder Never Forgets

"Suspenseful and heartbreakingly timely." —*Chicago Tribune*

"Introduces us to a delightfully unconventional pair of sleuths . . . O'Hehir is at the top of her form here . . . I couldn't put it down!"
—Sandra M. Gilbert,
author of *Belongings*

"One of the most intellectually delightful murder mysteries ever written."
—Vivian Gornick,
author of *The Men in My Life*

"O'Hehir sketches out characters in swift strokes, and the old people in this book are fully realized characters, both quirky and dignified. Best of all, the narrator's acerbic, funny, insightful voice makes what might have been just another cozy unforgettable." —*The Boston Globe*

"Fascinating, genre-bending mix of literary and crime fiction . . . A story that will move and captivate all who read it." —*Booklist* (starred review)

Dark Aura

Diana O'Hehir

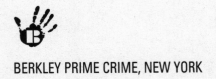

BERKLEY PRIME CRIME, NEW YORK

THE BERKLEY PUBLISHING GROUP
Published by the Penguin Group
Penguin Group (USA) Inc.
375 Hudson Street, New York, New York 10014, USA
Penguin Group (Canada), 90 Eglinton Avenue East, Suite 700, Toronto, Ontario M4P 2Y3, Canada
(a division of Pearson Penguin Canada Inc.)
Penguin Books Ltd., 80 Strand, London WC2R 0RL, England
Penguin Group Ireland, 25 St. Stephen's Green, Dublin 2, Ireland (a division of Penguin Books Ltd.)
Penguin Group (Australia), 250 Camberwell Road, Camberwell, Victoria 3124, Australia
(a division of Pearson Australia Group Pty. Ltd.)
Penguin Books India Pvt. Ltd., 11 Community Centre, Panchsheel Park, New Delhi—110 017, India
Penguin Group (NZ), 67 Apollo Drive, Rosedale, North Shore 0632, New Zealand
(a division of Pearson New Zealand Ltd.)
Penguin Books (South Africa) (Pty.) Ltd., 24 Sturdee Avenue, Rosebank, Johannesburg 2196,
South Africa

Penguin Books Ltd., Registered Offices: 80 Strand, London WC2R 0RL, England

This book is an original publication of The Berkley Publishing Group.

This is a work of fiction. Names, characters, places, and incidents either are the product of the author's imagination or are used fictitiously, and any resemblance to actual persons, living or dead, business establishments, events, or locales is entirely coincidental. The publisher does not have any control over and does not assume any responsibility for author or third-party websites or their content.

PRINTING HISTORY
Berkley Prime Crime hardcover edition / December 2007
Berkley Prime Crime trade paperback edition / June 2009

Berkley Prime Crime trade paperback ISBN: 978-0-425-22883-8

Library of Congress Cataloging-in-Publication Data

O'Hehir, Diana, 1929–
    Dark aura/Diana O'Hehir.
      p.   cm.
    ISBN 978-0-425-21753-5
  1. Indigo children—Fiction. 2. California, Northern—Fiction. I. Title.

PS3565.H4D37 2007
813'.54—dc22

                                                2007025049

PRINTED IN THE UNITED STATES OF AMERICA

10 9 8 7 6 5 4 3 2 1

*Many thanks to Mel, one more time,
and to good friends BK, Allison, Whitney,
Carol, Diana K., Annegret, and Mary*

The Egyptian material in this book owes to my reading of books and translations by a number of experts, including Maria Carmelo Betro, E. A. Wallis Budge, R. O. Faulkner, George Hart, Miriam Lichtheim, and Bridget McDermott. Any errors in reference or quotation are my own doing and not theirs.

🐧 Chapter 1

"She's not going to die," I say.

My friend Cherie, the Del Oro County sheriff, says, "Sugar, I wouldn't count on that."

"No, she's not going to." I hear myself getting passionate about it.

I especially don't want this pale, clean-profiled young woman to die because she looks, in spite of her fall, unmarked and brave, and like the priestess in my dad's *Egyptian Book of the Dead* who is marching solemnly off to the next world. You want to follow her and bring her back. And also because it seems that she's a friend of my father's. He is sitting beside her holding her hand.

"Make safe your shore," he says to her.

She has just fallen seventeen feet into a creek. I saw her fall. She hit badly.

She opens her eyes, which are a startling blue, and looks at my dad. Blood starts coming out of her ears.

"My baby," she says. "My indigo baby."

"Give us Lightland," says my father.

"Lightland." She closes her eyes. "Homeland. Coming forth by day."

I am here because of a phone call from my dad. This was a couple of hours ago and he was using his new cell phone.

I was in my office at Green Beach Manor and my father was twenty miles away, visiting our friend Susie.

"Carla, perhaps we should be troubled," he says. "I am here at Stanton's Mill. You know about Stanton's Mill. Where Susie has a house now? And these interesting babies are disappearing."

Daddy's cell phone is a gift from our loving friend Susie, and Daddy is now at Susie's new vacation house. My father, who has early-stage Alzheimer's, likes using his phone, although he is insecure about its operation. It tends to quit on him, even more than other cell phones do on the rest of us.

Susie is suddenly rich. That's her definition of it. "Oh, I just knew that Squeegee was basically a good person. And now he has gone on into higher things and has left me his house."

Squeegee is Susie's ex-husband, who drifted off many years ago to join a band. The house is a one-room cottage in Stanton's Mill, which is the town behind Conestoga.

And my dad is staying there for a few days with Susie. "The energy is very good here in Stanton's Mill," she says. "It will be healing for darling Edward."

Susie still has her organic-food store in Berkeley. She comes to Stanton's Mill for weekends.

"What's this about babies disappearing?" I ask my dad now, loudly enough that Susie, who is apparently behind him and listening, takes over the phone. "Oh, Carla, it is so upsetting. It's the indigo babies, those wonderful, talented children. And they are vanishing, one by one. Cherie will be around to get you." After which she severs the connection and I can't get it back.

Cherie appears twenty minutes later. Cherie Ghent is our new sheriff in Del Oro County. She is a minute fashion-model type, with curly blond hair, elegant clothes, and turquoise eyes. She doesn't look like a sheriff.

She is also my part-time boss, because I, too, am on the sheriff's squad of Del Oro County. I am a part-time deputy sheriff. I am quite certain you have never heard of such a thing as a part-time deputy sheriff, but I am not the only one in California. Cherie pointed this out to me when she persuaded me to take the job. "There are two others," she said, "both women; now what does that tell you about the assignment of sexual roles in our society? But if that's the only way I can get you, sugarbelle, I welcome it." Cherie has a heavy Southern accent; you must imagine anything she says slurred and softened and huskied up.

She is a lawyer as well as a sheriff and she was our lawyer briefly once. I liked her especially because she treated my dad with respect. Daddy's Alzheimer's is still not very bad.

Then Cherie and I had a falling-out about the fact that she stole my boyfriend. This became history when their affair ended, but it's only partly history. Partly it's alive and it's one of the things I think about when my batteries get low.

"What's this about babies?" I greet Cherie now. She wears a pale green pantsuit and is balancing deftly on spike-heeled sling sandals, with six strings of crystal beads swinging across her small, upright bosom.

I am at my Manor desk with a stack of relatives' complaints. My other job, my supposedly full-time one, is as assistant director of Green Beach Manor, the elegant senior residence where my dad usually lives. *Complaints* is one of my specialties.

And I have yet another job, a third one, actually my major occupation, a full-time assignment of worrying about my dad. He is getting older. He is, with Alzheimer's, arriving at the brink, almost ready to lose it, wobbling, the full dark curtain of forgetting spreading dust across his sweet life. I worry about him a lot.

"Give that stack of crap you're reading to somebody else and come along with me," Cherie says. "Believe me, darlin', this is serious." She can't pronounce the word *darling*, among other things. "I mean, it is not just babies, dear heart; I am not that densely into babies. And this baby problem here is questionable. But the atmosphere is way peculiar. Come on. Get your mittens."

In spite of how she looks and sounds, Cherie is very bright.

It's a California early spring day. The waxy buds are popping out on the magnolia trees; the jonquils are exploding underfoot; the ocean fog has cleared off and the air is full of pointillist dots of light. I'm happy to surrender my pile of irritations and follow Cherie out to her sheriff's vehicle, which is black with silver wheels.

"So," she says. "This is getting serious. You'll see. It isn't just the nonsense about those purple babies."

She is referring to the indigo children, who have hit Stanton's Mill big-time. An indigo baby analyst has arrived in town and has been interviewing babies to decide which ones qualify. Susie has heard a lot about this and is enchanted by the idea. "These wonderful, beautiful kids." Some of them, she thinks, are from another life. Or another planet. "Extraordinarily gifted. More than most children. Of course you, Carla, were special . . . and so was Rob . . ." She gets herself back on track. "Some people claim that they are attention deficit, but that is just envy. They are going to reclaim our world. Make it safe for all of us. And I learned about it *here*. Berkeley has become so corporate, people never talk about these things. Oh, I am so grateful to dear Squeegee. Remembering me all those years."

My personal opinion, from the rumors I've heard about Susie's ex, is that he simply forgot to change his will. The big mystery is how he happened to have a will at all.

"You can laugh all you like"—Cherie is hanging one elbow out the window as we drive down the coast road—"but this stuff is going to be serious. And, Carla, I need you."

"Okay, all right, you've got me." The Manor has been unusually repetitive lately.

"So, tell me," I say, "what gives?"

"Well, you know, this Anneliese Wertiger came into town and moved in with Susie's next-door neighbor . . ."

"Scope." People in Stanton's Mill tend to have odd nicknames. I know the town pretty well from having visited Susie there.

"Right. And she right away set up shop. Put a sign up outside. Something about healings. Or constructivist consultations. Or something. Tell me, Carla darlin', we got plenty of nuts in Berkeley but these ones seem more time-warped. Is it something in the water? The redwoods?"

Stanton's Mill offers an unusual combination of redwood trees, gully, and ocean. Most of the houses hug the sides of a redwood-shrouded gulch that winds around in back of Conestoga and cuts down to the sea. Conestoga people don't go down into Stanton's Mill much because there are no facilities there. The only store is a co-op, and you have to be a member before you can buy things in it.

"So everybody lined up for a consultation," I suggest.

"Believe me. And the place was littered with indigo literature. All kinds of pamphlets with purple jackets. And would you believe it, special glasses for seeing that indigo whatzit—sort of haze—around you? Whatzit called, darlin'?"

"Aura."

"Yes, darlin' Carla. That's why I need you. I can never remember facts like that."

One of Cherie's ways of controlling a situation is to appear dumb. When she is not.

"And the reason," she says, "we are hightailing it over there now is, there is this little blossom named Tamina. Who is only fifteen, but thinks she is Joan of Arc. She called me and said she had something important to impart. That was the word she used. Impart. The child is too bright for ordinary events.

"When the atmosphere here in Stanton's Mill is disturbed, she tends to go to the edge of this big rock they have here and wobble around and make speeches. The rock

is a collecting place where the Stanton's Mill people get together to argue. And I'm afraid little Tamina will be there
arguing back at them. Trying to impart.

"It has to do with these damn purple babies," Cherie
adds.

"So you can see why I need you. Hysteria accumulates
fast in a place like this."

We zip through Conestoga and head up a small rocky side
road behind the hospital. This side road is steep and dusty;
after six perpendicular miles, delivered complainingly by
Cherie's lumbering official vehicle, we arrive at the crest,
where we pause, pointing toward an overwhelm of sky and
trees. Below us, tucked into the wooded creases, lies Stanton's Mill. There are white-painted houses and cedar shingle
houses and picket-fenced gardens and magnificent tall trees
with fraying furry bark. The smell of redwood and eucalyptus is intense.

There's a creek. The ocean throbs half a mile away.

I know that this gulch actually is cold and damp, with
serious septic tank problems, but as we pause above it, looking down, it flickers up an image of the ideal town.

"You can't believe how they fight with each other,"
Cherie says reflectively, putting the official vehicle into
third gear for the descent.

"And," Cherie says, "this disappearing baby stuff is all a
bunch of the most absolute crap. As far as I can make out,
it's a total of three babies at most, and when I investigate,
each case turns out to be some story about the baby off to see
some auntie or grandma or something, but then the minute
I turn my back and go back to Conestoga, the rumor has

started up again. Separated couples do that. They fight like mad."

She's silent long enough for me to hear distant crowd agitation. Something muffled and anxious, like a preview of the French Revolution.

"Yeah," Cherie says, "listen." We descend, our wheels kicking aside roadway rocks and twigs, and the crowd murmur increases, gets to be a hunk of basic rhubarb-rhubarb movie noise: "Listen." "Watch it." "Something is going to happen." We wheel into the co-op parking lot, but the crowd event isn't here. It's somewhere over to our right.

Cherie noses the car against the building and sets the brake. She and I scramble out and scuff to an unfenced drop, where we stare down. She says, "Oh, hell."

A voice behind us says, "Darlings, surely not." It's Susie, arriving on foot from her house, which is somewhere down the hill. She has my father in tow, looking puzzled; he doesn't acknowledge my greeting.

This parking lot overhangs the gully. To our right and also jutting over the gully is a big spur of rock with a flat tennis-court-sized top; that's where the crowd murmur is happening. That scene is slightly below us, clearly displayed and arranged as if on a stage: people milling back and forth; a figure apparently making speeches and doing gymnastics at the mesa edge; other shapes dodging around it. Wisps of protesting sound drift over: "No, no." "Hey, right on." "Listen, cool it."

"How in hell do we get over there?" Cherie asks, and I say, "Down some steps and over to the path and up some other steps; it's complicated." We start out.

Cherie is an elegant, fit woman, but she's over fifty and wears high-heeled slingbacks. I am twenty-seven and have

Adidas. I hold her hand for the way down and push her on the way up. She doesn't weigh much.

The steps up to the Rock, which is what the Stanton's Millers call it, are homemade redwood; there's a splintery sagging rail. Cherie swears.

My father never fails to amaze me. He is eighty-seven years old but in excellent physical condition, and for a long time he made his living as an archaeologist by climbing things and hiding under things and scampering up them. And that's what he does now. While Cherie and I are struggling with the redwood steps, he passes us, lickety-split, and is triumphantly on the platform and diving into the middle of the crowd.

Cherie and I are closer to the crowd scene now, but the noise remains muffled. Muffled noise is not a good sign. It means that someone, or several someones, think sudden outbursts might upset the situation. So there is quiet that is sporadic, and punctuated by upheavals: "Stand back," and "Hey, Tammy, we get it," and "For God's sake."

I'm pushing Cherie as fast as I can but it's still too slow; the scene is delivered to me in slices between the stair boards, which are at eye level. What I see are feet, skirts, blue jean bottoms. Maybe up ahead are the little Tamina's feet—those rainbow-striped flip-flops. And that's the edge, where she's flip-flopping. Maybe she's doing a minuet step. Graceful, sort of. Other feet are in the way. I move more sharply, pushing Cherie.

We're still on the steps when the noise escalates to become screeches: "Tammy, for Christ's sake!" "Jesus, girl, watch it!" And then, high, delirious, in piercing ultrasound, "Stop it, stop, stop!" What kind of a voice is that? Male or female? I shove Cherie to one side and stumble up, scraping my knees, launching myself desperately along the remaining six steps.

And so I and my narrative are at the point where Tamina falls seventeen feet into the creek bed. From my place on the steps, at eye level with the platform, I watch her flip-flopped feet go over.

There's a tangle of arms and legs in my view; someone tries to run; someone else scrambles on hands and knees; voices squawk. I reach the top step and dive underneath some shapes and over some others and get to the edge of the drop-off.

There are too many people jostling.

But they're jostling quietly. Some stand with their toes right at the edge. All of these edge huggers are being careful. Everybody is looking down. The yelling has stopped; for a moment it's pin-drop still. I come closer and feel dizzy. If you stand too close to a precipice, you fantasize about letting go.

The view is down to the creek, which trickles gently, exposing uneven terrain. Half in the water and half out, a small figure spreads, arms outflung. Blond hair is splashed out and partly floating. The figure wears pants and a T-shirt. One of its feet is entangled with a flip-flop; the other foot pokes awkwardly up, ankle turned and sole exposed.

I am the one who turns Tamina's head, because I am afraid she is drowning with her face in the creek.

And my father, arriving behind me, is the one who sits beside her and says Egyptian poetry at her.

She says Egyptian poetry back. Even though there is blood coming out of her ears. Words like *sun-disc* and *purity*. She looks up at my father, with her strange blue eyes glazed. Her chest heaves and a stone pendant shaped like a tree slides back and forth there.

Cherie calls for an ambulance and a first-aid crew. She tells them to hurry.

Then she kneels beside the girl and calls her honey lamb and sweetie pie and asks her if she was pushed. Which Tamina does not answer.

Tamina is mostly in the creek, which means that Cherie is mostly there, too, with the trousers of her green silk suit and her slingback sandals becoming sodden. And my father is sitting with his butt in the stream, holding the girl's hand.

After a while Cherie gets up and goes to the creek bank. She tells me that this situation is out of hand. "I am the sheriff here," she says, and she fills up the time until the ambulance crew arrives by becoming Sheriff Inflexible Ghent and getting all the viewers off the viewing point above and down to the creek bank, where she makes them sit while she yells orders. "All right, shape up; I got the power to arrest you, y'know. Now, I want everybody to try an' remember. Just a moment of silence while you think, and then I'll begin with the person farthest on my left . . ."

She gets out a notepad and a pencil. What was Tamina saying before she fell?

There's a clamor. "Like, she had something important . . ." "No, no, something of import, that was what she said." "Something that would turn out to be important." "Didn't she say vital? Hey, dude, I think *vital* was in there."

"What happened?" Cherie asks. "Why did she fall?"

A woman in a flowered muu-muu says, "She was pushed." No, the woman doesn't know who pushed her; she didn't see; she just knows. This gets noted, plus the informant's name. And the names of those who agree with the lady's remark. Plus the name of the man who yells that she is crazy. Plus somebody who says Cherie should follow standard procedure.

Plus a cluster of other ideas. "No way that girl would jump." "Mano; she was enticed." "Enticed? I know when somebody's high on pot . . ."

Cherie says in my ear, "A good start, right?"

I shrug. All this is blatantly counter to standard rules about questioning and is probably dangerous. But right now it's producing something. Maybe the wrong something.

"You are not," Cherie intones with commanding venom, "to all talk at once."

I'm still thinking about this as the emergency crew arrives, a sure-footed bunch, three guys and a woman, jack-rabbiting down with a canvas litter, backpacks, and canisters. Cherie clears everyone off by threatening jail. She tells the crowd she has all their names. "And I got a real good memory."

"Cool it, darlin'," I warn her. That Southern charm is easy to pick up.

My dear friend Susie has joined us and has stayed unusually quiet. Now she emits a little sob, like a hiccup, and gestures at Tamina, being fitted with a plastic collar. "This lovely child. And so bright. She and Ed will do wonderful things."

I'm wondering if Tamina's future includes doing anything at all. She has achieved that paler shade of white, the one the manuals say goes with serious shock. A *dead white*, they call it.

⌐ Chapter 2

It is the next day, and I am back in Stanton's Mill, having returned from my job at the Manor.

"Stay good, now," Cherie says, dropping me on Susie's front porch. She is delivering me there because my car is in the hospital with a blocked carburetor; she'll be back on Monday. And I'm prepared for the weekend, fortressed with backpack, pajamas, notebook, and a small shiny gun, supplied by Cherie. "Wear it in the back of your waistband," she instructs.

I don't. I don't like it. I don't think of myself as that kind of sheriff. I am more the thinking, figuring, deducing kind. I stash the gun in the bottom of my backpack.

"And listen," Cherie says. "This problem here has turned out much fiercer than I thought but I'm afraid it's all yours; I got a set of meth crises back in Conestoga. Two murders, for the love of God, two knife murders. But about this here, you got to know—I guess it looks pretty serious now but you got to know it's maybe more serious than that. There's something I didn't tell you. When Tamina called me and said she had something to impart, she also said she'd been threatened."

"She said she'd been threatened?" I'm too surprised to do anything but repeat.

"Right. I know. Sounds weird. That was her exact words. 'Cherie'—she and I had gotten some friendly, she was an interesting kid—'Cherie, I've been threatened. They said they would kill me. I guess they didn't really mean it.' And then, before I could get cracking on asking, she signed off and I couldn't get her back. Next thing I know she's up on the Rock."

"So you don't know . . ."

"Baby, I don't know spit. But I am sure glad to have you here.

"This place"—Cherie gestures to include all of Stanton's Mill—"is full of rumors and secrets and counter-rumors; you'll never know what in hell to believe. Keep posted, sweet one."

She kisses me on the cheek and says to be sure to wear my gun "in the back of your pants now. And"—she dives back into the car and emerges with a stack of paper—"here are all the lists of everything—who was there and who said what. All summarized for you.

"Hey, printed out so clear a reader can practically understand it."

"Cherie is so absolutely brilliant," Susie says.

"Uh-huh." I do agree that Cherie is brilliant. She had better be, with all she has on her sheriff's plate these days.

"Do you have any idea how sinful Del Oro County is?" she asked me yesterday.

"Sinful?"

"Meth, sweetheart, crack, ice. Big effing surprise. These meth-making kids are killing each other. Really. I got these two little murderers in my two-seater jail right now. And I didn't expect it, who would have believed. I thought this part of California was all grass and ocean and the occasional artichoke."

Del Oro is one of the smallest California counties, but it borders the Salinas Valley, which feeds into the Central Valley, where a high percentage of the methamphetamine in the United States gets made. Or else sold. And the formerly rustic town of Modesto now has more car thefts per capita than anyplace else in the country.

"They do that here, too," Cherie says. "Steal stuff. But mostly they just make crystal and then knife each other. Or shoot. Your little friend Slimeball never even noticed."

Slimeball is Cherie's name for the sheriff whom she replaced. She replaced him when she researched his past and discovered a hidden high school car crime. She then went to Sacramento and arranged to get herself appointed sheriff in his place.

And she's well qualified for the job, with a degree from Northwestern and another from the University of California and a fifteen-year law practice in Berkeley.

"Yes, Cherie is just amazing," Susie says, picking up my thought.

We're in Susie's new house, the one she inherited from Squeegee. Squeegee was a terrible housekeeper. Susie has cleaned up some, exclaiming about dear Squeegee. "No one to take care of him, if he had gotten in touch with me . . ."

The indications are that Squeegee had several someones to take care of him, at least one blond someone, a brunette person, a gray-haired one. Though maybe these remains are from the squatters that happened later. Susie has been digging hair and other human detritus out of the corners, but she's not finished.

The house is a one-bedroom shingle cabin. There's an antique kitchen with a cream and green stove and a pint-sized refrigerator. The bathroom has a stall shower with an unclosable door. The view is down into the creek and across to the other bank and more redwood trees. The house is damp and very cold. "I love it," Susie says. "It's everything a vacation house should be." My father sleeps on the enclosed porch and I get the leather couch, which smells of marijuana.

"Probably oregano," Susie says, when I dig a leaf out of the seams.

I'll be staying here a lot of weekends now. "This situation is yours, darlin'," Cherie tells me. "You're our Stanton's Mill expert."

"Tell me about Tamina," I finally get to say to Susie after my dad has involved himself in TV.

"Little Tamina is so bright. Impressive. Wonderful. So full of life."

We observe a moment's silence. No one knows how full of life Tamina is at the moment. The hospital won't say. They agree that she is in intensive care and is being watched. "Holding her own," they say ominously.

"What do you think happened?" I ask, and Susie gets completely vague. "Oh, my goodness. An accident. Terrible. But of course, I can't believe that anybody . . . She was such a child of light."

"How old is she?"

"Old? Darling Carla, you know I don't pay attention to those details. Age is a fiction. An invented, arbitrary system. I hate to tie people to these . . ." Susie becomes aware of my disapproving stare. "Well. Fifteen, perhaps. Yes, I think so."

"People keep talking about indigo babies. Does she have one?"

"Have one? What do you mean?"

"Is she the mother of an indigo baby?"

"Good heavens, Carla. She's only fifteen." Susie amazes me sometimes. She combines a hectic free-spirited past with a deep-down, alarming innocence.

But she comes back to the main question. "Indigo," she says thoughtfully after a minute. "Well, yes, perhaps. She is extremely young."

I let this sit around for a while. "How do you know when a baby is indigo?"

"Why, of course. Anneliese tells us. Tamina was the first one."

I stare, waiting for enhancement.

"I mean, as soon as she got to town. Anneliese arrived and moved in with Scope. And then she came to the Save the Eucalyptuses meeting . . ."

I give Susie another inquiring stare and then finally decide I understand this. Save the Eucalyptus would be a special Stanton's Mill thing, not like Save the Redwoods, which everyone knows about. Redwoods are popular all over California, but eucalyptus aren't. Most towns are trying to get rid of their eucalyptus, which they say are nonnative weeds, and being unpopular everywhere else means that in Stanton's Mill you should defend it. *Eucalyptus are trees, too.* "Yes?" I say.

"Well, Anneliese made a speech about all the wonderful things we have here. And she got intense about the beautiful redwood and eucalyptus and oaks and pines and the wonderful other plants and the colorful, distinctive banana slugs, but also, she said, 'Dear friends, did you know . . .' Anneliese is very dramatic," Susie interjects here. "She stopped right in the middle and looked around the room—this was happening in the Co-op Community Hall—and then she picked up. 'You have among you, a gift from the heavens, from the stars, perhaps from another galaxy, who can say—a beautiful radiant indigo child.' And she pointed at Tamina. Who I guess was pregnant at that time."

I remember that Susie used to be an actress. She's using her acting to good effect now, with a pause between *beautiful* and *radiant*. And she's capturing the dramatic way Anneliese said this, with an upper-class Eastern accent. I decide that I'm ready to hate this lady.

"So, Tamina's baby is from another star."

Susie's hurt. "Carla, we simply don't know."

"And," I forge ahead, "she's not the only indigo child."

"Oh, of course not. Anneliese found several. Identified them. They are rare, of course—very rare, but this area is special. People brought the children to her—babies mostly—and she tested them and all that." Susie looks vague. "I think it's complicated."

I refrain from saying, "I'll bet. Also expensive."

"Anyway," Susie says, "several children got tested. It was all very interesting. People were talking about it. And . . ." She offers this defensively; maybe she has figured out that I suspect Anneliese of profiting from her Stanton's Mill experience. "And dear Anneliese—she is so impressive—she wouldn't test all the children that were brought to her. She said sometimes the atmospheres and the emanations are not right. But she can see the emanations—the aura, you know, the indigo aura . . ."

I say, "Ah."

"It isn't something you usually see. You intuit it. You have to have special powers."

This time I simply squint at Susie, who is talking about how you can train yourself to recognize auras, and that there is a book you can buy. In the middle of this, my father drifts in to interrupt. "I have looked at quite a bit of television. And they are talking about food. Carla, did you ask me about that young woman—her name is Ta-Ent . . ."

"Tamina." I have a dim memory that Ta-Ent is someone in one of the *Books of the Dead.*

"Exactly," Daddy says. "She had some ideas about Egyptian legends . . . and," he adds, "she didn't just jump off that platform. There was nothing about it in the documents. I knew from talking to her that she would never do a thing like that. And I was watching her. She was much too stalwart."

But when I try to tell Daddy that this is important and I would like to hear more, he says, "Oh, no." He is entirely too hungry right now to concentrate. "They were talking about hot dogs on television. Do you suppose we have a hot dog somewhere here?"

Susie, of course, has stocked up on tofu-stuffed hot dogs, and Daddy, who does not know the difference between tofu and pork, is perfectly happy with these. He puts organic mustard on his hot dog and tells me about how they ate hot dogs on the dig. In the Valley of the Kings. When he was finding his coffin lid.

That coffin lid, which now lives in a California museum,

became the high point of Daddy's career because the hieroglyphs on it solved some famous translation problems. "Yes,"
he says now, "and if your mother had only known . . ."
Maybe he means that she wouldn't have left him. And maybe
not.

My family is peculiar, with both parents being so old
when I was born. Daddy was sixty and Mother was forty,
both of them archaeologists and very different in personality—he warm and cute and scatterbrained and funny and
she ice-cold. When I was ten years old, she left us and went
off to work in Turkey.

We haven't heard form her since. I try not to think about
her.

And then, about three years ago, my dad started doing
things like putting his shoes in the refrigerator and asking
about the bus to Tell el-Amarna. He was developing
Alzheimer's.

My sweet, Alzheimered dad is doing okay lately. Belle,
the manager of the Manor, is happy to have him live in
her retirement establishment and happy to have him come
visit Susie for brief stints. And Susie loves to get over here
from Berkeley and away from the problems of her organic-
food store.

As for me, I also was planning to enjoy getting away during my weekends here. I wasn't planning on accident or
crime or both in Stanton's Mill. And now without warning,
I feel myself getting pulled under and pursued by crises and
duties, but also—well, yes, slightly emotionally involved.
That little Tamina drags too many questions after her. I
keep remembering her brave-child face, the dramatically
blue eyes. I'm conceited enough to think she reminds me of

myself at that age. And then there's the fact that people keep saying she didn't just fall. This is such a persistent view in town that my own father has picked it up and is handing it back to me.

![raven] Chapter 3

"Are you a member of the family?" the hospital wants to know.

After which they tell me, "No, ma'am, we can't give you any details; she is still in intensive care; she's holding her own."

I telephone Cherie and ask her to use some muscle. She says, "Why, darlin', of course I will; I'll get after that hospital again. But honest, baby, I think maybe the news is bad. They're acting awfully cagey. Darlin', I am so terrifically glad you're doing this. I think that interesting little teenybopper was pushed—no, I can't say exactly why; but too many people there are worried about it, as if they all have a reason . . . now why, I ask you, would anybody have wanted to push her? And of course, there was that call from her. When she told me she was in danger. Oh, and darlin' . . ." Cherie pauses, which is not a good sign in her conversations. It usually means she wants something. "I've had a call from Rob, and he is so worried about you."

I let this remark sit on the air waves. People's reactions to life events are unpredictable and erratic, and Cherie, who is gifted with one of the most blasé personalities in the world, has decided to feel guilty about her affair with Rob. I have no way of telling what Rob now thinks. Nor what he really just said to her. I've been quicker about mending my relationship with Cherie than about repairing the whatever-it-was with Rob.

"He thinks you get too involved in things," Cherie goes on. "Obsess about them."

"Rob," I tell her. "Right."

"So you'll call him and make him feel easier now, won't you, loved one?" When I don't answer, she goes on. "He really, really cares about you."

Oh, Cherie, shut up. I don't say this aloud.

Susie's couch doesn't provide the best sleep in the world.

The faint aroma of marijuana is pleasant, but there is also the smell of musty cracked leather, plus the ordeal of couch buttons in your back.

"How was your night, dear?" Susie asks the next morning, and I tell her, "Fine."

The pluses of staying with her outweigh the negatives. The pluses are her tender hippie care. She produces hemp waffles with organic maple syrup for breakfast. "Now I know they don't give you this at that Manor place," she says, handing me a sticky plate.

"Their waffles are a different shape," my father says. "I wonder how that little Ta-Ent is today."

"Oh, better, better," Susie lies enthusiastically. "Well," she adds, "I know they don't have hand-churned butter." Susie sometimes makes her own butter in a churn that works by foot, not by hand.

"She was quite troubled, you know," Daddy says.

Susie protests, "Ed, she wasn't," at the same moment that I say, "Tell me about it, Daddy."

I think Susie feels this is just too disturbing for my father.

"Perhaps something to do with the title inheritance?" my dad says. "That is confused. There are really no records. One of those archaeological problems that would be such a find if one could discover the original document. Maybe we talked about it? I think I talked to her quite a bit."

My father half remembers lots of things, often just enough to get a corner of memory. If you pull too hard, you tear it apart. "Please pass the maple syrup," he says.

When I tell him, "You liked her—Ta-Ent or whoever—didn't you?" he responds, "Who? What are you talking about?" and Susie says reproachfully, "The poor man needs his tea." She then produces honeybush tea, imported from Africa.

Susie's house doesn't get much sun; most Stanton's Mill houses don't, with their faces aimed at the opposite side of the gully. But there is a pleasant pervasive atmosphere of heavy greenery and the murmur from the stream plus an underlying ocean throb, from just a half-mile away.

"Now what will you children do today?" Susie asks.

I guess you could say Susie was born to be a mama and that maybe it's too bad she had only Rob.

"Dear Rob will surely come around to see you here," she informs me now.

I should watch out what I'm thinking.

Rob and I had our childhood romance when we were Berkeley children and then, later, we were lovers together over a garage in Santa Cruz. After that we were on-and-off and perhaps too used to each other, but we never really separated until Cherie came along.

The fact that Cherie is fifty-two and Rob is only thirty seemed to make it more interesting.

Susie would love to get him and me back together again now. She is completely oblivious to my remarks that I am not interested.

"I have other things I need to think about," I tell her, and slam out onto the enclosed porch, where Daddy has been sleeping.

He has tried to make the bed, pulling up Susie's Indian bedspread and piling the Persian cushions artistically on top. There are enough of those, in wild shades of red, green, and blue, with bits of mirror sewed on them in inconvenient places, to make a sturdy backrest. I climb onto the bed and settle back and reach into my pocket for my lists.

Down in the gully the stream murmurs. It makes a pleasantly busy sound.

I have three lists. The first is the list Cherie gave me on Susie's front porch—that of the people she questioned after Tamina fell. The second is my own list from memory of who was up on that flat rock along with Tamina. And my third list is Cherie's summary of indigo history in Stanton's Mill.

There are also, in list number one, some of the answers Cherie got from the people she yelled questions at on the Rock. These answers are pretty unhelpful, but I line them up and look at them.

So I have three pages of crumpled paper. I begin by

spreading them out against my raised knees and comparing to see if the names are repeated. And of course they are. There aren't that many people in Stanton's Mill. Several names appear all three places. The name of Beau La Roche seems important, because he's the manager of the co-op store and the person who called Cherie to tell her about Tamina. So does the name of Anneliese Wertiger and that of Scope (no last name). Anneliese and Scope live next door to Susie, but in Stanton's Mill that can be a lot of bushes and trees away.

I don't want to see them first; I'm already prejudiced against them.

"Do you think Beau La Roche is at work yet?" I ask Susie, who says, "Work? Oh, good heavens, darling, not yet; have another waffle."

I already know Beau from visiting Susie before all this started. You can't be in Stanton's Mill all day without going up to the store at least once.

I have more coffee and chat with Susie about what she should do about her field mice. "They are so cute. But so fertile. What is the point in nature making them reproduce all the time?"

Susie agrees that a cat is nature's way, but worries about the cat feeling lonely when she's not there.

A half-hour later I head off for the co-op store. It is sharply uphill. Everything in Stanton's Mill is either uphill or downhill and reached by paths that are rutted and rocky. In addition, there are two surfaced roads, one that comes down from the hilltop and one that runs along the edge of the creek. The one on the creek floods every winter.

The co-op store is the one with the parking lot where Cherie and I parked yesterday. The store itself is made of cedar planks. It's a pleasant, small, low-slung California building behind a patch of leggy geraniums. The inside of the store is drafty, which doesn't matter since the door is always left open and no Mill resident ever admits to feeling cold. Despite drafts, the store smells pleasantly of garlic and onion and cinnamon; there are bins of produce with wobbly signs: OUR VEGETABLES ARE NEVER SPRAYED! YOU BET! NO BIO HAZARDS! ORGANIC ALL THE WAY. There is a glass case full of cheese and another of natural health medicines; pine shelves display homemade nut butter and conserve and jam. I've already tried the jams, which are good.

There's an open cubicle at the back for the manager. Behind that is a door into the meeting hall.

"Carla, well, greetings." Beau is a slender fiftyish man who has nominated himself the Stanton's Mill eccentric. Being an eccentric in Stanton's Mill is difficult. He has decided to be the opposite of the flower-child hippie that is the Mill norm; he has opted for academic. He wears a tweed jacket, a plaid shirt with a couple of ballpoint pens in the pocket, khaki pants that bag at the knees. He's handsome in a tired way.

I know him pretty well from previous visits. Normally he's verbally speedy; today he seems repressed. "Carla," he says again. "Here on business," he interprets.

"I'm sorry about the girl," I tell him. "She sounds interesting. Unusual."

He says, "Yep," and installs himself behind his desk, up on a slightly raised platform.

He settles in, creaks out a drawer to put his feet on. He sighs. "Yes, she was a bright child. I knew her pretty well; she clerked here sometimes . . . Yep, she was good at it," he answers my question. "Harder than it looks because people bring things in—their jams and all—and don't keep records. She was okay with that. But she was nervous."

"Like standing on the cliff."

He gives me a once-over with large dark brown eyes. "She went there to make a speech. That's one of our quaint local customs. Making speeches on the cliff edge.

"But, sure she was nervous. She had pressures."

When I ask what kind of pressures, I get another appraising look. "What inhabitant of God's playground doesn't?"

I say, "Huh?" and he rethinks. "Her mother is—well, not exactly simple. Thirty-seven years old, stupidly innocent. And that Anneliese, who's not innocent, was leaning on her. And there was a boyfriend. Innocent again. They do a lot of that around here."

I'm firming up to get more questions in, but Beau picks up, "Want a drink?"

I think he means tea, but he doesn't. He produces a bottle with a Russian label, which I decline; he pours himself some of that and finds an orange organic liquid for me. "Parsnips," he says of his own drink. "Real good on the free radicals.

"Tamina," he resumes. "This indigo stuff had her on edge."

"She had an indigo baby," I prompt.

He puts his parsnip drink down and gives me another solemn surveillance. Cherie thinks he's smart. No, that wasn't what she said, she said sensible. So far I can't tell. "If you were fifteen years old and some sophisticated-looking older female told you your baby was spiritual-special, you'd believe them, right?"

I start to say I thought everyone knew, and then I revert

to "Susie said . . ." and then, because his lined face stays uninflected, I do a précis of Susie's description of the community
meeting and Anneliese's identification: Tamina's unborn
babe, the perfect indigo specimen. Beau says, "Duh. You
ever live in a place like this?"

"Visiting Sue."

"You been here four times, maybe? You can't believe how
things get scrambled in this town. The whole venue is a vast
arena . . ." Maybe Beau used to be a teacher; he seems back
to practicing that now. "Do you know that children's game
called telephone?"

"Where somebody whispers something to the person
next to them and that person repeats it . . ."

"Right. Well, this entire town, every single person in
it . . ."

I stop him with, "So everybody in Stanton's Mill believes
in indigo babies and then repeats it and gets it wrong?"

He surveys me. "Christ, I am a blowhard," he mutters,
and follows with, "Maybe. It seems glamorous, at least part-
time. And Tamina was beautiful and the baby looked all
right, for a baby."

I say, "So where's this baby now?"

Beau shrugs. "Yeah. That's the telephone part of it."

So we have the first Disappearing Indigo Baby.

I get ready to ask, What did you think? What did Tamina say? How long did she have the baby? Did you see it;
did she bring it in to work here, et cetera, when Beau takes
a final swig of his parsnip brew and says, "Child, all this is
making me nervous." I translate this into, "So, scram," but
he reaches for his phone and signals for me to stay. "With

that kid in the hospital," he says. "She was an unusual kid."
He lapses into ordinary English. "She was great. I don't
know, *defiant*. In a good way." He punches some numbers
into his phone.

I subside against my chair, an uncomfortable handmade
one composed of slats and splinters and a defeated tapestry
cushion.

Beau is apparently calling the hospital. He asks for a
nurse, and then a doctor, and then Intensive Care. "Tamina
Kerry," he says, supplying me for the first time with Tamina's last name, and after that, "Yes," several times, followed
by, "Yes, yes," and "I am," and "I'll wait," and "Okay," then,
the clincher, after a pause, "I'm her father."

I am staring accusingly at him, which gets me no place.
He holds the receiver to his ear and rests his elbow on his
desk. His other hand lies on the desk, and has started shaking. He waits and I wait; he says, "Yes," some more. Followed
by, "I see," "Okay," and "All right." Then he says, "Yes." Then
he says, "Yes," again, after which he adds, "Yes I am." There's
a pause and, "What?" and "When?"

"I know you didn't know to call me," he says. "Yes, I'll
be in."

He hangs up the phone and rests his head on his hand.

It's not the time to ask more questions.

I gather my notebook to get out of there, but on the way
out I spot the clerk, who wears a white jacket and is draped
across the cheese display case with her mouth open. She
must have arrived while I was talking to Beau. She is my
good friend Sunshine, who works occasional mornings at
the Manor.

I grab her by the elbow and pull her outside.

"Sunshine," I say, and add, "Shit."

She says, "Yeah." I'm surprised to see that her little oval face is tear-streaked, moisture tracking down from each eye. Her nose, ornamented with a single turquoise, is dripping. She also has a bolt through her eyebrow.

Somehow I hadn't thought Sunshine would grasp an overheard conversation. Or maybe I didn't expect her to react like this.

"Sunshine, *mi amor*," I say, which is mean of me, because she replies, "Huh?" and looks at me helplessly.

She's a sweet youngster and does the best she can on her job chasing around at the Manor. But I've never had any of the fictions about her that I've begun having about Tamina. Fictions like I've begun thinking of her as a younger version of myself.

"Listen, Sun," I say, and then, "all right, let's sit down here," because she really does seem upset. I'm upset, too, but Sunshine is shaking and her nose has begun running a steady mucus stream. I shovel her onto a bench and camp beside her, half holding her up. She sniffles persistently and I finally produce a bedraggled Kleenex. But she doesn't blow her nose on this; she clutches it and says, "Oh, wow."

I won't wipe her nose for her; the turquoise makes it too difficult.

"She was such a good kid," she sniffles after a while.

I pat her on the shoulder.

We're interrupted by Beau, banging out of the store toward the parking lot. He has posted a sign that says, BACK IN TEN. He goes by, hunched, staring at his feet, without looking at us.

"Tamina was a good friend of yours," I venture after a while.

"Good friend? I mean, way more. Best friend. I mean, she was lots younger than me, like two years, but we sort of, you know, bonded, and she told me everything and I told her and we were way close."

"So you knew about the baby?"

"A' course. But everybody did, everybody knew about Penelope Ta-Ent—isn't that a great name? And Tammy was real crazy about her but Tammy was real young, you know, and so she sent the baby to stay with her grandmother—no, maybe it was an auntie—for a while.

"And that bothered her. It got her upset, I mean. And there were some other things, too. Like, when they thought she was in on the meth story."

I'm still absorbing the fact that there was a baby whose middle name was Ta-Ent. The name my dad has been using to talk about Tamina. And the name of somebody in a hieroglyphic Egyptian document. Did my dad name Tammy's baby? Or did she pick the name up as a glamorous interesting label? "What?" I finally ask. "What meth story?"

"And," Sunshine says, disregarding my question completely, "Tammy was never into meth. Never. Not even pot. Well, not much. But for sure not meth. We never even knew anybody that made it. And there's a lot of that around here."

I say, "Oh for God's sake." I've not been paying close enough attention. I've not been taking notes. I've had a whole batch of new facts fired at me within the last twenty minutes and I will never be able to sort them out. In addition, back in Susie's cabin is the list of names I was working on.

I should grab Sunshine right now, when she's feeling

shook up and communicative, and find out who's supposed to have been making meth.

I'm still wrestling with these concepts when the intrusive racket of a motorcycle, which has been sawing into our conversation for the last minute, finally explodes into the parking lot. It is a small, dusty motorcycle straddled by a young man, who dismounts. He wears no helmet and is rangy and dark-haired, and has orange-rimmed goggles. He shouts out, "Oh. Hey, wow. Geez. Sunshine."

She says, "Oh. Wow. Arby." She had slowed down on the crying, but now she starts up again.

They coalesce, with Sunshine getting cuddled and kissed. I can't tell whether Arby is her boyfriend, someone else's boyfriend, or just a member of the community. "Let's take off," he says, scooping Sunshine close with one arm and giving me a dirty look.

I don't interpret the dirty look personally. With his goggles down around his neck on a strap, he emerges as a very young guy with dark hair and a few teenage spots. The dirty look is just for somebody (a) older, and (b) not Stanton's Mill, and, possibly, (c) not connected with the Tamina tragedy.

He helps Sunshine onto the front of the motorcycle, puts his dark glasses back up, and blasts the two of them out of there.

🜚 Chapter 4

Susie is a confirmed natural foods, organic, cholesterol-free cook, mostly vegetarian. She likes fish, but will eat only the less intelligent ones.

I've told her that the less intelligent fish are obviously the ones who let themselves get caught, but she doesn't listen.

Now she is cooking a rice, lentil, and sweet potato stew. "We need it. To restore our equanimity."

When I tell her that Tamina is dead, she says, "Oh," and has to take the pot off the heat and sit down.

My father says, "Dead? Someone died?" I have trouble explaining until Susie says, "The one with the amulet," and then he says, "Oh, I am so sorry. So very sorry. I spoke to her a good deal. Sometimes, my dear—I remember this, I don't always remember things. But sometimes I almost thought she was you."

I put a hand on his shoulder.

"And," he continues, "I don't believe she died. I think she was sacrificed. There's a difference, you know. In spite of the amulet."

My mind flicks onto that carved thing at Tamina's throat. Yes, of course that's what it was. A carved *djed* symbol. Unusual, most people want the *ankh*. She must have gotten it from Daddy.

A *djed* looks like a tree with a set of crosspieces on it. The scholars aren't sure exactly what it represents.

"She wasn't supposed to," Daddy says solemnly. "That was a protection. To foil the sorceries of the enemies." He pulls out another chair and sits beside Susie. "An exploration into the world of the turquoise trees. Have they found her body yet?"

Susie says, "Don't think about it, dear."

"Daddy," I say. "Honey." I've only just pulled myself together to absorb what he's been saying. "I want to know more. About protecting her? Tell me about that. I think it's important."

But my father gets a look on his face that I recognize. It's a stubborn look, mouth compressed, eyes half-closed; I'd almost call it mulish. "I can't possibly do that. It was privileged."

We stare at each other for a minute until Susie announces that we all need a little glass of chardonnay. "It will do him good, you know."

So maybe it will do all of us good. She puts the bottle and some glasses in the middle of the table.

"Oh, dear. That lovely young life. Oh, my dear."

She adds that she doesn't understand the workings of the Higher Power.

I should be asking more questions. Get your questions out early, while people are still upset or surprised, before they get a chance to brood. But all the things I can think of to say make me feel sick. I pour some chardonnay while Susie steals my cell phone and calls Rob. He is, after all, her son.

"Well, then, darling, soon," she says, in the tentative voice she uses with him. She's a little afraid of him, because he is so organized and she is so not. "We need comforting."

Well, I'm mad at Rob and he isn't high on my list of comforters. After she signs off, I take a swallow of wine and say, "Tell me about Tamina's family."

"Family," says my father. "A concept of major importance. She could have written a letter and put it in the container."

"Family?" Susie asks, sounding baffled. I supply a lead-in. "I know that Beau is her father, but her mother, what's she like?"

Susie thunks her glass down loudly. "*What* are you talking about?"

"Tamina's family," I say reasonably.

"Beau her father? Whatever gave you that ridiculous idea?" When I just stare, she says, "Beau wasn't any more her father than . . ." She gestures at the window. "Than that tree there."

I wait for a couple of beats and Susie finally says, "Her father was Jimmy. Jimmy the Jumper. You know. The rock-and-roll one."

Our area is rife with famous musicians whom no one outside Del Oro County has heard of. But Jimmy the Jumper got into the *Chronicle* a couple of times when I was in school. He was an old-style rock-and-roll musician, long hair and craggy face. Sweet-looking, if you like the unkempt style.

Susie sighs. "He was an attractive young man. Oh, dear. He wouldn't be young anymore, would he?"

My question, "And where is Jimmy now?" just elicits a despairing shrug from Susie, but to my surprise, she picks up on the next issue. "And her mother. That's Happy Dawn. Happy Dawn is very beautiful.

"But she had a little drug problem. She sells jam. Sometimes on Saturday. You've seen her. Out in front of the store."

"That's Tamina's mother?" The woman who sometimes is in front of the co-op with her jam is pretty, something like her daughter, I now realize, but I avoid her because she offers her plaid-jacketed pots with an imploring, "Hello. I've been clean now for thirteen months." It's mean of me, but I don't want to be included in her recovery program.

"That would depress Tamina, all right," I say, and Susie objects, "Carla! How can you? Happy Dawn is so brave to admit her problem that way. I always buy her jam."

"Jam," says my father thoughtfully. "Do you know, I would really appreciate some lunch."

Susie's food is always delicious. Some people might cavil about the shortage of protein, but not I. I eat assiduously and finally direct another question at Susie. "Why did Beau say he was Tamina's father?"

"I have no idea."

"Was he a friend of Happy Dawn's?"

"We are all friends here, Carla." Susie has very quickly fitted into the Stanton's Mill ethos.

I give her as close to a withering look as I can. I really love the lady. "Susie. Come on."

She sighs. "I wasn't here sixteen years ago, dear. What a shame. I would have loved it. And sixteen years ago really wasn't the best time; the best time was more like thirty years ago. Such a wonderful atmosphere of freedom. And universal love."

I think, but do not say, Yes, universal, oh, boy.

My mean meditations are interrupted by the arrival of Rob, who bursts through the door saying, "Mom, what do you mean, you need comforting? What am I supposed to do, bring you a . . ." He's stopped by the spectacle of me. He stares for a minute. "Hello, Carla."

"Hi, Rob," I say politely.

My father chimes in, "Why, young man. Yes, of course I know you. The name will come in a minute."

"Hello, Ed," Rob says. "Carla, hello."

Rob and I have had difficulty speaking to each other ever since the Cherie episode. What could be a long empty conversational patch is interrupted by Susie, who says, "Rob, darling, you mustn't be mean about comfort; I feel so bad, that lovely child going . . . oh, it was so terrible, over the cliff."

"What?" says Rob. "What are you talking about, cliff, what cliff?" He fires this off as if he takes the idea personally.

"She fell," Susie explains. "Toppled. Off that cliff. There." She points up and out the window. "Little Tamina. One of my friends here. And Edward's good friend here. Maybe you met her."

Rob says, "Son of a bitch."

"Rob, dear. So you know her?"

"No, I didn't know her. But I had a patient a couple of days ago who said he pushed somebody off a cliff. He was extraordinarily overstimulated, of course." Rob looks at me. "Sky high."

"Pushed someone," my father says. "Someone pushed her. Or at least bumped. I am quite sure I saw it. I was there, you know. But it wasn't him."

"Darling," I say to my dad, "who? You can remember. I know you can. Try really hard."

"There is an envelope of silence that accompanies those who walk by day," my father says.

Susie shakes her head as if she has a gnat caught in her ear. "But darling. I mean, is it relevant?" Which is an amazing question for Susie to ask. She's addressing Rob.

"What," he asks, "the guy I was talking to? Yeah. It was a guy from here. I mean, from Stanton's Mill. Of course he was dangerously hallucinatory. Imagining things. He talked to Ulysses S. Grant while he was in Emergency."

"And he thinks he pushed someone off a cliff?" I ask.

"That's just one of the things he thinks. Thought. We brought him down, he's recovered. Did a lot of sleeping and waking up and crying. He was pretty bad. A combination of mushrooms and methamphetamine. One gives you visions and one makes you high as a kite."

"Meth," I say. "Interesting. Do you get a lot of that?"

Rob says it's not exactly interesting; it's the latest new old thing around here; there's lots of meth; it's a cottage industry. "You can make it on your electric two-burner."

"It is a stimulant and quite dangerous," Susie says critically. "So bad for the psyche."

"Did you believe him at all?" I ask Rob, who answers, "How do I know? I didn't have any idea what he was referring to. But it stuck in my mind. Weird. Weirder than Ulysses S. Grant."

"And who is the guy?"

"Well." Rob stares at Susie. "Mom. You've seen him around. A kid, really. With a bike and a guitar. Works sometimes at the co-op and hangs out with, I guess she's called, Sunshine?"

I say, "Oh, for God's sake." At first I think the interlocking of facts around here is eerie and then I decide that's what you get in a small town. A very small town. Everybody is related to everybody, everybody in love with everybody, everybody fighting and having sex and trading suspicions. You want a murder candidate? Grab a pin and shove it into the list somewhere. Bingo.

"Boy, he sure recovered fast," I say. "I saw him today. He looked okay."

Rob seems only minimally interested. He says that's the advantage of being a kid.

"Rob," I say, "why don't you have a glass of chardonnay and then come for a walk with me?"

Rob is very willing to come for a walk, which in Stanton's Mill is better defined as a scramble. Rob feels sheepish and awkward around me, as he should. And he thinks that whatever time we spend together being confidential may help. After all, he and I are each other's oldest friends.

Directly uphill from Susie's takes us by the co-op, but we

don't have to go inside the store, from which a conversational babble emerges, indicating a full house. I circle the parking lot and climb a few rocky yards more and find a nice damp log. A dry log is probably not a possibility in the Mill.

Rob sits beside me. He puts his knees together and looks uncomfortable. "You're working with Cherie on this?" he asks.

I say, "Uh-huh," and squint at him to see how he looks pronouncing the name *Cherie*. My psychic acceptance of that Cherie-Rob event isn't complete. I've spent a lot of time reminding myself that Rob and I were just friends and that is not a restrictive category. Rob is a free agent, why shouldn't he have a romance with somebody; I had a few of those. And so on. None of this stuff has adhered too well.

I seem still to feel that Rob was mine and he let me down.

"Yeah," I say. And describe the progress of the Stanton's Mill events, beginning with Cherie wanting me to investigate the indigo children and progressing in my story through Tamina's fall off the cliff, through Beau, Sunshine, and company, to the present. And Arby.

Rob has never heard of indigo children and is appalled. He advances the opinion that most people are idiots. He says Arby was hallucinating and was extremely vague. "First he thought he did it. And then he thought somebody else did. And then that he saw somebody fall or somebody rise. And somebody that he called the Prof knew something. After that he was Satan's handyman."

"Another straightforward, reliable witness."

"How are you, Carla?"

He asks this in a concerned voice, which makes me decide to ignore him. "How old is Arby?" I ask.

Rob takes a minute.

I think, Oh, shoot. I've just squelched an overture. That's the trouble with these old relationships. I have shut Rob up when he tries to make an overture. Now I feel guilty.

Rob sighs theatrically. "Arby's young enough to be one of our kids. If we had kids."

I stare at him. I don't say, "Cut it out, Rob. You're thirty and I'm twenty-seven." What I say instead is, "And he takes a mix of mushrooms and methamphetamine."

"I never knew him to do it before. I had to wash him out for a half an hour. Plus some shots."

"Listen, Rob, wasn't there a story published someplace about methamphetamine?"

"Yeah, in the *Chronicle*." He looks thoughtful. "That was about four months ago, I guess. And yeah, it mentioned Stanton's Mill. But also some other places. That little town of Cedar, just back of Oakland. And downtown Oakland, too."

"Somebody said Tamina was involved some way. People were mad at her."

He moves irritably. "Involved? This place is ridiculous. Sure there's meth here, I guess, but only some; it's just because we're close to the Salinas Valley and then the Central Valley. Pot is the big industry here. That story was just a general roundup. The reporter could have gotten most of it off the Internet."

"Nothing somebody could get mad about and want to get even for?" I ask.

"Oh, for God's sake." Rob has a short fuse on speculation.

"You better dig up the original stupid newspaper story and look at it." After a minute he adds, "I don't know, Carla, I wonder if all this poking and prying and speculation is good for you.

"And my mom," he adds quickly.

A long-standing battle between me and Rob is his urge to control versus my urge to control. Each of us grew up with a parent who needed help and each of us was the main help-supplier. It's the role we feel good in.

"The way I see it," I continue. I'm going to ignore this control question and keep on talking to Rob because he is, if he can stop feeling defensive, the only person around with normal responses. "I think Tamina was pushed."

"You don't know that. It was her own idea to go and wobble around on that cliff."

"She told Cherie she had something important to tell her. After that she went to the Rock to make a speech. And then she died."

"Right away?"

"She fell right away.

"First," I go on, "there was this indigo baby thing. And then Tamina's death. And she had a baby that was supposed to be indigo and it's off somewhere. Sunshine said she cried a lot."

"Proving zilch. Listen, Carla. I hate this. It's so diffuse. Do some more fact checking on the baby situation. In general, not just the way it links to this Tamina child, but in general. To everybody you can ask about it. Then collect your rumors here in Stanton's Mill; I'm sure they'll turn out to be nothing much. Write Cherie a report. And get back to the Manor, where you know which end is up."

I don't say, Oh, shut up, but I think it.

And we start down the hill toward Susie's house.

He tries to hold my hand, but I don't let him.

I'm feeling strong and innocent, which is the way you feel before something bad happens.

♩ Chapter 5

In Susie's living room my father is stretched out on the leather couch, the same fragrant one on which I've been sleeping.

Susie is bent over him, doing caretaking things to his forehead. "A little accident," she says.

"Someone threw a rock at me," Daddy says.

"Now, Edward. That was an accident. It was meant to scare a raccoon."

Long experience in countries rife with uprisings and feuds has made my father realistic. "Perhaps it was an accident but I don't think so. The rock had a message tied to it."

It takes several moments for me to understand all this. I babble around for a while, "A rock? Someone threw a rock?" and so on, and then I rush over to his side as if there were something I could do about that now, and say, "When did it happen? Are you dizzy? Do you still hurt? Let me see."

Susie is administering a pack of frozen peas. She feels me observing her work and says defensively, "Of course I don't believe in frozen food. But sometimes in midwinter . . ."

"Are you all right?" I ask Daddy. "Did it tear the skin? Do you have a headache?" I kneel beside the couch.

Susie moves her frozen peas aside and lets me inspect: a red spot, not too bad.

"And the message was for me," my father continues. "It was addressed, 'Hey, Great Egyptian King.' "

"What else did it say?" I ask, and he shakes his head, dislodging the pea package. "The rest of it was not for me, because it said, 'Hand over her diary,' and some other things. And I do not have a diary."

"Oh, sweetheart." I caress my father's shoulder since I don't feel safe caressing his head.

"It was an accident," Susie says.

"I don't understand the rest of the message," Daddy tells me. "Perhaps you'll look at it?" He reaches behind him into the depths of the couch and comes up with a battered square of paper.

The message is written in pencil. It's hard to tell whether the writer really is semiliterate or just wants to appear that way. The paper is crumpled, from having been wrapped and tied around the rock, and the results are smeared. The word *Egyptian* is misspelled, emerging as *Egyptan*. But the rest of the message is what bothers Daddy: "Git redy to anser if you can't come up with it. There's no money there. And forgit about what you think you know. You don't. You are an old man with Alzhimers."

"It's pretty peculiar about the money," I say.

"The whole thing is peculiar. And the spelling bad."

I'm highly suspicious of that spelling. Who writes *get*

as *git* unless they're pretending to be Li'l Abner? And the printing tries to look labored, but doesn't really succeed.

"You sure you don't have a headache?" I ask, and Daddy is cheerful. "Sure, I'm sure." He loves sounding colloquial when he can remember how to do it.

I call Cherie to say that my father and I will drive home with Rob; she doesn't need to come here and get me the way she promised at the beginning of the weekend. I give her the story of Daddy's rock. She asks me to be sure and save the paper. "We'll get those slimy bastards, darlin'; all my love to my sweet good Crocodile; is he okay?"

Crocodile Dundee is Cherie's nickname for my father; she thinks he's the adventurous type.

"The way up and the way down are not one and the same," I inform Rob during our drive home.

Rob has a serviceable red Honda and is being polite. He's not impressed by my misquotation. "So what does that mean?"

"Just lightening the long road home." He doesn't like it when I get literary. And of course, he understands that I'm talking about us and our relationship. "You were part of that class, too," I say, intending to deflect the conversation and remind him of a joint experience: Philosophy Survey, Santa Cruz, 2002.

He says, "Well, shit," and asks my dad how he is.

Daddy, from the backseat, says he feels fine. "Really, my head is better now than it was before."

"Sons of bitches," Rob says in my ear. He adds, "How could it happen? They're crazy about him here."

In a while he adds, "This is a weird place."

A few miles later he tells me, "I never stopped loving you."

I start to say, "Why don't we just drop that subject," but don't say it. Which I guess is a brownie point for me. I'm relieved when we arrive at the Manor.

The Manor is a grand old California fake baronial mansion, now an elegant retirement center, where my dad lives and where I live and work. It seems that we have been missed. Belle, the director, comes out front to greet us. "So, old sport," she barks at my dad, "line up here, let Grandma look at you. Good God, Buster"—she has spotted the abrasion on his forehead, which has begun turning purple—"what has your child been letting you do?" Belle is a rangy Calvinist specimen who affects a gruff approach to the world; she runs the Manor capably.

And I don't feel like explaining. "Daddy is all right; he'll tell you about it," and I bid a polite farewell and thank-you to Rob, and go upstairs to my room, where I unpack my backpack and gun. And think that I am old enough and educated enough to live more elegantly and have a roll-on suitcase instead of a backpack.

The next morning I find that my pile of Complaints has multiplied in my absence,

Complaints is one of the things I do as assistant director of the Manor, a job I slid into because I wanted to be near my dad. I suppose I should say it's my full-time job, with deputy sheriff being my part-time one, but lately I have tended to short-change Job A for Job B. My other Manor duties involve Billing and Morning Meds. Billing is the usual procedure everyone knows about, and Morning Meds is pushing a cart along the corridors, checking to make sure my charges are still alive, and then dispensing a lot of Tylenol, Pepto-Bismol, and Preparation H. I also do Lost Objects and anything else my boss, Belle, shoves in my direction.

Belle loves my dad and allows me a good deal of latitude.

Complaints mostly come in four kinds: (a) complaints from relatives that their elderly loved one is inadequately tended, (b) complaints from relatives that their elderly loved one calls them too often, (c) complaints from relatives about the food (too bland, too boring, too rich, too spicy, too much), and (d) complaints from residents that someone is stealing their jewelry, shoes, mail, money, Tylenol.

Last year I wrote a set of responses, one for each kind of complaint, and my job now is mostly matching complaints and answers, except for (d) the residents who think they're being robbed, and their letters go to Belle. These cases get investigated, but they almost always turn out to be baseless. Sometimes counseling, for the complainant, is suggested.

"I am dying," I announce to the person who interrupts me at this work. "I will sit here and desiccate and no one will know."

My interrupter is an elegant old lady named Mrs. La Salle. She is my favorite Manor resident, after my father. She wears inventive jewelry and looks like an ad for something expensive.

"I've been here for three hours," I tell her.

"You should find another hobby." She takes me by the hand. "Come outside."

Mrs. La Salle lives here only part-time; some of each month she spends in San Francisco, where she writes something that she won't talk about. Since she knows everybody in San Francisco and Marin and used to work for *Bay City Upbeat*, I suspect her of doing a gossip column for one of the San Francisco journals.

But maybe she's writing a book about the Manor.

We settle onto a garden bench near a statue of the Hans Christian Andersen mermaid. She smooths the knees of her raw silk pants, displaying a large amethyst ring, set high and with lots of diamonds. "So tell me everything interesting. Where you have been and what you know. Your father said something about Ta-Ent, who, I take it, is an Egyptian goddess."

I start talking and am encouraged by Mrs. La Salle's interest. So I keep on talking. She indicates attention with small appreciative noises. When I have pretty well finished "The Saga of Stanton's Mill," she says, "Yes indeed." Then she says, "Your principal duty, of course, is to your father."

"Of course." I announce this crossly. Today has not been a good day.

"You realize that the best evidence for murder is that note to him?"

"Certainly."

"Because"—she pauses dramatically—"it shows the girl knew something. Something they're worried about."

"Yes, but who's they?"

"They is whoever. And if she knew something, it is possible your father knows it, too. The message shows they think he does. They also think he could talk about it, which is bad news. Has he mentioned it to you?"

"He's tried." I feel a sinking in my midriff. If I knew of

some way, any way, of making him remember clearly. All I can do is wait. Wait and poke.

"People that think you know something may come after you."

I tell her yes.

Mrs. La Salle waves her hand; the amethyst catches light. "And the second most important thing is the lists you have of people that were up on that overlook."

I like Mrs. La Salle but I don't like her outlining my work for me. She's smart. She thinks fast. That isn't always so great.

"Daphne," I say firmly, "this is all confidential."

"Oh. Certainly."

Is she planning a column? To include my stories in her book? "It's truly confidential, Daphne."

"Yes, of *course*." But her response is delayed enough to seem suspicious.

"Well," she sighs, standing up and surveying the lush contradictions of our garden, where palm trees and ice plants fight for territory.

"Carla," she asks, "do you even know who the other babies are that presumably disappeared?"

I inspect the gravel in the mermaid walk. No, I don't know about the other babies, just Tamina's. I've only been doing this for three days. Maybe four. I haven't been thinking about those others. "We're working on that," I say. Suddenly I'm dying to get upstairs to my lists and my telephone.

"Well," she says. "A fascinating story." She turns around, set to go back to her apartment. This lady has superb posture. I hope I can do as well when I'm seventy-three.

I tell her, "Thanks for your help," and sit back, feeling

snide about her for being so together and so smart. Then I accuse myself of being a card-carrying bitch. Maybe it's just the mood I'm in at the moment, but I decide that the only person in the world whom I can like unreservedly and without thinking an occasional mean thought about him is my father, and maybe I respond to him because he's damaged.

I have a compressed and contorted new e-mail list from Cherie ("Drlng: Nw tgs I thot of"), which takes me a half-hour to decipher. After I'm done decoding, I call her and assail her about the purple babies. That's what I have started calling them in my head. "Cherie, we've got to start getting specific. Who is supposed to have had a baby? Who says it's missing?"

"Why, darlin', I put all that on my list. And some in my e-mail."

I don't say, *No you didn't, you didn't put much of anything on that list except names.* When Cherie understands something, she sees no reason why other people shouldn't understand it also, immediately and without a lot of boring explanation. "E-mail is unreliable," I say. "Tell me again."

"Well, different people complained about different babies—I mean, they said those babies hadn't been seen for a while and the reasons offered for their absence were evasive—is that the right word, darlin'? Anyway, Molly Kinsolving complained about Tamina's baby and she was the same one who complained about Lana's baby . . ."

"Hold on." I have stashed the phone in the intersection of my shoulder and ear and am scribbling furiously. New name: Lana.

"And Happy Dawn complained about Beau's baby—"

I have to interrupt here. "Beau has a baby?"

"Grandson, darling. Lived with him."

"Oh, uh-huh." Most of the small children in Stanton's Mill would be grandchildren. The chief residents of the Mill are flower generation, like Susie. And they had their own kids and those kids . . . Well, I know in general where most of those kids are. Off someplace, like Oaxaca or Tangiers. And having had babies, which they sent home to Grandmom. But Beau as a grandpa with a resident baby—a resident indigo baby—well, I think, that is on the ridiculous side. And it's also ridiculous the way information keeps piling up in elaborate unstable structures that teeter and then collapse. "Who's Molly Kinsolving, Cherie, for God's sake? And who's Lana? And why haven't I heard about them before?"

"Why, darlin', you have. Molly Kinsolving is Molly Littlefeather, who said Tamina was pushed off the Rock. That was in my notes."

I decide not to inquire why Molly Kinsolving is Molly Littlefeather. I remember her statement at the time Tamina fell and that she was a fat lady in a flowered muu-muu. I say, "And she complained about Tamina's baby and she also complained about Lana's."

"She did. And then, guess what, it turns out she's an indigo parent herself. Or grandmama. Her daughter had a baby and Anneliese said yes indeedy, it had the aura."

"And did it disappear?"

"Well, the daughter's in Iraq, so for sure that baby's off someplace."

"Okay, okay," I concede, scribbling resentfully. "So, who's Lana?"

"Lana went to live in Placer County."

"Taking the baby with her?"

"I don't know. That Molly Littlefeather is a bit of a blabbermouth. Talks about scraps of everything. All I know about Lana is she was older than most of the ones that had those babies, those indigo babies. I guess Lana was in her beginning forties and she made clay pots."

"You can't support yourself, even in Stanton's Mill, making clay pots."

"Right. I think there was an ex-husband someplace.

"And," Cherie continues, returning to her list, "Happy Dawn complained about Squeegee's baby."

"Squeegee's dead."

"Well, dear, he didn't used to be, did he?"

"And he had a baby?"

"According to Happy Dawn. But she's not the most reliable witness ever."

"Oh, God," I tell Cherie. "What a mess. This is hopeless." After a minute Cherie supplies a final fact that there is someone named Heather, a cousin of Sunshine's, who lives in Lompoc now. But she had this boy baby that Anneliese said was indigo. "Did I really not put all that in my notes? Oh, hey, careless me."

I reposition the cell phone. I now have a notepad that looks like the document the chicken walked across. But with the Squeegee possibility, it dawns on me that maybe Cherie left a fact out on purpose. Maybe she was being nice and trying to spare Susie's feelings. I'm amazed. I know Cherie has a lot of virtues, but I didn't think that kind of compassion was one of them.

I decide to be irritated. "Cherie, this is ridiculous. It's very confused."

"You can say that again."

"Well, I'm going out to the Mill tonight." I've been reluctant about trusting my recently repaired Toyota to a safari down that rocky Stanton's Mill defile. They don't have street lights there.

"Good luck, darlin'. Let me know if you need help."

I hang up feeling weird. But not enough so to welcome the eleven more complaints that are waiting in this morning's mail.

There's plenty of choice about whom I'll interview in Stanton's Mill, but maybe I'll center in on Happy Dawn, who ought to be able to tell me about two of my problems, Tamina and how she was feeling, as well as Tamina and her Disappeared Baby. Happy Dawn is Tamina's mother. Correction: was Tamina's mother.

I'll be intruding on her right after her child has died. But that's when you're supposed to intrude. The sooner the better, from the standpoint of getting frank responses.

I think, oh shit, while I shovel my papers into a folder. I'm an investigator. Her daughter is dead. Her daughter fell. Maybe she was pushed. I have to find out.

Night has descended on Stanton's Mill when I arrive. It is about 6:00 P.M. In the rest of the world the sun is setting in the west; at the Mill it disappeared behind the hill an hour ago. The shadows are long and dark and wet; various nocturnal creatures beep and cheep in the undergrowth. I switch on my brights. The trouble with brights is that they highlight all the wet splayed stuff that sprawls out into the road. They make it look more menacing.

Susie has described Happy Dawn's house as a sweet little white-painted cottage. "Just down the street from me, and then turn to the right and then cut down the hill on the lane and then off to the left. No, right."

I decide that the English translation of these directions is "a little shack hidden off among the bushes."

"You can tell it because it has some of those striped buoys hung up in front."

"Striped boys?"

"Those things they put on the side of boats."

Susie adds, "And, oh. I'll make a casserole for you to take over."

I tell her there won't be time for me to stop off and get a casserole. The tradition of bringing food to assuage grief apparently lives on in the Mill.

I get completely lost looking for Happy Dawn's house. Susie doesn't know right from left and it has gotten truly dark. Finally I'm attracted to the house more by lights and over-heard conversation than by recognition of landmarks, but I do spot the striped markers outside. A lot of people in the Mill seem to have them. Them and abalone shells.

The porch of Happy Dawn's house is unstable and its railing, when I try for a minute to lean against it, threatens to give way.

There is no doorbell, but there are some big brass things, maybe ship's gongs, and a mallet. Together they make a substantial racket.

Happy Dawn comes to the door. She says, very fast and all at once, "Oh, you came to the wake; it's happening right now. Hey, that's so great of you; we don't have her here; they wouldn't let me take her, and she looked so beautiful but they still wanted to keep her. But I mean it's so great of you." She moves aside to let me in.

I deduce that in Stanton's Mill a wake is the true Irish variety, with the body of the departed present, and that Happy Dawn is telling me that the hospital wouldn't release Tamina to be here. I think I feel relieved about that.

Happy Dawn has a round innocent face and long fair hair like her daughter's. She has a pink ostrich feather looped over one ear and is wearing a dark green shift with embroidery on the front. She doesn't look as old as most of the flower generation at the Mill; maybe she was a later import.

She doesn't ask who I am. Either she knows or she's stoned or she doesn't care.

A gentle smell of marijuana pervades the room, which is furnished in Goodwill couches and chairs with the stuffing coming out and piles of crumpled carryout cartons and old magazines. There's a Formica-topped table with stainless steel legs. A jug of wine sits on the table along with a large photo of Tamina and a pot of rhododendrons. Four people sit around, one of whom is Sunshine and one of whom is Beau. The remaining guests are the heavy lady who has been identified as Molly Kinsolving or Molly Littlefeather and a fat man busy dropping ashes on the floor from a hand-rolled cigarette. His hair ends in a drooping pigtail.

Molly Kinsolving/Littlefeather is a sturdy lady with short curly gray-brown hair and a tanned jowly face. She again wears a muu-muu-type garment, this one with Mexican embroidery. She also is smoking, but using a wineglass for an ashtray.

"Snoop Lady," Beau greets me. "Thank you for coming to mourn. What good does mourning do? Who knows, but it's

one of our quaint customs; Tammy would have been glad."
And he chides the fat guy, "Scope, for God's sake, quit that
stuff, dropping ash all over the place. Have some respect,
this is a house of mourning."

Happy Dawn extends the jug. "You want some wine? A
joint?"

I locate a kitchen chair and sit on it, balancing my backpack on my knees and reaching behind me to fuss with my
gun, which pokes me in the spine. Yes, I wore it today.
Daddy's rock made me decide to do that.

"This is Carla," Beau says. "You all know about her."

Happy Dawn and Scope stare. Molly Littlefeather extin-
guishes her cigarette with a fizz. Everybody appears mussed
and has red-rimmed eyes. Pot will do that, as well as grief.

I try to remember the dynamic among these people.
Molly K/L ratted on Happy Dawn—she phoned Cherie
about Tamina's baby. Happy Dawn fingered Beau—she told
Cherie that Beau had a grandchild and that the grandchild
was missing. And Happy Dawn also complained about
Squeegee, who isn't here, or anywhere.

Oh. And Molly called Cherie about someone named
Lana, who was old to have any kind of baby, much less an indigo one, and who went off to Placer County.

Then Molly herself turned out to be indigo. That is, she
was an indigo grandmother.

Scope, smoking silently, is the one who lives next door
with Anneliese, who started the whole indigo baby craze.

Sunshine, off on the sidelines, has no baby, as far as I
know. But she has a cousin named Heather, who is in Lompoc, California, maybe with her indigo baby. Or maybe not.

I resist the impulse to get a scrap of paper and do a dia-
gram, with arrows.

* * *

Sunshine is sloped in a corner with her back to the wall. She looks mashed and sad and crumpled. I feel my protective instincts rising. "Sunshine, you better take tomorrow off."

"Oh, I did already. I mean, today and yesterday."

"Sunshine has been so great," Happy Dawn says. "I mean, she helped. I mean, she really, really organized things." Happy looks down; her chest heaves; she suppresses a hiccup. Her transparent blond hair hangs in her face.

"And you really need that, Happy," Molly Littlefeather says. "If you'll be honest about it." Molly has a husky, overused, insistent voice. "Honey, you don't take care of yourself. I say it straightforward, like a friend, you're careless. You could get things better organized. You just let it all pile up. Or accumulate. Or drift away." She waves a hand at Happy's messy main room.

Scope, who has provided himself with a saucer, carefully jogs off the burnt end of his joint. "Cool it, Molly. Her kid just died."

"Being helpful, chum. I like to be *helpful*. Get some *order* started." Each time Molly stresses a word, she squares her substantial shoulders and smiles. Tanned, muscled arms project from the short sleeves of her muu-muu.

Beau says, "You can be helpful some other time."

Sunshine says, "Her kid, Molly. Her little girl."

Molly's husky voice goes down a peg. "Yeah? Well, and so *okay*, Tammy was her kid. And my personal opinion, even in a moment of grief, is that some of this was preventable. And Happy, if she had really thought about it, could of . . ."

I've never seen Sunshine react to anything much, but now she gets mad. "Molly, shut up; you're a busybody and a creep."

A free-for-all is forming. "Sunshine, good for you," Beau tells her. "And Molly? Hey, shut up. You got off on being so pious about the indigo kids and how could they be so careless and then your own daughter turns up with one. So wind it down."

Molly gets out of her chair. She delivers a soliloquy standing, sturdy legs in Birkenstocks planted firmly apart. "Yeah, Beau? Well, what business is it of yours anyway, who appointed you general guardian and eyes and ears of us? Are you so good you can be the boss of me? And of other people? And you going around saying you're her father."

"Yeah? So maybe that would be okay. Being her dad, that would really be okay. Molly, now that we're into it, who asked you to go poking your nose in everywhere?"

"Right," Sunshine says at the same time that Happy Dawn emits an audible sob. Scope slams his saucer on the table. A major upheaval is in the offing; everyone freezes and looks at everybody else.

Then Molly sits back on her chair and appears to think for a minute. She puts a hand on either metal chair-arm. "Well, hey, I guess you know I worry. I worry way too much. All these things around here. Those indigo kids. And then finding out about my Jewel Marie. That her Tiffany is indigo. I worry about that a lot. My Jewel is simple; she got talked up into the army. But that Tamina, she had everything; she had everything good. A lot of people don't notice. I notice. That girl had everything. I look around and see things. It helps sometimes to speak out. That's my nature."

Scope sighs and says, "Hey."

For some reason, Molly's speech is accepted as a kind of apology.

Everyone alters his position.

Scope, who has to reposition a large stomach, says, "Happy Dee, now, I guess, I wonder what happened there at the end with your kid. Did she go over of her own free will? I just wonder."

"No way," Sunshine says solemnly.

Beau asks, "Yeah, but did anybody see anything?"

"*Her* dad did." Sunshine is pointing at me with a small smudged index finger. "The Prof. He knows something, anyway."

I tell myself, *Oh, for God's sake, not again.* Every time we're in a life-or-death crisis, people credit my father with special knowledge. And maybe he does have special knowledge. He thinks he does. Oh God, I hope he hasn't been talking.

As if he knows things that he himself isn't sure of.

"He doesn't," I say. "He doesn't know anything. He's an old gentleman who still tries to read books."

"He knows something." Sunshine tips her chin back; she's not letting go of this. "He was special friends with Tammy. She told him stuff."

I say firmly, "Sunshine, you aren't sure, you're just guessing, if you're a friend of Tammy's and a friend of mine and a friend of my dad's, and you say you are . . ." I stop to get a breath and reload. "Then," I pick up, "you'll stop spreading fantasies, because that's what you're doing."

Sunshine gasps. "Fantasies?" She makes the word sound dirty. Maybe she has it confused with heresies. Or terrorist activities. "Oh, my God, of course not."

Molly doesn't look like the type to get abashed, but maybe she was abashed anyhow a minute ago, because she now speaks up for the first time in a while. "You think he wasn't up on the Rock? Sure he was there. I saw him. Like I said, I observe. When I know a thing is so or when I see a truth, well, I just got to say so. And that old professor gentleman was up on that Rock and for sure he was around to see something.

"I see a lot that people don't know I see," she adds, looking pleased.

Beau says, "Well, there's somebody else that knows, more than the Professor does. Arby knows."

"Arby? No, not Arby?" That's Sunshine, sounding horrified, at the same time that Scope inquires, "What happened to Arby? He fell off his bike?" and Happy Dawn says, "That little louse."

"He went to the hospital," Beau announces. "A whole lot of people heard. I'll bet Molly here, Molly's the town Internet, I'll bet she heard. Arby was in the hospital, raving around. Like he'd had too much substance."

Happy Dawn says, "Oh, God," and buries her face in her hands.

Scope struggles to his feet, sliding his belly out of the way as he rises. He lumbers over to Happy Dawn and pats her on the shoulder. "Listen, Happy Dee, I'm giving you all my sympathy, y'got it?"

Happy Dawn is sniveling. "If you hadn't brought that Anneliese into here . . ."

"Babe, I didn't bring Anneliese no place. She showed up on my porch like a bad dream come true."

Happy Dawn is crying harder. "And if there hadn't been all that stuff about the indigo children . . ."

"That has nothing to do with anything." Scope is still patting her shoulder.

At the same time Beau rises. He tinkers for a minute with the cuffs of his blue shirt. "Correction, Happy darling," he says. "It has everything to do with everything. You all will find out."

🦅 Chapter 6

I am back at the Manor and our receptionist Rebecca has called me from Manor Reception. "Carla, there's somebody here to see you."

Her voice is edged with caution, so I ask, "What kind of somebody, Becky?" I prompt, "Male or female?"

"Oh, male."

"And?"

"Well. Young. A man."

"Oh, for God's sake." I have only five Complaints left. I shove these together and take off for the front office, where I find a male with greasy black curls and a dirty checked shirt slouched across the waist-high marble counter.

He lifts his head and he is Arby, he of the hospital confessions. And also Sunshine's motorcycle cowboy from the co-op parking lot. He looks at me flatly.

Arby has high cheekbones and might be handsome if he washed his hair and found a clean shirt.

"I need to talk," he says. "Like, I mean, to you?"

He has, of all things, a string of yellow Greek worry beads, which he is clicking around.

"Okay," I tell him. "So talk."

He gestures at Rebecca's office. "I mean. Like. Private?"

Rebecca is making faces to indicate *No*.

"Follow me," I tell Arby, who is clicking his beads. And I lead him down to my office. Actually, it's the beads that make me decide it'll be okay; he won't try to murder me.

"How are you?" I ask politely after we both get seated, I at my desk and he in the facing chair.

He says, "Well, shit," and examines his feet, which are clad in rainbow-striped flip-flops, the twins to Tamina's. Maybe this is significant or maybe the co-op store had a sale on them.

"Everything sucks," he announces.

I resist the impulse to ask, "In what way?" staring neutrally and pretending to be Dr. Melfi from *The Sopranos*.

He clicks some beads around his string. "Like first," he says, "Tam dies."

I wait during three more worry beads. "What I need to talk to you about," he says, "is, I went to the hospital when I was high and said a lot of dumb stuff and now everybody thinks I did something dumb and, well, Tam was my girlfriend, did you know that?"

I tell him, "No."

"Well," he says, "Sunshine says you're okay and you're investigating, and, well . . ."

"Arby," I say, "the doctor that saw you in the hospital—he understood that the stuff you said was a fantasy."

He interrupts me with, "Hey, yeah, okay. Right. Fantasy. I guess. I don't remember. But now. Well. Hey."

I resist a comment about pulling teeth. "Yes?"

"Now, like nobody believes anything I say."

"That will pass," I promise, trying to put an older-comfortable-woman sound into my voice.

"Yeah, but wow. I mean. Like. There are things I *want* to say."

I resist rising from my chair and going over to shake him and deliver a lecture about the importance of words. And also asking how Tamina, the Egyptian poetry fan, ever put up with him.

Then I hear the worry beads clicking faster. This kid is scared. And he's very young. Tamina was fifteen.

"Are you the baby's dad?" I ask.

He stops clicking long enough to gasp and put his head down on his hands. "Oh, God."

"And you know something you should be telling me? I'm the deputy sheriff."

He doesn't answer this. Maybe he's crying.

"It's okay. It'll be confidential." I don't add, *Unless there are criminal consequences*. I think that and keep it in reserve.

He says, "Oh, God," again.

"Well, if you do, I'm interested." I add, "I really want to know. I want to know what happened to Tamina."

"Oh, wow," he says. "Tam was so great."

After a minute's silence I offer, "My father liked her a lot."

Arby says, "Your dad. Oh, God. Your dad; I feel bad about him. I did something dumb there, too.

"Real dumb. Like, I thought it was for Tam. Know what I mean?"

"What did you do to my dad?" I ask, my voice carefully uninflected.

"And I had to do something for Tam," he continues. His eyes don't focus too well and he is certainly being spasmodic. Probably he's on some sort of upper or downer now. "Like, it was important. Like, she's a major person in my life. Tam was always there for me."

"Tell me about my father," I say, and he says, "Hey, she was a major person. Like, *major*," and I give up on my father as a subject.

"Tamina, in what way?" I ask, using my most neutral Dr. Melfi voice. But for a while there's no response, except for some hiccups.

Finally Arby raises his head. His face is tear-smudged and scowling. "Do you believe in Jesus?"

"Do I *believe* in Him?"

"Yeah, Jesus."

I revert to being my father of ten years ago. "I believe that there was a Jewish leader named Jesus."

"Sun says He can forgive all our sins."

"Arby," I say, "it will help you if you speak."

Sun, I guess, is Sunshine. These kids are awfully young.

There's a small commotion at the door. It's my father, who apparently has been on the doorsill for a while, listening. He smiles at me. "Why, darling, that sounds like the 'Admonitions of Ipuwer'; I'm so glad to hear you quoting from it; my impression is that you don't use your Egyptian knowledge enough; you know, if you don't access those stores of information . . ." He stops and surveys Arby. "Good evening, young man. I know you, and the name . . . the name will come to me in a minute. Don't tell me; you are part of the group from Amarna."

Arby stares despairingly at my father. "Oh, Jesus, Prof."

"And you were a friend of that beautiful young woman; I think her name was Ta-Ent, yes, also the name of a famous traveler across the landscapes of the dead. She talked to me and I'm sure she talked to you."

"Oh, God, no," Arby says, sounding choked. "She didn't."

"She had a great deal she was concerned about," my father continues calmly. "And she confided. That helped her to feel better. You have a nice string of worry beads there. Perhaps they are a help."

"Arby," I say, "if you want to tell me something . . ."

Suddenly this guy is angry. He clutches the beads and contracts his fists, which are large for the rest of him. "Holy shit!" he says. "I don't know nothing. Want to tell you something? Who said I know something? It was that witch Anneliese thought I knew something. And I don't."

I tell him *okay, okay*, and repeat, *Listen, I'm interested.*

My father says, "You know, you are behaving like someone who does want to talk. That is very interesting."

Arby doubles over in a slouch. He clicks the worry beads as if they're staving off an incipient vomiting attack. Finally he straightens up and says "Okay," and stands slowly and precariously, saying "Okay" some more. He gives me a dirty look. To my dad he says, "Listen, old guy, you don't know anything. But I'm real sorry for anything I done. Did. I mean to you." Then he slouches off out my door. I can hear his footsteps dragging down the hall and the worry beads clicking.

"A troubled young man," my father observes. "I wonder, did I upset him in some way?"

I am wondering the same thing about myself. Yes,

Daddy did something. He implied Arby had knowledge. Arby didn't want to have knowledge; he thought that was dangerous.

And for me, what was it? Not really agreeing on Jesus? Using the phrase *want to tell*? I think that in Arby's script you're not supposed to want to tell.

Maybe the Manor atmosphere finally got to him.

Or was he high on something that then wore off? At the end he seemed to be slightly oriented, as we say. He remembered which way to turn to get out the door.

The person I have to see now, it seems to me, is Anneliese Wertiger.

Her name keeps coming up. She's important.

Not that there aren't a lot of people who are important. But the idea of Anneliese nags at my subconscious.

I wait until the next evening. My life at the Manor has switched from my stack of Complaints to my stack of bills. Not that Complaints aren't still arriving. But I like to vary the kinds of torture.

Bills are somewhat worse than Complaints. I'm glad to climb into the Toyota and head for Stanton's Mill.

Furthermore, Susie has told me that she has a bread pudding for me after I finish with Anneliese. Susie's bread pudding is the kind you think about on a cold and stormy night.

I know that Scope and Anneliese's house is next door to Susie's, but I've never located it. It's the usual Stanton's Mill story of a dwelling being camouflaged by its greenery, which in this case is four redwood trees and a flock of juniper bushes. Just as Cherie had promised, there is a sign, quite a handsome one, offering CONSULTATION, INDIGO CONSCIOUS-NESS, SPIRITUAL MESSAGES. But the sign has to compete with the redwood tree where it hangs, and it's hard to see.

The house is a low redwood house, my favorite kind.

It has a nice wide battered porch with an overhanging roof. And here, on the roof overhang, the INDIGO CHILDREN AND SPIRITUAL CONSULTATIONS messages finally get properly advertised. There's a series of wooden signs, one after the other, across the front, in different shapes, some oblong and some scrolled, but all in wood with gold lettering. And as I'm climbing the three steps to the porch, a final sign blasts on. It snaps to life above, just for me. It is neon, it is purple, and it makes the usual neon insect noise. INDIGO SPIRITUAL HERE, it says. Its searing light stains the whole porch and goes on and off, to dizzying effect.

The woman who stands in the half-open door is probably Anneliese. It's hard to be sure what she looks like, with the purple light barrage. But I can tell she's tall and thin and doesn't resemble the Anneliese I've been imagining, which would be another fat lady in a shift. This woman waits for a while and leans against the door for a while. I think she is staring appraisingly at me.

There are lights on inside the house; I can see through the uncurtained windows to a wood-paneled room with bookcases and more signs, some in sparkle-highlighted script; they talk about CONSCIOUSNESS, LOVE, FEELING, THE TRUE YOU. There are Peruvian blankets and things hanging from the ceiling.

*   *   *

The woman shifts slightly. "Why are you here?"

"Whoa," I say. "How about, 'Hi. How are you?'"

Silence. This lady is not into chumminess.

"Or," I add, "you could try, 'My name's Anneliese. Who're you?'"

She keeps her face in shadow. "I *know* who you are."

"I'm just a fellow traveler, Anneliese. Just another innocent human being." I'm getting slightly drunk from the purple neon, which keeps right on jumping. "Just asking my way around the topography."

"Bullshit."

A justified remark. To my surprise, she stays in the half-open door. She doesn't slam it in my face, which maybe shows a desire to keep communications open.

"My name," I announce placatingly, "is Carla Day and I'm the deputy sheriff. I've got some questions connected with the death of Tamina Kerry."

Anneliese waits some more and pushes the door a fraction more closed.

I put my foot in the door gap. "Where is Tamina's baby?"

"What makes you think Tamina had a baby?"

This really gets to me; it seems like the ultimate in the many Stanton's Mill reversions and contradictions. "What in hell do you mean?" I hear my voice getting squeaky.

Anneliese lifts her shoulders. I think she smiles. "You don't know *anything*, do you?"

I take several deep breaths. My foot is blocking the door, so we're partly stalemated.

"You don't know anything at all. You're a babe in the woods."

"Guess what?" I say. "We've gotten off to a bad start. You're right. As yet, I'm uninformed. But I'll *get* informed." Some people respond cannibalistically to the modest approach (which is the way I would react) and some other people love it. Anneliese apparently veers toward this latter group. Everything about her relaxes fractionally, including her hold on the door.

She steps back a millimeter and gives me another once-over. "Well," she says finally. "You're just going to be snooping around in the underbrush anyway. Come on in."

Inside, Anneliese is revealed as a handsome woman. She's upright and slender, with severely parted glossy dark hair, scooped back into a chignon. Maybe she's around forty; she has good skin, arched dark eyebrows, a form-fitting tan silk dress. She wears a long string of hand-carved beads. She looks like a combination between the Dragon Lady and the front cover of *Vogue*. Neither of those women ever seems friendly.

She clicks something to turn off the outside neon.

"Thank God," I say, which doesn't get a rise.

The living room, which must really be the reception room for Anneliese's business, is dominated by the indigo sparkle-printed signs and by a display of purple-covered books. The hanging objects are stars, large, paper, and purple. The Peruvian blankets also are mostly purple. The couch and chairs must belong to Scope; they're black leather.

And Scope himself appears now, preceded by some coughing from the back rooms. He slouches in, shoving one foot in front of the other as if his shoes are too big. He's mussed and frayed and his shirt is rucked up and his belly hangs out. He's out of synch in this organized purple room. "Shit," he says, pausing by the bookcase.

Anneliese pays no attention. She sits down and rests her arms on the arms of her chair, copying the pose of one of Daddy's Pharaohs.

The final item of living room decor is a framed photo, larger than life, of a sturdy man in a round black hat. He has white hair and a loose nightshirt-type garment and the kind of kohl-surrounded black eyes that seem to follow you when you move.

"So you want to know," Anneliese says, "you want to know, do I really believe in indigo babies, and how much money have I made off the idea and why do I call myself a spiritual consultant. And how old am I and what do I know about Tamina?"

I decide this is an excessively together lady. "I think you're wasting your talents here in Stanton's Mill."

"They have been richly used in Stanton's Mill."

"Are you hiding out here?"

Scope crosses the room noisily and settles down with a loud leather squeak. "You bet she is. She has an irate husband looking for her somewhere. If she were my ex, I'd be an irate husband, too."

Anneliese ignores this. "You can find everything you need to know about me on Google."

"No, I can't." Actually I haven't tried, but I feel safe denying it. "All I found on Google," I say, improvising further, "was a website with a description of your books."

"Oh, you found that?" She looks pleased.

"You wanna know if she ever killed anybody?" Scope asks. "The answer is yes."

Anneliese doesn't even bother to say, "Cut it out, Scope."

"I researched indigo babies eight years ago," she says. "When I was on the staff of a prominent mental health facility."

"Mental health?" I ask.

"A good private place. Not one of your anonymous state outfits. It had some younger patients. And there were births sometimes. It was at the appearance of the occasional unusual baby . . ."

I'm expected to prompt here, so I do. "Yes?"

Anneliese leans forward and fixes me with a piercing glare. "A baby that immediately, almost on the delivery table, one instantly recognizes."

I manage "Yes," again.

"It took many years, in that exclusive setting, for me to investigate and test . . ."

I reflect that all this will be checkable. Somewhere there must be a record that Anneliese worked for the interesting, exclusive mental health facility. And did research on babies.

"The hospital must have been very grateful to you," I say. I want her to tell me more, to say the name of the hospital.

Which she doesn't intend to do. "Yes," she agrees. "Certainly."

"And your research is written up?"

"There was a certain pattern about these births," she says, sidestepping briskly. "When they would occur. The phases of the moon. Tides. Storm systems. You're familiar with these ideas. If you've kept in touch with your father's work."

"Yes, sure," I say. Actually, the ancient Egyptians were pretty practical about this stuff. They were interested in when somebody died, not when they were born. They figured that happened nine months after impregnation.

"Oh, how I wished, after I arrived here, that I had known your father then." Anneliese sounds peculiar saying this, as if she's reciting a motto instead of talking. I look to see if she's serious and she hawk-eyes me back flatly.

"Oh, wow," says Scope. "Drama time."

"Your father is an exceptional personality," Anneliese informs me. "A divinely gifted one."

"Was he an indigo child once?" I venture.

She's scornful. "Of course not." When I don't produce a question here, she says, "Indigo babies are a recent development, a response to our particularly turbulent times. Yes, they've existed before this. But in other periods of enormous need. Your father was born at a quiet time."

"The end of World War I," I remind her.

She's unfazed. "Exactly. The end of that war. With the world entering a period of prosperity."

I contemplate a short history lesson about impending bank failure, the Depression, world unemployment, and the rise of Hitler, and decide against it. I say, "Yes," again. Then I pick up her topic. "You were a psychiatrist at a mental hospital. Was it Langley Porter . . ."

She looks at me sharply. Maybe it's the word *psychiatrist*. Maybe she did something else less prestigious. Maybe she doesn't like Langley Porter. She simply says, "No," and waits a little while. Then she picks up. "And when I left that setting . . ."

I make a mental note to check up on her in a whole lot of records. Names of hospitals. Publications about babies. Lists, lists.

"So when I left, I decided to make the indigo children my life's work. And the first baby I identified led me on a wonderful path that ended here."

"Aha," says Scope.

"Who was that?" I ask.

"The child is no longer at Stanton's Mill. These children find other destinies."

I say out loud what I've been thinking: "You certainly are sure of yourself." What I mean is, *Don't you know we're investigating the disappearance of these kids? Aren't you the tiniest bit troubled about that?*

"Michelangelo was an indigo child," Anneliese says. "So was Jesus of Nazareth. It depends on the point in history. I can draw you a chart of when they appear. There is a kind of wheel, a cycle of the crises in the world's development."

"She moved in on me," Scope says. "I met her at the bus stop in Conestoga and the next day she was on my front porch. How's that for brass?"

"You needed me," Anneliese says, untroubled. "The town needed me and still does. It has been a rewarding relationship . . . And now, Carla . . . that is your name, isn't it? Not the best possible name for you, somewhat austere and Latinate, I think your father could have done better by dipping into his Egyptian cultures . . . well, then, Carla . . ."

She's getting ready to announce that my time is up, so I squeeze in a question. "What happened to Tamina?"

"She died."

"Yes, but why? Was it related to the indigo babies?"

"Everything in the web of events is related to everything else. Now"—she is half out of her chair—"this interview has tired me and used too many of my powers. And Susie is waiting for you."

I remind myself that she knows Susie is waiting because she understands Susie, not because she has special occult knowledge.

On the way out we pass under the big talismanic photograph. I stop to appraise it. It's pretty spooky, so big and
so intense. I gesture. "Who's the rabbi?"

"He's not a rabbi but he is a spiritual leader. He is very
advanced. Very fine, very special. For a few people only. You
are not sufficiently advanced yet to understand him."

"Yeah," Scope says. "Be grateful for that."

He precedes me to the door and whispers, "Come talk to
me later," and tries to screw his face into a wink. Anneliese
is right behind him and he doesn't do the wink very well.

‌ꓶ Chapter 7

"Well, hi, stranger," Molly Kinsolving/Littlefeather greets me. "Welcome to my humble home. I sorta thought I'd be seeing more of you."

It's an accident that Molly Littlefeather is my next site of inquiry. I wanted to talk further to Happy Dawn or to Sunshine, but neither of them is home.

"Hello, Molly." Molly K/L lives in a house that I suppose you could call quaint. It has a steeply sloping roof and a sweet little brick front porch and some well-tended geraniums. Geraniums do all right here in the soggy shade of Stanton's Mill.

"C'mon in," Molly says, standing aside and waving invitingly. Inside her house, the décor is no longer especially quaint, since somebody has been busy with plasterboard and pink paint. There are paste-on moldings with a Greek key design. "I got some papaya juice," she says. "Very yummy."

Her living room has the usual Goodwill tan furniture, but spiced up with ruffled pillows. And there is an enormous poster-sized wall picture of a rustic scene involving a house and lane and distant roofs, plus a lake, mountains, drifting smoke from chimneys. The space over the mantel is occupied by two rows of photographs.

"Well, I just knew you'd come," Molly says satisfiedly. "So you pull up a chair and set for a spell. That's what my grandma used to say."

People say things like that in movies, but I wonder if anybody's grandmother ever actually talked that way. "Why did you know I'd come?" I ask. The papaya juice is good.

"Sweetie, I have very good perceptions about people and I just knew that about you. You had that *I am interested in that lady* look. A lot of people react to me that way. And you look like you need to poke into things."

"Why did you change your name to Littlefeather?" I ask, not pausing for this. Molly seems to rejoice in her bluntness, so I guess I can be blunt in return.

"Hey, dear, Kinsolving—well, in addition to not being the most musical name in the world, it went with a guy that, he and me had decided to not be together anymore. And Littlefeather is real sweet." She sips her drink. "Good, huh?"

"Delicious. And—"

"So how long have you been a deputy sheriff?" Molly interrupts me.

"How long have you lived in Stanton's Mill?" I ask, very fast. Molly tries to grab an interview out from under you the minute you stop to breathe.

But she's perfectly happy to be urged to talk about herself. "Ten years. It was the Kinsolving gentleman that brought me here; he was more like the rest of the people in this town—sort of flaky, you know—I'm more the straight-forward type? But I stayed on, because I got my flaky side, too, and it's been okay, pretty good years. It's always great to feel you're aiding the community.

"I'm the Avon lady here. A lot of the Mill, they like herbal and that natural face stuff and that's perfectly okay, but some of them like to smell good, and that's where I come in. My clientele keep telling me what an asset I am."

She gestures uphill in the direction of the rest of Stanton's Mill. She lives down near the creek. This means that her little house is cold but is pervaded by the soothing gentle noise of running water.

"And how does it feel to be an indigo parent?"

"Grandma, darling, just grandma. Well, if you must know, big surprise. That Jewel Marie of mine, I never knew what she'd be up to.

"Gorgeous little baby.

"And now," she adds after a pause, "Jewel is off driving a truck in I-raq. You heard about that?"

"And the baby?" I ask.

"You mean, like, where is she? Not like some of those others, they got some dim relative someplace they all of a sudden came up with, our Tiffany's in one of those baby centers and the army pays. You know? The army takes care of its own."

"So," I say after a minute's pause, "do you still think some of the babies disappeared?"

"Well, dear, I don't know. I'm not ready to say I was all wrong. This is a funny place here, this Stanton's Mill. I know about my little grandkid, my Tiffany, I know where she is. But some of these others? Now there I'm not so sure.

"But we talked enough about this. Come on, bring your drink along. I want to show you my clay sculptures."

For a minute I'm confused. I thought it was Lana in Placer County that did ceramics, but then I remember that pot making is a widespread Stanton's Mill affliction.

Molly leads the way through a bright red bedroom. She's a more inventive housekeeper than Happy Dawn; she has installed a canopy over her bed.

Beyond the bedroom is a paneled hideaway with shelves filled with painted clay objects. I stare for a minute and realize that all of them came from prefabricated molds. There are sets of toadstools. A family of pigs. Gnomes on one shelf, rabbits on another. And a squadron of angels circles the room on the top shelf.

Molly surveys from the doorway. "Good, huh?

"I had to send around to get different kinds," she explains. "Categories. I like to group them together. Almost every mold company makes angels, but not everybody makes pigs."

I compliment her on the colors. She has been inventive with colors and also with designs. The larger animals are embellished with stars and curlicues. "Does . . ." I start out. I want to ask what the rest of the Mill thinks of this kind of art, but I'm not sure how to put it. I'm pretty sure molds would be disapproved of here.

But she guesses where I'm headed. She shrugs. "Y'know what? Those people you were with last night? Most of them don't like my work.

"They think they know about art and they don't, not even that Anneliese. I mean, I went to a celebration at her place. I think she called it a ritual. She invited me after she identified little Tiffany.

"And I got to admit, it was real impressive. They had the room darkened, with purple curtains. And this chanting and this guy she talked about afterward; she said he was her guru. He was tall and weird but there was something about him—I don't know—I thought maybe I knew him. And a lot of that singing and some kind of a drum. And then there was another guy—at least I think there was; it was hard to be sure. Actually, it was weird but it was real interesting; that Anneliese is real talented. She can put on a show, know what I mean?"

"You noticed about Tamina's baby . . ." I start out, wondering how I'm going to tie this inquiry into the rest of the conversation.

But with Molly, sequence doesn't matter.

"Yeah. Tamina. Now, she for sure could paint, know what I mean? But about her baby. Everybody jumped on me. Called me a busybody. That's what they say around here when you notice things. And all I did was call Cherie and say, first there was this cute little baby. And then there wasn't.

"Went off to visit its grandma or its auntie or something, they said. Well, nobody around here ever heard of a grandma before that. But then, afterward, well, I guess I was wrong.

"So what the hell. That's what you get for being civic-minded."

"You didn't believe it about Tamina's grandmother."

Molly shrugs elaborately. "Listen, dear, I know it from Morrie—that was Mr. Kinsolving that I used to be married to—some of these people lead real unstable lives. I guess she had a grandma. I guess that's it."

"And what about Lana?" I ask.

"Lana? Oh, well. She went off to Placer County. I was real

friendly with Lana for a while. She and I went to that indigo
ceremony together and the guru told us about the great indigo age and how we will all be saved and will be different.
Nobody poor, or owing taxes, or invading Iraq, or any of
that stuff. It was real impressive. And then Lana moved to
Placer County and I haven't seen her, even though I thought
we were kind of friendly, know what I mean? And . . ." A gesture has revealed her wristwatch; she stops to survey it. "Listen, dear, this has been great; I have really liked talking to
you, but I got this appointment; I was so fascinated talking to
you, I let time slip by. I gotta get to Conestoga. I got a date
there. I got a date with a friend." Molly presents this with sat-
isfaction.

She is steering me toward the door. "Yeah," she says.
"And listen, dear, you know, the thing about me? I'm real
good at noticing stuff. Other people don't notice so much,
but I do. And I really don't see why some people should
make money off something and other people not, know
what I mean? Like, make a whole lot of money off something that just sorta happened to them?"

I would like to ask Molly what she means, but she is con-
ducting me very firmly toward the door. "It was real nice to
meet you and I'll look forward to doing it again. They do a
lot of talk about spiritual values around here. Well, it's a
help to meet someone that doesn't keep criticizing my spiritual values, know what I mean?"

Chapter 8

I have conferred with Susie about whether my dad should
go to Tamina's memorial, and Susie is amazed. "Carla, darling, of course your father should go. Death is an integral
part of life; he knows that."

"Yes, but will it upset him?" To which she points out
that he is much tougher than I am about Integral Facts.
"You're the one that gets off your trolley," is the unflattering
way she puts it.

So Daddy, happily expectant, is sitting beside me as we
drive to Tamina's memorial. It is a beautiful northern California morning, the fog just worn off, the sun beginning to
burn hot, the roadside growth still green from a late heavy
rain. Daddy has the car window open; he inhales deeply.
"Today we are going to help her start on her soul's journey,"
he says. "Don't you think that's what we're doing, Carla?"

"That sounds good."

"It's unusual to make a ceremony of it so early in the afterlife, though. This will be something new."

I tell him I thought a ceremony was what they usually did, a big parade with mourners, and he corrects me, "Oh, daughter, no. You've forgotten. That's much later, after the body is prepared. Mummified." Daddy makes a huffing noise; he gets upset when he thinks I've forgotten my Egyptian facts.

"She was interested in all that," I say in a pacifying voice. "Tamina was. Interested in Egypt."

"Oh, yes. Oh, very. She read a lot. Wanted to be something. A priestess, perhaps it was? Or maybe a chantress, does that sound right? Or possibly a psychologist. They did not exactly have psychologists in ancient Egypt, although I guess you could call a priest who was willing to treat the mind . . . I must check on that . . . I think I could check at home in that red book . . ."

My wandering dad is starting to wander off the chart; I try to lure him back. "And she learned some of the Egyptian poetry. Ta-Ent did."

"Poetry? Oh, yes. Quite a bit. Protection, you know. Some of it is protection against monsters and terrors. Monsters, you know, that pursue your knowledge. She needed protection."

We're almost at Conestoga. I pull over to the side of the road; maybe *monsters* will be an opening for my other, heavier questions. Did Tamina know something that could have gotten her pushed off a cliff?

"Why are we stopped?" he asks in alarm, and I say, inspired, "Jelly Bellies," producing a bag from the glove compartment. "What kind of monsters was she afraid of, Daddy?"

He's solemn, fussing with the plastic package. "The usual ones."

"Like what?"

"They exist in the afterlife. The jackal. She was especially afraid of the jackal."

"A jackal?"

"A sort of small slinky dog. He is usually the judge, but this time he's the keeper of secrets."

"And that's a danger the soul must pass—the keeper of secrets?" My father thinks I don't remember the *Book of the Dead*, but actually I remember it pretty well, and this idea is new to me.

He assumes a spectral voice, which means he's quoting: " 'Oh, you dark one, you of the damaged face, you shielder of secrets, surrender your sacred care and let me by.' "

I tell him I don't remember this passage, and he says, "*She* wrote it."

"Tamina wrote it?"

"She was very talented."

"Yes, I'm learning that." I start the car, trying to fill in my picture of the clean-profiled blond child. *Shielder of secrets, surrender your sacred care.* Pretty good stuff. And *damaged face* is suggestive. Strange but sophisticated. Could I do that at fifteen? I simply can't remember.

I guess I could. At fifteen I was actually in Egypt. With Daddy and Rob. Daddy and Rob dug and I made lists of artifacts.

"So she thought she would have to pass a shielder of secrets in the afterlife."

My father crinkles paper. "I think it was in this life. A danger in this life. That's what she had the *djed* symbol for. You know that I gave her a *djed* symbol."

I think. Yes, of course, the little blue item that looks like a tree with crosspieces.

"In this life? Why in this life?" I hear my voice get too interested, and know this will scare him off.

Which is what happens. He moves a fraction away from me on the car seat. "I have no idea, not any, you know. I am not good at these things; I cannot talk about it; that material is dangerous, really dangerous. It would hurt someone dear to me. Carla, I am not good at these things. I used to be good at them. When I was at Thebes, I could have told you . . . Oh, how I wish we could go to Thebes again."

"Sweetheart, so do I."

Here's a lesson for you, Carla: don't push, I caution myself. Not with him or with anybody.

I wait a minute while both of us recover. I feel better, and when I look at him, he seems to be better, too; he's industriously eating Jelly Bellies.

We climb the hill into Stanton's Mill with me irritatedly trying to speed, which isn't possible on that incline.

Of course there are no parking places left in the co-op parking lot and we have to park down at Susie's and climb the hill on foot, with my dad being cheerful and me being distracted. A lot of things are happening, and I'm apprehensive about this memorial, which is bound to get emotive.

The meeting hall is jammed, but apparently there are seats for my dad, who is treated like a favorite; several people hail him and point. He proceeds across the room, shepherding my by one arm. "They call me Prof," he says. "I am popular here."

I don't remind him that someone from here threw a rock at him, even though that's on my Urgent list.

The hall is decorated almost festively. There are boughs of greenery and heaps of passion flower and wild mustard and a cluster of orange candles arranged like an arched cathedral window. An argument is now happening about these candles: "Hey, for God's sake, you never heard of fire laws? You don't believe in fire?" The protester is Beau La Roche, resplendent in a white suit. The candlelighter apparently is Happy Dawn, who is crying. Beau puts his arm around her. The candles are snuffed.

An enormous photo of Tamina, holding a sheaf of lavender and with the wind fluffing her hair, occupies center stage of the small platform. Surrounding it is more greenery and a lot more passion flower and a little pile-up of objects like teddy bears and jars of jam and a few blue things, which I identify as Egyptian statuettes. I'm too far away to be sure, but I think they are the figures called *shabhti*, servants buried with the dead.

I look around the hall. Folding chairs sit more or less in rows. We're in the second row; behind us are several familiar faces. Susie, three rows back, gestures and mouths words and looks affectionate. Cherie, in a dark green suit and buttercup yellow shirt, blows a kiss. My friend from the Manor, the elegant Mrs. La Salle, sits beside Cherie, which surprises me. She's a writer; maybe she senses a story. Molly Littlefeather, attired in a dark blue embroidered smock, waves enthusiastically. Scope, farther back in the hall, stares stolidly. Anneliese Wertiger stands at the back, erect and alone. Perhaps there's no one she wants to sit with.

The building vibrates with the noise of a lot of people talking at once.

On the platform Arby dangles his legs over the edge and twangs at a guitar; some chords drift by, maybe "You Can't Always Get What You Want." Sunshine, beside him, opens her mouth as if she's singing, and then stops to bury her face in Arby's shoulder.

The piled-up noise gets worse.

Finally Beau climbs to the platform and positions himself beside Tamina's photo. "Hello," he says at the crowd. He has a mike on his collar. "Hello." The meeting room quiets slowly; finally just a few voices are left, plus one burst of laughter.

My dad reaches and takes my hand. I must be sending out nervous signals. Daddy is good at picking up stuff like that.

There's a commotion in our row. Someone is pushing; I look along the row and see that it's Rob. He negotiates the whole line of chairs and manages to wedge in next to me, using half of the same chair. "Hi." His hand squeezes under my hand.

I don't know how I feel about this.

"You think," I whisper, "you can shove back into my life?"

He whispers, "Oh, God, can I?"

People tell us to shut up. I let the hands stay the way they are.

Beau is saying this is a sad occasion and the community has lost something precious. He invites anybody with a remembrance of the brilliant child we have lost to talk about her. Talk freely. Beau usually sounds ironic and maybe he still does, but not much.

The speeches that follow aren't at all original, but they're heart-wrenching just the same. People stand awkwardly in front of their chairs and try to talk. Some can manage only a few words before they have to stop. Arby tries to sing, but can't. Sunshine reads a poem in which *soul* rhymes with *goal* and *gone* rhymes with *dawn*. She gets through three verses of this in spite of a shaky voice, and says at the end, "Tammy never jumped; she wouldn't; she was a real good poet; she would of hung around to tell me this poem is terrible," and then she bends over, saying, "Oh my God, oh my God."

Silence follows; Sunshine has been the first person to refer to the cliff edge. Finally there's a disturbance at the back of the room, someone moving and talking; the sound of footsteps purposely proceeding forward.

It's Anneliese. "Friends," she says. "My good friends."

She gets the room's attention and moves along the aisle to mount the platform, chin up, shoulders back.

In a clear, carrying voice, she projects, "Hello, dear friends. Let's not dwell on the negative; let's discuss the positive." She allows a second's pause. "What a beautiful gift she was. What a luminous young intelligence. How well I knew her, with her vivid interest in the indigo. She spoke to me about the value of indigo consciousness and the special role it can fill in the emerging world. She was an inspiration, a true motivation. Let me give you all an example of her role here in Stanton's Mill . . .

"Tamina used her marvelous energy to help people," Anneliese continues. "Conestoga Library, Del Oro County Senior Center, you name it, they called her Bright Light. She had a charming illustrative story about a sparrow lying on its back in the middle of the road, feet in the air. Asked why, it said it heard the sky was going to fall. 'Oh, and your spindly legs will hold it up?' 'Well,' the sparrow said, 'one does what one can.' "

Anneliese's other stories about Tamina are well told and circumstantial. Some of them strike me, even in this solemn moment, as a little improbable, and I wonder if she's been consulting an anecdote book. But hell, we all do that when we have to make a speech. I certainly did it when I was working for Habitat.

She finishes with a smile for Beau and a smile for the audience. "Now," she says, "we don't know what happened, do we? Whether there was a terrible accident or whether Tamina decided to take her future in her own hands? She was a strong, vibrant personality. And liked to make her own decisions. Many gifted people have done that. She was an artist, a true artist, but she was very young. And she had given us so much. Let's take a minute to think about her." Anneliese stands for a while, hands folded, head down. She is wearing a simple black dress. It fits nicely, accentuating her small, shapely bosom.

The hall is silent except for the squeak of chairs being adjusted and the grating of several throat clearings. Finally Anneliese lifts her head and draws her breath in loudly. "She was with us then," she announces in a low, carrying voice. "Didn't you feel her? Tamina? With all her power and energy and love? The wonderful mother of a wonderful indigo child? I felt her." Anneliese tilts her head and stares up.

She waits a minute until the rustles and chair squeaks start again. Then, scooping her black skirt behind her, she gracefully descends the stairs, pauses at the bottom for a second appraisal, and proceeds slowly to the back of the hall.

There's a long silence. A voice behind me says, "Wow."
Another voice says, "Real cool." Maybe I'm imagining that
somewhere in my row a mutter happens. "Stuck-up bitch."

Arby still sits, hunched like a pelican, on the edge of the
platform. His elbows are bent, his head bowed, his hair in
his eyes. Suddenly he yells out, "No," and slams a hand
against his guitar. He climbs to his feet.

"She wouldn't," he says loudly. By this time everyone is
watching him. "I mean, she wouldn't." He thumps at the
guitar belly. "I mean, on this cliff-jumping thing. She
wouldn't of jumped off. She knew better. She knew different." He is stopped by calls of "Right on," "Okay," "Yeah,
man," and only one of, "Hey, cool it."

He's still standing, looking unable to sit down, when
Happy Dawn captures the stage by clambering the three
steps up to it. She wears a long white dress with an embroidered blue cape; high-heeled blue sandals show as she
climbs, her ostrich feather curves over one ear. She reaches
the platform and turns, wobbling, as if she's not used to
high heels. Beau, still on the stage, steadies her for a minute,
then unclips his mike and hands it over.

She holds the mike in her hand and stares vaguely down;
Beau clips it to her dress. He kisses her on the cheek.

"What I mean is," Happy Dawn begins. She looks as
though she may cry. But she doesn't. "I mean." Her voice gets
louder. "Did you all know what a brain my Tammy was? Her
dad was a real smart college professor, and that's what it was."

Oh, hell, I tell myself; here's the third opinion on who
Tamina's father was. When I tune back in, Happy Dawn is
talking about genetics. "And she showed it real early. I
mean, that that brilliant man was her dad and she got his

genes. You all know the story about the chess game, how
Tammy used to go down to the co-op to watch them play
chess, and when she asked if she could play, they just
thought she was a cute baby-child and said, 'Why sure,
baby girl, why not?' because she was only six. And it
turned out she knew how. Just from having watched those
guys at the co-op, she knew how. She could play chess and
real soon she could beat everybody. She was perfect at it.
She was too perfect; she knew that; she was too perfect at
everything; she knew it wasn't a good idea to be so perfect, and when she got older, she pretended to be just ordinary. She told me being ordinary was the best cover-up.
But she wasn't. She never was ordinary. Maybe you all
didn't know. Underneath she was always this superbril-
liant person that never fit in. She was an artist, a real
artist; she painted, did you all know that? And she wrote.
I guess everybody knew that. She wrote poems and she
wrote plays. She finished school real, real early. Just fifteen, think of that. She loved the idea of all the stuff she
could do. She wouldn't have gone off that cliff. She valued
herself. I mean, Tamina. Really.

"She liked to scare people because she got mad at how
dumb the world was. That's why she wobbled around on the
cliff. She went there to talk to people and she wanted to
scare that dumb world. She would never, never have gone
over. She knew a lot of things people didn't think she knew.
She kept telling me about how much she knew. Lots of
things.

"Like she knew somebody wanted to hurt her. She told
me about it; she was afraid of someone.

"It was because she was smart that it happened."

Happy Dawn puts both hands in front of her face, she begins rocking back and forth; her feather, partly dislodged, gets caught in her sleeve. "Oh, God, she was so wonderful. And some bastard pushed her. She didn't go off that cliff all by herself. I swear to God, she was pushed."

♈ Chapter 9

Cherie catches up with me in the co-op parking lot. She puts an arm around my neck in an affectionate semistranglehold. "Well, lover girl, what are you going to do about all this?"

"I'm chasing it. I've got hold of a whole lot of strings. But it's like that thing we used to make in school, cat's cradle, was it? Which string do you pull?

"I wish I'd known her," I add. "Tamina."

Cherie squeezes, her gesture halfway between an embrace and a choke. "Baby, me, too . . . Well, I got total faith in you, darlin'."

My father, holding my arm on the other side, speaks across me to Cherie. "Aren't you going to kiss me?" Which she does. A big smack on the cheek. "Crocodile," she says—they're mashing me between them—"you always make me feel better. You smell of peppermint."

"Peppermint Jelly Bellies. Would you like one?"

The crowd in the parking lot is milling back and forth, bumping into each other, looking somber and talking loudly. A lot of remarks float by about, "Wow," and "Hard. Real hard," and "Yeah, something bad, for sure. Right?"

Cherie moves her arm from my neck and reaches for my hand. With Daddy at my arm, we make a cozy triptych.

"We'll go down to Susie's," she announces.

Susie, who has pulled up behind us, chimes in, saying that she has a warm coffee cake. "And of course, I'm expecting you. You're coming."

"Sure we will, sure we will," Cherie agrees. And then, I think, she tries to line us up in a row. I'm not quite sure why she's doing it, because it's at this point it happens.

Subconsciously I've been waiting for something to happen.

Something bad.

Well, at first nothing really occurs except that there's a piercing soprano scream. One of those screams that the newsreels let us hear when they're doing the sounds from the latest massacre in a current war zone. No words, just powerful volume, ululation, horror, protest.

Action on the parking lot stops. Just for a minute. Then everybody turns and babbles. People push. More screaming happens, not as loud. People start running.

That first noise came from behind us. And the person screaming apparently is Sunshine. She is bent over now with her hair in her eyes and her mouth still open and her hand on her chest. Her other hand clutches a corner of the shirt of someone who is collapsed on the tarmac.

The person on the ground is Arby. The shirt that Sunshine is grasping is partly blue. The rest of it is red. Apparently

Arby is bleeding. He must be bleeding a great deal. His collar is soaked red and so is his shirt and the top part of his pants. Blood is coming out onto the ground to form a dark stain under him.

"Je-sus," says Cherie. "My God." She stops holding my hand. She pulls out her gun, which I guess was in the pocket of her pantsuit.

My own gun is in my waistband, where I've been told to keep it. I don't pull it out. As I've said, I don't like guns.

Cherie grabs me with her other hand and pulls me back to where Sunshine and Arby are. "Let go of him, Sun," she commands.

Sunshine is gasping and hyperventilating; maybe she can't let go.

"Just let go, sweetheart." Cherie kneels down beside Arby.

Arby is lying facedown. When Cherie turns him over, I discover that he has had his throat cut.

If it didn't sound like an inherently ridiculous observation, I'd say that he'd had his throat cut neatly. In a straight line with no jagged wavering. It's possible to see this because his throat gaps and he has bled an enormous amount. The front of his shirt is drenched and there is a big crimson pond sinking into the wood chip and gravel surface of the walk. One hand is caught under him, and that is dyed red, as if he's wearing a red glove.

He must have been hit from behind, I sort of half think. I'm not really thinking much.

Cherie puts her gun back in her pocket and drags off her neck scarf. She jams this into Arby's throat, somewhere near where the wound is.

I have wrenched out my cell phone and am calling 911. "Tell them fast," Cherie says. "Ask for real fast. And a blood support. Say it hit an artery." She leans over and tries to push her hand in against his throat next to the scarf. "God.

"Nobody leaves," she says up at me.

I pick this up with an announcement: "Nobody is to go. Everybody stays where they are. Sit down, all of you. Just sit down on the ground and wait."

A few people do this. I have an inappropriate thought that, for once, the Stanton's Mill terrain isn't sopping wet.

But of course, I also think, it's too late. Too late to tell people to stay, because some of them, who's to say how many, have already disappeared. The parking lot was too crowded for driving, but you could easily slope away on foot into the underbrush.

I have a minute, while I stand staring severely at the populace of Stanton's Mill—some sitting on the ground and some not, some complaining and asking what happened and wanting to know who in hell am I to tell them what to do, and all the other things they're saying—I have a minute to think that this isn't what I expected. Or sort of expected. It's seems awful to remember, but during the memorial I was feeling that something more was certain to happen. I didn't think *murder*, I just thought *something*. And I was wondering whom it would happen to. I had picked Happy Dawn as a candidate. And from an entirely different standpoint, Anneliese seemed a possibility. I didn't think about Arby.

"I'm the sheriff's deputy," I say loudly at the crowd.

"Is he going to make it?" I ask Cherie.

She looks down. I can tell from the way her body is braced that she's pushing at his throat hard.

* * *

The ambulance crew arrives, the same crew as when Tamina went over the edge, four kids looking frazzled. The head one says, "Jesus Christ." They set up an intravenous stand. They take turns kneeling over Arby and adjusting and poking tubes and getting spattered and saying to each other, "Hey, is that intravenous flow working?"

I have my hands full with Sunshine. I have given up trying to police the other populace of Stanton's Mill and I just work on her. "Bend over," I tell her, then, "Lie down," then, "Take deep breaths, Sun; can you do that—try real hard."

Sunshine clutches me spasmodically, but mostly she just shakes. Finally, with her teeth chattering as if she's been stored in ice water, she asks for my dad. "Please. Tell the Prof. To come." She does this three times. At first I don't understand.

So my dad, who is right behind me, arm in arm with Susie, comes and sits on the ground next to her and puts a hand on her shoulder. He remembers her name. He says, "Sunshine."

"My dear," he says. Sunshine leans against his knee and shakes.

The ambulance crew is considerate and doesn't pull a black covering over Arby's face. I look at him before they take him off and he is very pale, lying on his back, face toward the sky, his throat and shirt soaked red but his face almost clear except for some red spatters. He looks about twelve.

You had something you wanted to tell me the other day, I think at him. *I should have found out. I should have been a better interviewer.*

I try to remember back over our conversation, but don't find any clues.

Then I try to think ahead for what I'm going to have to do.

When Sunshine feels better—if she feels better—I'll have to find out what she knows. Because Sunshine knows something. One of the answers as to why Tamina died or whether any babies are missing. My dad also knows something, probably the same things as Sunshine.

He speaks up now from where he is sitting beside Sunshine. "Yes," he says, looking at me; maybe he can read my face. "Yes, dear, I have trouble. Trouble with my memory. But I can help here. I am needed. I should stay in this town. Being here will jog my memory. And I can help. I was supposed to help little Ta-Ent. I know you will want me to leave, but I'm needed."

I stroke his shoulder and decide we'll argue about this later.

"Can you guys leave me some pills?" I ask the head paramedic. And this fellow, a skinny weathered youngster, gives me a straight-out stare and then produces a small bottle.

I look at Cherie, who looks awful. Blood is splashed on her yellow blouse and on the cuffs where they hang out of her jacket sleeves; you can't see blood on the dark green jacket. She has a red smudge in her short blond hair. She catches my eye and makes a kissing mouth to signal sympathy. I send the same signal back. The two of us have a bundle of work ahead of us.

I tell Sunshine I'll drive her home. I kiss my dad and send him off with Susie.

I've known all this time that Sunshine lived in Stanton's Mill but I never wondered about what kind of a house she had. For me, she was just a sweet kid who showed up at the Manor occasionally to help out. But tonight I discover that Sunshine lives in a shack. Not even a white-painted shack, the way most shacks are at the Mill. Hers is an unpainted weather-beaten wooden one with a lot of rust stains.

Two minutes of knocking on the door produces a woman in jeans with a bandanna scarf tied around her breasts. It's chilly for this outfit, and it looks accidental, as if she hasn't finished getting dressed.

She stares at me, blinking. At first I think she's drunk, and then, after I wait a few minutes, I decide maybe not. Some people have that squinty, questioning look because life has been consistently mean to them.

She's nothing like Sunshine, I think at first. And then right away I amend my opinion, Yeah, sure she's like Sunshine, just give Sun twenty years of the same bad breaks.

"Sunshine has had an awful experience," I say, and the woman stares.

I try shock methods. "Arby was killed." I'm assuming she knows who Arby is.

Her face closes up.

I say, "Are you Sunshine's mother? I've got to put her to bed," and she says, "Unh," so I shove past her over an uneven door lintel, and into the house. The front room has a rucked-up shag rug and two wicker chairs that have lost their legs and have bricks holding them up. Open food cartons marinate on a table. Sunshine's mother, since I guess that's who this is, follows, saying, "He died?" The news has just worked down to her receptors.

"Where is Sunshine's room?" I ask forcefully, and she points.

Sunshine's room is a closet that she has tried to fix up.

There is an Indian bedspread and a stuffed monkey and a
Bono poster. I drag Sunny into her cubicle and ask her
where I can get a glass of water. I force a couple of my pills
that the paramedic gave me into her. She says she has to
have her pajamas, which I find, and then she says she needs
her polar bear, which is under the pillow. In bed, she has a
session of shaking. "Hold that bear hard," I tell her.

Finally her eyelids half close. I put an extra pill on a table
with the water.

"You've got to listen for her," I say to her mother, who is
in the other room. At first I think she hasn't heard. Then I
decide she doesn't want to hear. But finally she looks up at
me, and her eyes, gray like Sunshine's, are red-rimmed and
full of water. Her face is wet. She says, "Oh, God, oh, God."
After a minute she asks, "Why is life so goddamn awful?"

I have one more pill, which I was saving for myself, but I
leave it with Sunshine's mother. I tell her to take it and get
into bed right away.

I decide I'll call Susie and ask her to check on both of
them in a couple of hours.

Back at the Manor I discover that I wouldn't have needed
my knockout pill anyway, because Rob is waiting with a
bottle of brandy.

He says, "I figured you could use it." He has already
poured me a toothbrush-type glassful. He says the news of
the knifing was all over the hospital.

I discover that I'm glad Rob has brought me a bottle of
brandy.

He asks, "Are you okay?"

I tell him Sunshine's mother wanted to know why life

was so goddamn awful and I couldn't tell her anything. "Not even, 'Maybe it will get better,' or 'Write down your feelings.' Nada."

Rob just says, "Yeah."

"So what good are people for each other if they can't do anything at all?"

"Listen," he says, "that kid—Arby? I really don't think he pushed her. You know, he sort of said he did. And then he changed his story and thought he didn't. He said, 'What's the matter with me, am I crazy?' And then he said, 'I was supposed to help her. There was something—something she had to'—here he got all confused—'something she had to,' and he apparently couldn't think of the word; he kept saying 'restitute' and then saying 'no, no, that's not right.' 'She'd found something wrong, terribly wrong,' he said, 'I was going to help her.'

"Here he got really confused. I guess I should have been taking notes, but I didn't realize at the time."

"Of course not," I say. "You didn't know how serious it was going to be. That there would be a death. That Tamina would die."

"And then Arby said, 'The Prof was supposed to help.' The Prof is your father; I guess you know. 'But,' he said, 'the Prof isn't so . . .' And then he got sidetracked. Maybe he wanted a word like *coherent* or *organized*. 'But I didn't help,' he started up again. 'And if I had helped, I didn't do anything. And she was counting on me to . . .' And he got off into, 'It's all my fault; I could have stopped it.'

"And he kept saying, over and over, 'It was my fault. My fault they killed her. I sent her over that edge.'

" 'I was the one that did it.' But of course he didn't mean that."

Rob and I are in the Manor library. Around us are the redwood shelves and the rows of old, mostly green-bound books. Some of these books are matched sets and some are haphazard. We're sitting on the floor; there is a Tiffany-type lamp on the table above us. I say, "What's this about my dad, Rob?"

"I'm not sure. He was involved in some way. Knew something."

"Jesus, why does that always happen? Any mess that comes by they try to pull my father in, too."

"You dad has that receptive atmosphere. People want to think he can help."

I'm silent, thinking. "And this is such a sad sort of case. It's my first case as a deputy sheriff, you realize that?"

"A part-time deputy." Rob sounds a little as if the title irks him.

"Don't knock it. Ten-fifty an hour. But the *case*. The case is so sad. Indigo babies. And then fifteen-year-old babies that have them. And worry about them. And get killed."

There's a silence while I stare into my brandy and suppress the impulse to drink it down, glub, glub, the desert traveler staggering into the oasis.

"So," I finally resume in a measured voice, "my father. I guess he's in danger."

"I guess so. With this and the rock in the head."

Have I really been not thinking about that rock? "He's supposed to know something and Arby was supposed to know something and Arby got knifed?" I put my brandy glass down on the rug and say, "Shit.

"And they think my dad can remember," I go on. "When he can't remember what he had for breakfast. Maybe he should wear a sign around his neck: TOTALLY UNRELIABLE."

"Carla. I'm so sorry."

"I ought to send him safely away," I say. "He's started talking about how he has to stay in Stanton's Mill. He can help. He's needed.

"That idea of being needed is important to him.

"He hates not having a job. Not being Dr. Edward Day. He hates not remembering. Sometimes he knows about the Alzheimer's or senility or whatever it is and gets depressed and it gets worse. And then he's better when he decides he has a duty.

"Damn," I say. "Damn, damn."

We're silent. Staying with Susie is not being "safely away." Susie is all love and emotion and feeling and doesn't understand danger.

We both have more brandy and leave some nice round bleached rings on Belle's good furniture.

The reason we're careless about the furniture is that we now start lying on the rug and being affectionate. The Manor has thick Oriental rugs that get vacuumed with good-smelling powder, and it feels good to be cuddled and stroked and squeezed into the rug pile and told by Rob that he always loved me, that Cherie was only a passing aberration. I am too tired and drunk to tease him about the word *aberration*; I kiss him back. He's a good kisser. Yes, he's very good; he's always been very good, and I would do something more about that if I weren't so sleepy I can hardly keep my eyes open.

"Oh, my God," I say, "oh, Rob; I forgive you for that whole mess." And then I fall asleep.

Later that evening, when I have awakened and staggered up to my own room, I remember saying that and decide it isn't really accurate. But I'm not sorry I said it.

⌋ Chapter 10

My dad is still at Susie's. I tell him he has to come back to
the Manor with me; he has to come back tonight. Stanton's
Mill is not safe, I say. Lethal things are happening here.
Arby got murdered. Tamina was murdered.

"Yes, I think she was," my father agrees.

And he had a rock thrown at him. A rock with an ugly
destructive message.

"The rock was Arby," he says.

I stare at him. "How do you know?"

"It was revealed to me, dear."

"But, Daddy," I start to say, " 'revealed to me' is not good
enough." And then I think about it. Well, yes, Arby in that
encounter in my office was saying something like that.
Maybe a scrambled message that went, "I threw a rock at
you, Prof, and I'm sorry." Maybe he was telling my dad that
he had leveled an antagonistic act at him. He regretted it.

"That's still unsatisfactory." My words also sound that way. Unsatisfactory.

Daddy looks at me. He is sitting on the marijuana couch and I am on a kitchen chair. He gets up, which takes a while because that couch is low and soft. He has to hold on to the couch arms and wobble himself upright.

"It's destined," he says. "That I be in this place. In Stanton's Mill. That I help. Daughter, you understand destiny."

Yeah, yeah. Destiny.

I've run into destiny with my father before. When I wanted to keep him from doing something. He managed to do it anyway; he managed to be any place he wanted to be. There is a local cabdriver, Henry, who thinks my father is a wonderful, smart guy and I am nuts to pretend he's senile. Henry will come anywhere and get him. He will even do it for free, though he usually tries to sock me with the bill afterward.

Not only is there a destiny of Henry but there also is hitchhiking. My father out on the side of the road with his thumb up and his white hair afloat can get anybody to stop.

And the kitchen staff at the Manor adore him. Everyone adores him and the whole public of Del Oro County will give him rides to any place where he feels he has a destiny even though his daughter has told him to stay clear.

I've seen it happen several times.

"If you are concerned about protecting me, which is stupid, but if you are, my friend Cherie will protect me," Daddy says.

I brood on this, at first resentfully. Why is Cherie better than I am at protecting him? And then, suddenly, gratefully.

Ah-ha, yes of course, oh my goodness. Cherie. Not just Cherie herself, but her staff. Cherie has two new deputies and I think, since she loves my dad so much . . . Yes, I will ask her. Probably she will assign a deputy to watch over him, at least part-time.

That is better than dragging him back to the Manor and having him brood and suffer and rebel and run away every second day.

"If you are worried about someone being safe, you should worry about little Happy," my dad says. "She has been over the lake of fire, and that makes for carelessness."

"Little Happy?" I ask. There is an Egyptian god named Hapy, and at first I think that's who Daddy means. And then I realize he's talking about Happy Dawn, Tamina's mother.

And he's right. Happy Dawn has been over the lake of fire, which makes you terribly unhappy. And careless. And the lake of fire made her talk too much at the memorial.

She has publicly announced that she knows something about Tamina's death.

For sure I need to see Happy Dawn before I go back tonight.

Night has fallen when I finally set off on my excursion. Night at the Mill is a serious proposition, given its steep, rocky roads, zero streetlights, houses hidden among the underbrush. The Mill has wildlife, which emerges at night and croaks and squawks. Something enormous and white flings itself at my windshield; I decide it's an owl, which ought to know better. I get lost twice in the quarter-mile between Susie's house and Happy Dawn's. Yes, there are only two roads in the Mill, but there are also driveways, which look like roads. And when I finally arrive at Happy Dawn's house, I'm unsure that I've reached it, because the house is completely dark, and I'm still unsure until I climb out of the car and circle the house twice.

Of course, Happy could be out for the evening. But the place feels closed up. The brass gongs still hang above the door, ready to be banged on, but I don't use them.

I reach out to jiggle the screen door and it opens toward me, unhooked and unlocked.

I should stop right now. The resident is not home. Her front door is closed. Whether the door is locked or not, it is still a legal barrier against invasion. I should just quit.

But I don't quit. I reach toward the front door, which is a nice old-fashioned ornamental one with an elaborate tarnished brass handle and a lever you can depress. I depress the lever and the door opens inward, easily, creaking slightly. A big handful of mail tumbles out of the mail slot and onto the floor inside.

Should I now proceed on in to Happy Dawn's deserted house? Of course not. As a sheriff's deputy, even a part-time one, I'd be compromising the entire Sheriff's Department of Del Oro County. I think about this for a while. And decide maybe Cherie will never know. I'm prepared to deny everything.

So I sidle in, closing the door quietly behind me. When I see Happy again, I'll give her a lecture about safety and locking your front door.

Probably there's a Stanton's Mill tradition that it's uncool to use locks.

Her mail is a magazine, some envelopes, two grocery fliers, and three Target and Costco ads. Happy has been gone at least a couple of days.

I don't turn on the lights. I have a flashlight. With that and the modicum of moonlight sifting through the sticky uncurtained windows, I can see a room that looks much the same as the last time I was here, for Tamina's wake; there is still the same mismatched leaky stuffed furniture, that kitchen table with steel legs, the piles of trash, the orchid plant that is now deader than before but still not quite gone. Other things are different. The orchid has gotten surrounded by wobbly sparkled sympathy cards. I tuck the flashlight under my arm and read several of these. One is signed "B" and says, "Darling, you have my love." A couple from "Nonie" and "Cissy" say girl things, like, "She was always there for us." An anonymous card contains a silver ink drawing of a star labeled, "The brightest star." One which I appropriate by putting it in my pocket says, "Pride goeth." This is written in wobbly printing that looks as if it had been done left-handed; the card is an ordinary flowery tribute. I hope Happy Dawn was too absorbed or generally upset to understand it.

The large picture of Tamina from the memorial service has migrated here and is faceup on the floor. There are several scatter rugs, one balled into a heap. There is laundry, also in heaps, and some clothes looking ready to be packed, such things as sweaters with their buttons buttoned and rolled-up socks.

I remind myself that I should be looking for facts about Tamina's death or about Arby's death or about the indigo babies. Or—a new one—about where Happy Dawn might be now, since all the signs indicate a Happy who has taken off after wedging everything she could into a suitcase.

Maybe she left a message, I think, and then I tell myself to have some sense. Who would she leave it for? Her daughter is dead. I go into the kitchen, Happy's territory, where she makes that jam that she sells along with the message about being clean now: "I've been clean for whatever number of months." The kitchen smells of blackberry.

Who was it who said, "Most people lead lives of quiet desperation"?

Working with a flashlight lets you see only a little round space at a time. Now my illumined circle picks out the kitchen table, containing six empty jam jars and a half-open package of Aunt Fern's all-whole-wheat bread and a calendar open to the month of April. There are squares for each day, and in day-before-yesterday's position there is an inked-in telephone number.

I copy that and scout around through the previous pages. There are other phone numbers, which I copy; I'm particularly interested in two out-of-state ones. There's a note of something happening in Petaluma. And of a "Friends of Bill W." meeting. "Friends of Bill W.," I know from my work with Habitat, is a code name for Alcoholics Anonymous.

After I finish in the kitchen, I do the bedrooms, which I didn't have a chance to see on my previous visit. The one that seems to be Happy's is messy and mostly pink, with flowered sheets scrambled into the sort of heap you make when you sleep restlessly. There are magazines—*Glamour* and *Eve* plus a couple of colorful crumpled journals with names like *Divinations* and *The Other Side*. I guess Happy, along with everyone else in the Mill, is delving into the paranormal. There are no books.

I rout around in the bed and on the table, but I don't find anything else written.

The next bedroom, obviously Tamina's, has a Far Eastern decor, with a gold-and-red Javanese bedspread, a small red Chinese rug, and an overflowing bookcase where books are stacked three deep, some upright and some on their sides. I grab a few and get *The Sagas of the Icelanders*, and *The Remains of Elmet* by Ted Hughes, and *The Idiot's Guide to Ancient Egypt*. There's a whole shelf of infant care books. *The Remains of Elmet* turns out to be poems by Ted Hughes along with photographs. Who has been pushing Tamina intellectually? My father did, a little. Beau probably has, too, and of course, there were teachers at school. And maybe others. I put the book back, again feeling sad for the loss of so much inquisitiveness and brightness.

A search for something written by her delivers journals (My Very Own Diary) from 2004 and 2003. ("Today I am TWELVE YEARS OLD!" "2003 begins with a blast"). The desk drawer holds a small collection of letters. Apparently she has a grandmother in Wenatchee, Washington.

And in a bottom drawer I find an Italian daily calendar. I mean one where the months and days are named in Italian: *Gennaio, Febbraio, Marzo; Domenica, Lunedi, Martedi*. It's a pretty little object, with a spiral binding and black cover. A trophy, I gather, from some exciting trip to a San Francisco restaurant. There are a few notes in the weekday spaces: Sunny, Robert, Beau, Arby, co-op, the kind of elliptical notes people put on a calendar. And at the month of *Marzo*, there's a line of hieroglyphs across the top of the page.

I have to think and squint, but finally I recognize a few of them. These are Egyptian hieroglyphics. My memory comes back reluctantly, slowly. Those are the symbols for *hidden*, or *hiding*, or *not seen*. That combination, that *hidden* and *not seen* combination used to be one I liked, because it seemed pictorial, involving wavy lines and an eye, the sort of shapes you associate with hiding or not seeing. The whole quote, I think, is a kind of spell: *Let me stay away, let me keep away from that which has been hidden.* Or maybe, *Damaged, or hidden.* Something like that.

I remember Daddy's remark about the jackal, and how he gave Tamina a spell against it.

I stand holding the calendar.

She was in danger and she died.

I shove the calendar in my pocket.

Then I put everything away pretty much as it was and proceed to the front door, where I debate whether or not I should lock it, and don't.

Should I now go down to Susie's for tea and sympathy? I decide on the co-op, which is still open.

"Greetings," Beau addresses me out of the semidarkness. "Neophyte Investigator, how are tricks?"

He is alone, sitting behind his raised desk at the far end of the store. The lights are dim and the store is cold, but I see the glow of an electric heater beside him, and I head that way.

"So, Beau," I say. "Holding the fort. As usual."

There's an undercurrent in this of, *Boy, are you a cool*

customer, which he picks up. "You know what?" he says. "You don't have the slightest idea about me."

"Too true." I climb the couple of stairs to the desk platform and capture an uncomfortable revolving chair. Beau reminds me of teachers whom I knew well at Santa Cruz; that makes it easy to be flip with him.

Also, he looks like somebody out of that world. Somebody emblematic, by which I mean that the person stood for something, some idea or point of view.

After a minute's thought a picture comes to me and it turns out to be that of William Faulkner. Which applies. Beau probably drinks himself cross-eyed, too.

"Beau, why are you here in Stanton's Mill?"

"Why am I . . . For God's sake. Sweet Cakes, I live here."

He adds, "I've lived here for eighteen years. I have a job here. What in hell are you after?"

I suspect Beau knows what I'm after—the occasional bit of the picture that seems peculiar.

"Where's Happy Dawn now?" I ask.

"Lady, you sure know how not to stay on a subject. Happy is gone. Don't you think she should have gone?"

"Yes, I do." We let that sit for a while.

"And if I knew where she went," he continues, "I wouldn't say. The fewer people know the better."

I agree, "Right," and he asks, "Do you want a drink?"

After I'm holding some kind of raspberry-smelling liquid, I say, "I think my dad saw what happened to Tamina on the edge of the Rock. Also, I think she told him something. Or maybe gave him something to read."

"And he can't remember any of it."

"He remembers some. His recall comes and goes."

Beau says, "Don't we all," and sips at his drink. He adds,

"Maybe she wrote it down. She wrote all the time. Other people got pieces of her literature. No telling what's a revelation and what is teenage stuff. She was only . . ."

"She was only fifteen," I interpose.

Beau shrugs. "She liked your dad. She might have given him something that mattered."

He leans back, watching his empire. The rest of the store is dark; a small fluorescence glows above the cheese display; the electric heater blows a comforting current. The cheese case and the tiered jars of jam and homemade lemon curd and honey catch the light from the heater. Stacked against the wall next to the jam display is a cluster of straight sticks like ski poles; these are tied with red thread and boast a set of red flags. "Beau"—I point—"what on earth are those?"

Beau says, "Huh? Oh. Fireworks."

I tell him that fireworks are illegal and he says, "So what?"

He adds, "Here we celebrate Bastille Day *and* the Fourth." This is followed by a minute of silence.

"Yeah," he says finally. "About Tammy. Maybe she did. Keep a journal. And after the baby came, I think she wrote in it every day. She wrote reams. And she probably showed it to your dad. She kept saying about him, 'He's all there still. The real him. You just have to ask.' "

"She liked you, too."

"She was in and out with me."

I say, "So talk about her, Beau," and he shakes his head. "I don't know much."

Suddenly I'm energized. Of course Beau knows a lot. Whom Tamina liked and feared. Who might have killed her. "Listen, you can't kid me. This was a bright kid. Wanting someone to hang out with. She talked to you. About

philosophy, the *New York Times*, the books she read." I remember Tamina's bookcase. "She read everything. Specu-
lated on it all. Had ideas about books. About life."

"She talked some."

"So tell me."

"Maybe later, Snoop Lady."

My throat gets hot; I feel myself getting fired up. "Don't
you want this killer caught? The person is evil. He kills
kids." (I arbitrarily assign a sex to the killer.) "He's dangerous. An evil lurker in the underbrush." Now I'm enmeshed
in my image. "Beau, for God's sake, what's the matter with
you?"

He turns his chair. I haven't seen him angry before this.
His face pulls into tight Germanic grooves, like the ones in
a Medieval etching. "You have *nerve*. Anybody ever tell you?
Snoop Lady, who the fuck are you to come and lecture me?
You don't know me. Or what I'm thinking. Or feeling. You
don't know anything much."

Well, touché, Beau, my friend. I've been presumptuous.

I mutter, "Okay, all right, sorry."

Maybe we should both have a time-out.

I change the subject.

"So tell me about the indigo babies, Beau."

"Tell you? What's to tell? I guess you're up on all that."

"You have an indigo grandchild."

"I have . . . I have a what? Oh, for God's sake. What red-
hot intelligence told you that?"

There we go again. I won't even try to maintain confi-
dentiality here. "Happy Dawn told Cherie, and Cherie
told me."

"Well, forget it. Happy was stoned. Or mad at me. Or getting Tammy off the hook. Or Cherie got it wrong."

He waits a minute, contemplating this series of possibilities. "You don't get it about this place."

"What don't I get?"

"Half the time the people are . . . well, embellishing."

He lets this statement wait for a minute and then amends it. "Lying, but . . . only sort of lying. They invent a lot. It's hard to define. With the outsider, they embroider. Or don't much care."

He contemplates this series of possibilities. "I guess you find this confusing."

"You can say that again."

"And we're an inbred community."

"Oh," I agree. "For sure."

"Well, what I can tell you . . ." He pauses and drinks some of his raspberry wine. "They don't really hate *you*. If that's any help."

I keep quiet. Not being hated seems a beginning.

"They hate a lot of outsiders. Most. You know, going to Conestoga is called 'going over the ridge.' As if it were the other side of the known world.

"But," he continues, "you're related to the Mill. A little bit. Because of Susie. You're only partly an outsider."

"Big deal," I say. It's ridiculous, but I feel mildly encouraged by this appraisal.

In my Manor room, I scroll off a long e-mail to Cherie detailing my interviews with Sunshine's mom and with Beau. I don't say a word about searching Happy Dawn's house. I list my fears about my dad and raise the question of a deputy—part of a deputy—to keep an eye on him. I say that things are feeling hot in Stanton's Mill. "Hey, Cherie," I finish. "Come on. Send supplies. Send help. Use your Big Lady muscle to get facts. Hospital records, statistics. I need them."

🦉 Chapter 11

Cherie calls me the next day and we make a date for lunch at the Best Western in Conestoga.

I get to the Best Western twenty minutes before she's due.

She'll be on time. She just gives the impression of being someone who is always late.

I am here early because I want to interview the desk clerk. The number Happy Dawn wrote down on her calendar is Best Western's switchboard number.

The clerk is chewing on a toothpick and admiring his cuff links. I remember from a previous stay here that these are jade, and that he likes them, so I pretend that I do, too. "Hey. Great jade there."

This clerk is skinny and his teeth stick out. He's pleased. "Yeah, right. Pretty good, huh?" He shoots a cuff.

We have a conversation about where he got them. He

went to Chinatown in San Francisco; it was a complicated outing. His name is Skippy.

Finally I see a chance to pose my question. "I wonder, do you remember a lady; she came here maybe two days ago . . ." I describe Happy Dawn, and when I get to the pink ostrich feather, I strike pay dirt, "Oh, sure, right, kind of a pretty lady, sort of; but boy, I didn't think people still did that feather stuff . . ."

And to my amazement, it turns out that not only does he remember Happy Dawn perfectly clearly, but that she is a tenant here. At the Best Western. She's staying upstairs. He reaches for the phone.

"Not right yet," I say. I'll wait until after I've talked to Cherie. Maybe my approach will be clearer by then.

Cherie appears ecstatic to see me. She gives me a series of abrasive hugs, pushing a large silver belt buckle into my crotch—she's about four inches shorter than I am.

She's wearing her new sheriff's uniform, tightly fitted, with zippers in the places that make it adhere best and the waist cinched by a belt decorated with Indian silver castings. "Figured I had to give in and shape up and wear the damn thing." She revolves for my inspection. "The little hoods are scared of it."

I tell her the uniform looks good on her.

She's also wearing aqua and green braided sandals with four-inch heels.

"Listen, baby," she says, "I've got some scoop on Arby. It almost looks as if he was killed by the Aryan Guards."

"He wasn't messing with them." That's just an instinct on my part, but a pretty firm one.

"Well, the knife . . ." Cherie begins. "Mind you, they haven't found it, but the autopsy guys can tell from the kind of wound and the real neat cut, one swoop and no sawing, right across the throat . . . Yeah, babe, I guess it is grim . . ." She shrugs. Cherie combines her bandbox china-doll look with an inflexible toughness. "Anyway, they drew me a picture of this knife and it's just like the one the meth hoods use. Not that they're the only guys who use a knife like that. You can get one at any good hardware store. Murderous little item. Curved, you know. They hone the blade down real fine."

I say, "Um," and, "Maybe too easy an answer?"

"I agree, babe. Real easy. But sometimes the easy one is the right one. Well, the other thing I got is some shreds about Tamina's baby.

"I got to the hospital and researched their records, and okay, fine, girl baby, et cetera, nothing weird—Penelope Ta-Ent Kerry—your dad helped name her, right? You know that—right on the birth certificate, Penelope Ta-Ent Kerry. Cool, right?

"And the next time we hear of this baby, she's three months old and Tamina brings her in to the hospital. Apparently she fell off the bed; the hospital reports that Mom, which is Tamina, didn't think she could roll over. And Mom is more or less right in that; three months is early for rolling over.

"But it could happen. A precocious baby could turn over at three months, and she could wiggle off the bed. Little Penelope wouldn't be the only three-month-old baby that ever did that. But the hospital is still suspicious. Bruises, although no broken bones. Bad signs.

"So they watch the mom—Tamina—real closely at the

examinations and interview; they got a lot of notes on it, and she seems just like a concerned mama. She's only fifteen, of course, a baby herself, but right up on her infant-care knowledge. And real worried. 'Oh,' she goes, 'the book said . . . And I was asleep; I guess I was asleep; now I got to get her a crib with sides; I'll do that right away—oh God, it's so awful. Of course I know the book's not always right.'

"The hospital reports she was affectionate with her child. 'Wow,' she said, 'she's such a great baby. So bright. And responsive.' So they just red-line her and give the baby back. But—get this—they give her back to the combined guardianship of the mom and the maternal auntie, whose name is Anneliese Wertiger."

"Hell," I say.

"Yep. The daddy, incidentally, is reported on the birth certificate to be a gent named William Jones, formerly of San Francisco, whereabouts now unknown."

"Sure," I agree. "Bill Jones, address unknown."

Cherie and I have arrived at the dessert part of our meal, which is a tasty (unlike most Best Western food) rhubarb crumble. We're silent for a couple of minutes, cleaning up the remains of the whipped cream. Finally Cherie provides the perfect opening by saying that she wonders about that silly little Happy Dawn. "I mean, darlin', she seemed like she knows everything. And talks about it. I, for sure, for certain sure, don't want another murder in this case. Maybe you should try and get her out of there."

I enlighten Cherie about Happy being upstairs, and explain that I found her by following clues, really simple ones.

I say nothing about frisking Happy's house. Cherie looks at me sharply but doesn't question.

"So get her away," she says. "Maybe she thinks she's safe here, in the big modern hotel, but she's way too close to Stanton's Mill. And somebody took her here, and they'll talk. She was sounding off at the memorial as if she were being paid to blab. I know she's a mom whose kid just died, broken heart an' all, but she was the same as saying, here I am, come kill me. God, what makes people do that? Get her somewhere else."

I think for a minute and decide she can stay in my dad's apartment at the Manor. As long as he's away in Stanton's Mill. "You for sure will get a deputy to watch him in the Mill, now won't you?" I confirm, and she answers crossly, "Babe, I said so. Shee."

She surveys her face in her pocket mirror. "Never mind, dear one, I got funds. If you don't spend the state's money before the end of the year, it melts."

Happy Dawn has a room with a view of a cornfield and an oil derrick. She comes to the door holding a bottle. She has been crying. She lets out a squeak when she sees me. "Oh. I thought—like—the boy with more ice. How did you . . . I mean, *who* are you? You were back there when . . . I mean, I saw you when she . . . Oh my God, everything reminds me of it."

"I was at your house. For Tamina's wake."

It's no trick to persuade her to leave. I guess she's been lonely.

* * *

In my car she has a meltdown of crying and wondering if she is doing the right thing.

I decide not to be subtle. I say, "Tell me why you're sure Tamina was pushed."

To my amazement, she stops crying and produces a coherent sentence. "She knew she was going to."

"Someone threatened her?"

"Someone promised."

"Who promised?"

"The seer . . . Oh, Jesus, oh, Jesus." We have only just gotten out of the Best Western parking lot and already Happy is hysterical. "I shouldn't tell." She tries to get out of the car, but it has kiddie locks on the doors and I have secured them. "Oh, my God. I couldn't see, but you know, so wonderful, purple."

And then, before I can get onto this and try to drag her back to coherence, she's off on another trail. "And Tamina had a baby book, did you know that? A book where she wrote everything down. All about little Penny and how she talked . . ."

"What happened to Tamina's baby book?" I ask, not hoping.

"What happened? I have it with me."

"I wouldn't leave that behind," she adds, in the voice of someone explaining important things to a not-very-bright child.

I get Happy Dawn into my dad's apartment. She is impressed. "The Prof's own place. Look at all the books." I wash her face and shovel her into an almost-clean smock from her suitcase and cut the gum from her hair and reposition her ostrich feather and ask if she's feeling better.

"Dear, so much. You are so sweet. What's your name?"

This is promising and I'm about to ask if I can see the baby book. But she wants to look at my dad's bathroom and his kitchenette and I have to take her down to the library to inspect the big TV.

Maybe I should peruse the baby book in private, but I'll take what I can get. "Okay," she says finally. And we go back to the apartment, where she drags one of her fiberboard cases into the middle of the floor and throws stuff around.

A pink imitation-leather-bound volume with a clear plastic window in the cover gets unearthed. Behind the window is a snapshot of a baby with its eyes closed. "See. That was my Tamina's Penelope. Penelope was the one in the fairy story that waited and kept weaving something or other. She had blond hair.

"Both Tammy and I are blond, so that is important.

"Be real careful with that book now. My Tammy is so proud of it."

I take the book and sit down, thinking sadly that Tamina's mother still refers to her in the present tense.

Tamina's narrative begins on the third day of Penelope's life. *She looks at me, and I know that she knows. Those eyes—the clearest kind of transparent blue, as if you can see through to the back of the soul. And I—spreading wide my narrow hands—*

Tamina sneaks bits of Emily Dickinson into her meditations, even if they aren't suitable.

Happy Dawn, crouched fetally in my dad's easy chair, has

been watching me read. "It makes you sad, doesn't it?" she announces.

And this new person that I looked at before and didn't understand and who I now see is entirely different—and the body is only an interem—interim??—spelling??—indicator of the spirit, isn't it? This person is so interesting and informed and who has spotted that my Penny is that kind of special aura keeps saying that there is a better way and I know that there is and if I were not so selfish I would be willing . . .

"It's kinda hard to read, isn't it?" Happy asks. She has started watching a hospital soap on my dad's TV, but she's also watching me. "I mean, I was trying to read it, but I was crying all the time, know what I mean?"

"Yes, Happy, I know." She doesn't seem to mind that I give her the sort of halfhearted attention I sometimes give my dad.

Back to Tammy's baby book. It's all here except for the real details. I imagine those real details; I can deduce what happened. Anneliese spoke to Tamina. She identified little Penny as an indigo baby. She said that an indigo baby needs to be protected.

Anneliese was working on Tamina to make her baby "safe." Give her up, in other words. But then what?

What do you do with a superbright and handsome baby that you are shipping away to a secret destination? Where do you send it? And why? What's in it for you?

Money is the root of all evil. I get a strong odor of snake oil from Anneliese. The lady is an experienced capitalist. A saleswoman. An operator, a maneuverer. She would do things that leave a trail.

I comb Tamina's musings diligently, translating school-girl effusions about "o my bfl chld so prfct hrd 2 blve," dodging blurbs about weight, length, how the hair is curly, the eyes still blue, "and I ws so hping they'd sty blu, not just that Mama and I have blue eyes . . ."

When Tamina lapses into straight prose, I know things are getting serious. *And now there is something new, this disease that I seem to have, which maybe is a bad disease, why didn't I think of that when I couldn't remember about her falling. Maybe it runs in families and if I knew who my father was. My father, and why didn't I think of that. But she is a girl baby and girl babies should mostly look like their—I mean, you are the echo, the im-print, the future of me and all that you are is the best that I could be and guru says and I do indeed believe guru that . . .*

And, oh great goddess, she said that it was in Crystal that it all started. That there was a baby that was the baby. And in Crystal. I thought that so important. Because of course Crystal is special and has powers, just the way indigo has.

Oh great power, I know enough to defy the evil doers and hide what I love from them. And you will protect me and Sekhmet that presides over pregnancies will continue me under her care and restore me, specially if I listen to my DUTY.

The word DUTY is written in red ink and decorated with pink scallops.

Now suddenly, no warning, we have a line of little shapes, weird and yet familiar, squarish shapes, slightly backhanded but geometric. I am cross-eyed from having read too much and not having thought enough. It takes me a minute to rec-ognize hieroglyphs again.

I spend maybe two minutes staring at them. Until fi-nally. Oh, for God's sake, and bingo. A word here and an-other one there. My dad would be cross with me, but I'm doing all right; that knowledge doesn't go away. An invocation: *Oh, great god (goddess) be with me . . . favor me . . .*

I recognize only some of Tamina's square shapes, but I have a recourse, a hieroglyphic dictionary upstairs in my room. I'm squeezing a marker between the pages of the book when I'm stopped by Happy Dawn's voice. "Don't go," she says. "I'll really be worried if you go. I'm sort of scared, you know?"

I cancel my plans for the rest of the afternoon and lead Happy to the library, where I organize her with Mrs. Levine into a game of dominoes. Both ladies are pretty good—Mrs. L, who is a dear old bald sweetheart, wins one game and Happy Dawn racks up two.

So it's later on, evening in fact, before I can sit down with my hieroglyphic dictionary and Tamina's baby book.

My hieroglyphic dictionary is English to hieroglyph. It's simple and straightforward—words designating people, animals, work, furniture, food. Nobody has managed a beginner's dictionary that goes the other way—hieroglyph to English. Daddy has on his bookshelf a set of articles, mostly in German, which organize the hieroglyphs by basic shapes, and after you have that figured out, you could maybe translate them. But I never learned how to cope with the German scholarly phraseology. If I can figure out where the verb is in a German sentence, I'm doing great.

I start the dictionary in the section on people. I try *baby, woman, man, scribe.* Nothing. Not there. Not in Tamina's square, neat renderings. Tamina wasn't talking about woman, man, scribe. Not even baby.

But here, maybe, is *face.* Yes. A straight line and a curved one. And Tamina has put a red mark there, which shouldn't be part of the hieroglyph. What was she trying to say? A face with a mark, a defect? A face that she wants to eliminate?

It seems important.

Then there's more. I stare. I squint. I close one eye.

A line of script, the first word of which looks familiar.

Tamina has written a prayer. Or a curse? A prayer for her own well-being?

If I don't do this she will suffer.

Oh, great god Thoth, please forgive me for what I am about to do.

Please be with me. I make this sacrifice in your name.

Well, sort of. Some of that is prayers, ones that I remember from my long-ago Egyptian studies.

And then a passage in English:

Oh, great God—the word *God* is in red ink with pink frills—*she said that it was in Crystal that it all started. I thought that was so significant. Because of course Crystal is special and has powers just the way indigo does.*

And it would help and protect my Penelope so much.

Anneliese has been very powerful. She helped at the hospital after Penny fell. And I felt so guilty. I like the idea of Anneliese and Crystal.

⌐ Chapter 12

I like the idea of Anneliese and Crystal, too, but don't get to make the full association for a couple of days.

I've started researching Anneliese's past. Her past that she spent at what she calls an "interesting, exclusive" mental facility. Which she won't divulge the name of. Where she discovered the true value of indigo.

I suspect the worst of Anneliese's past.

I fold my laptop under my arm and head toward the library with plans to tackle the Internet in pursuit of that psychiatric hospital.

"Hello," Mrs. La Salle says three-quarters of an hour later, "what are you doing? You seem to find it depressing."

"Shoveling fleas," I tell her dismissively.

She looks over my shoulder, which she has not been invited to do, and says, "If it is an Internet problem, I am very good at the Internet."

Mrs. La Salle does not look as if she would be good at the Internet. With her straight carriage and perfect white hair and good jewelry, she appears to hail from some century where the most advanced electronic gadget is a key on the end of a kite tail. I try to ignore her.

"If you are getting too much or too diffuse information," she remarks, "it is because you have not made your request specific enough."

I continue tracking and she continues sitting beside me and interfering until suddenly I have had it and scoot my mouse onto the floor.

"You can break it that way," she remarks, collecting the device. But instead of giving it back, she hangs on to it. "Come on, let me have a try."

"Oh, go ahead," I finally say. "Take over. Have fun. My God, what difference does it make?

"I'm trying to find out something about Anneliese Wertiger," I throw at her on my way out of the room. "Anneliese and what mental hospital she worked in. Do you know how to spell her last name? W-E-R . . ."

"Yes, of course," Mrs. La Salle says.

I go off for a bathroom break. I am hoping to return to a lady completely lost and wandering around in a wilderness of revolving computer pinwheel symbols. But I find her clicking purposefully and making approving noises like "Hmmm" and "Oh, yes." And shortly I am sitting beside her feeding her the few facts I know.

"So I accessed her name on Google," she says, and then does that. "Yes, yes, and after that her publisher . . ." Which I hadn't bothered with but which apparently produces a handsome ad for "Indigo Auras," and instructions on several ways of sending money. "Well, then, so there was this book, let's try bookstores . . ."

"Yes, it is curious," she says after a few minutes of maneuvering, "there really is nothing further back than eight years ago; now on one occasion we have a middle name . . ." And she tries Anneliese Susanna Wertiger, Susanna Anneliese Wertiger, and other combinations. "So, nothing," she says, almost triumphantly at the end of this. "That lady just evaporates eight years ago. Nothing earlier than 1998. And that despite the fact that I'm sure she's an attention hound; she loves publicity. Something is truly amiss. Have you any other pointers?"

"Hospital," I offer. "She said she worked in a hospital."

"Oh, good. And what did she say about the hospital?"

I fail to see that this is good. In fact, I think it gets us nowhere. "What she said was a string of meaningless adjectives. Intended to show how superior she was."

"Tell me."

I try to reprocess Anneliese's remarks. *"Prominent private mental health,"* I say. "Those were her words. *Private,* she stressed that. And *interesting, exclusive.* That's what she said. It sounds ridiculous. Like an advertising flyer."

"Exactly," Mrs. La Salle says. "How good that she should remember so exactly. And you should remember so exactly."

I look at her questioningly. She feels me doing this, even though she's crouched over the computer. "Because," she says, "I think that is exactly right; it sounds like the hospital's publicity flyer. Probably literally from their flyer. And she remembered it word for word, and you did, too. Both of you have perfect recall."

I start to say, "Well, ter-rific," and then don't, and sit

back, feeling fairly squashed by the fact that I share this virtue with Anneliese Wertiger.

"And what's so good," Mrs. La Salle says, "is that that's the way Google remembers things, too. It picks up exactly the diction of a blurb and can locate an entry that way.

"When you put that combination of words into your request, the search engine will come up with the place that used that nonsense in its publicity.

"Now, do you think," she begins, "and you may have to guess on this one . . . was it in California? Or outside of?"

"Good God," I say. There were no clues about that in anything Anneliese said. No indication of place at all. I try to remember back to my conversation with her, but she didn't converse that much. Any clues in her house? I do a mental review of it, room by room, shelf by shelf, paintings, pictures. And finally, yes, there was that one picture, the one of the guru, a picture that may have been taken in California; the guy has a wild-looking coastal landscape behind him. Of course, all Northwestern coasts look alike, but still . . .

"Try California first," I say. "Maybe."

Mrs. La Salle types busily. She's giving Google a long list of instructions.

"Well, good," she says finally, after a couple of what are apparently misfires. She is surveying the crowded page in front of her. "Or almost good." She seems to have a list accompanied by small pictures. "I guess more than one mental facility used some of that same luscious description.

"But . . . but. One name leads all the rest, the way the poem says. Does the name *Crystal* mean anything to you? There's a Crystal Health Facility."

"Crystal?" It takes only a minute for that to surface. Of course. Crystal. Anneliese stressed it, Tamina stressed it.

"Yes," I tell Mrs. La Salle. "Crystal means something. I think maybe it does. I'll look into it. Oh, for God's sake. Thank you. Thank you so much."

I feel noble telling her *thank you* like that. It is difficult to wholeheartedly thank someone who has horned in on your project and taken it over and done it much better than you could have.

"So," I say to Cherie over the phone, "Crystal Health Facility. Did you ever hear of it?"

"Sure," Cherie agrees, somewhat too readily, I think. I want this to continue being a discovery process.

"You did?"

"Sure. I got an old legal client there. At first she wanted me to get her out. And then she wanted me to help her stay in.

"She's nuts. Bipolar. And maybe paranoid, too. Both at once. She's still there."

This is proving too easy. "I think that's where Anneliese was. You know, I can't trace her earlier than eight years ago. So, maybe . . . Anyway, will this former client talk to me?"

"Jenny? Sure she will. She loves to talk. And she's smart, when she's not nuts. You'll like her. I'll e-mail a note to her. And write you something to show them at the hospital.

"Hey, good, turning that up," Cherie adds. "Must have been way hard to do, huh? You really are a brilliant genius, lover girl."

There are plenty of times when I miss Cherie and wish she weren't so busy pursuing meth offenders.

Chapter 13

My dad says he is doing just fine. No, he doesn't miss me. He sounds surprised at the suggestion. "I have my dear friend Susie. And I have been going to gatherings they have here; it is some kind of a shop where they have vegetables and gatherings. There were shops like that in Cairo, except that this one is cold."

I tell him that I am taking a trip to Oakland and he says yes, he thinks he remembers that place; did one get there on a boat?

"Susie is concerned," he says, "about the people that used to live in this house." After that, our phone connection breaks off and I can't renew it.

I decide not to worry about this statement. Daddy often says things that are hard to relate to.

* * *

The Crystal Facility is at the top of a hill overlooking the Oakland harbor.

The full Crystal blurb, in addition to *prominent private mental health*, is as follows: *"Convenient, elegant, fully professionally staffed and reasonably priced—Welcome to our health center, perhaps this is the place where you'll settle in to regain full health, freedom from substance or alcohol abuse, freedom from fears!"*

I had expected an upscale part of the East Bay with a view and lush vegetation. And it isn't.

It does have a view, but the prospect is of the lower part of the Oakland harbor. Visible are three of those cargo loaders that look like dinosaurs, two large container ships, and many stacks of containers painted orange, yellow, or brown. It's too far away to see the names of the companies that will claim these shipments, but I'm sure most of them are bound for the Far East.

The road up to the Crystal Facility is utilitarian and well paved. Recently someone—probably Crystal management—has tried to improve the neighborhood by planting palm trees, skinny new-looking ones that still have their tops tied together with wire.

The building is half a mile from the port, but it has the same square cement look. Probably it was once a maritime office building. There was a picture in the Google spread that wasn't exactly misleading, just too small to tell you anything—a modern-age cement front and a couple of the palm trees with their headdresses untied.

I pull up in front of the building—there's plenty of parking—and turn around to take in the prospect. I like industrial views. But I guess if you're a resident of Crystal, you might not agree, and would rather be soothed by rustic woods and robins.

I have some theories about what I'm going to discover here. I'm kind of looking forward to it, learning the low-down truths about Anneliese Wertiger.

The front hall of the facility is approached by a flight of stairs and a ramp and is guarded by a cheerful man in a yellow sport shirt. His name, pinned on his front, is Barry. At first he looks young and then he doesn't. Final verdict: about fifty. He grasps my hand. He smiles sincerely. "Oh," he says after reading Cherie's note, "Cherie, one of my loves. And Jenny. You want to see Jenny. Of course. Yes, of course. Let me check now." He punches some computer keys and scowls at a screen. "Jenny, yes, certainly. Well."

After a minute he announces enthusiastically that Jenny is great today and of course I can go up. He will just get Edna to take us.

The inside of Crystal is more fixed up than the outside. There are tan halls and blue carpets with some kind of insignia. And Jenny has a pleasant wide room with a good view of the shipping.

She's a large, old bleached blonde sprawled sideways in an easy chair who doesn't respond to Edna's comment, "Jenny? Guess what? You have a visitor." She keeps her side view at me and watches the container ship. She seems to be chewing on something. "Who're you?"

I resist quoting Emily Dickinson, "I'm nobody! . . . Are you nobody, too?" which Tamina would have liked.

Jenny is some age over seventy. "Cherie sent you?" she asks, lapsing into thought, chewing on her lipstick. "Weird little thing," she recollects, still eying the view. "I sort of liked her."

I've brought a box of candy and a bakery package containing six éclairs. The candy was Cherie's suggestion. "Cherie liked *you*," I say, with more enthusiasm than I'm feeling.

She examines the Godiva box, runs a finger over the gold lettering ("Humph"), and sticks her nose in the baked goods. Finally she tells me, "Thank you," and turns fully in my direction.

Her face is white and red, white for powder, red for lipstick and the two blobs of color on her cheeks. There is a lot of sticky-looking mascara. She wears an electric red shirt and seersucker pants. She examines me. "So. What is it?"

"I wanted to talk to you about somebody who used to work here."

"Uh-huh. Well, I been incarcerated ten years. My first husband put me in. Then I got a second husband, and he lived right here. We holed up together here, in this room. We were the romance of floor three. This is the third floor, you noticed?"

I tell her that if she's been here for ten years, she will certainly know this lady. "And Cherie said," I continue, inventing industriously, "that you had really good powers of description."

"Sometimes I do. When I'm all right. You know I'm not always all right?"

I blink, to show agreement. I feel my way to a chair. None has been offered, but I think it's time to sit.

"They say it's manic-depressive. I read up on it. You stay here long enough and you're more informed than they are. Doctors. Take a look at you and think they know everything. Well. My second husband died, too; you know that?"

I blink again.

"So. Here I am and I got used to it. And now I got one of the best rooms. Well, then, tell me. What was it you wanted to know? . . . Oh, yeah. About some doctor. Or was it a nurse? Social worker? We got 'em all."

I'm not going to confess my private suspicion, which I've been coddling on my way up here. That Anneliese was at Crystal not as a doctor or a psychiatrist but as a patient. "Her name is Anneliese Wertiger."

Jenny squints at me suspiciously. She says, "No."

"No?" I ask.

"No. Nobody named like that has been here. I got, like Cherie says, a good memory."

It's perfectly possible Anneliese used another name, which would go with my suspicions.

"Susanna," I suggest, offering the middle name that Mrs. La Salle turned up.

Jenny says no.

I begin on a description. "She's tall. Good posture. Dark hair, done in a bun at the nape of her neck. Regular, sharp, even profile. Good-looking, in a rigid sort of way—"

Jenny interrupts me. "And you think she was med staff."

"Well . . ." I wait a minute and come out with another "Well . . ." *No, I think she was in your category,* I parenthesize to myself. *There was something off about her. Too upright. Too rigid. Tensed against the rest of the world.*

"Sweetheart, you do a perfect description of Ann Warner. And Ann Warner was not medical. Nor support. She was the bookkeeper."

"Bookkeeper?" I have to repeat it. The last thing I would have thought of. Bookkeeper. Trusted. In charge of money.

And then, in no time at all, I have constructed a meaningful fiction. Anneliese as the bookkeeper who stole the cash. I don't know that any cash was stolen, but I love the idea. "How was she at that job?"

"Good, I guess. She was smart enough. This is a small place, everybody knows everybody."

"But did she . . . was she . . ." What I want to ask is, Was she fired for stealing money? Cooking the books? Fiddling the taxes? I finally think of how to phrase it. "Wasn't there some kind of financial situation here, about eight years ago?"

"Oh, yes. Damn right. And you know what? She was the heroine of that. She discovered it."

She discovered it? *No, she didn't,* I think. *Oh, come on. This is Anneliese we're talking about.* I stare at Jenny. I can't produce any way of following up. I brood on it for a minute and finally ask, "Did you like her?"

"Like her?" Jenny makes this sound like an aberrant question. "No. She wasn't the kind you liked. But she was smart. We used to talk sometimes. I miss that around here.

"Not too many of these idiots are informed, like me," she adds, modestly making herself head of the category.

"Tell me about the scandal."

She pauses to open the bakery box and grub around. Finally she extends it. "Be my guest."

The éclairs come equipped with supporting paper doilies. The result is messy but pleasant. Jenny eats voraciously, commenting that ever since she stopped taking her Depakote, she gets hungry like a normal person. "It's weird, manic-depressive. If that's what I've got. Or bipolar; that's what you're supposed to say. All kinds of famous people had it. The composer Schumann, maybe Edgar Allan Poe, maybe Lord Byron; I got all their works in my bookcase; I read them all. Makes me feel better."

She gestures toward the window. "Y'know? You might think I wouldn't like it staring down at all that machinery? Well, I'm different from lotsa people. I do.

"It reminds me of my good old days, when I would be down in a scene like that and maybe meet somebody. Y'know? I was a dish." She sticks out a wide, well-corseted pair of breasts.

"Okay." She licks her fingers. "Ann Warner. They all went off to Pelican Bay and she was the only man left standing.

"Not tax stuff," she answers my question. "That wasn't what they got indicted for. Insurance. Those big insurance companies don't like being cheated. And I guess Ann found out a whole lot of stuff and reported it. And because she reported it, she didn't get a sentence. I wasn't told the details. Naturally. We peons just got reassured, about us. *Do not worry, oh, peons. Your bills won't go up.* But you hear things. That she was part of it—the plan or whatever—and then ratted so as not to get charged. You can do that, can't you?"

I said I didn't know, but it sounded like what Anneliese would try. "I wonder why she changed her name?"

"Yeah, right. You want another éclair? No? Well, I do." Jenny waves a pastry in demonstration. "I been off that Depakote for a couple of weeks now, and boy, does your appetite come back." She licks her fingers. "And your brain."

I say, "Jenny, were there ever any babies here?"

"Babies?" She makes it sound as if I've asked about crested pterodactyls. "What in hell would a baby be doing here?"

"Nobody ever came here with a baby? Or had a baby afterward?"

"Gawd, no." After a minute she says, "Well." Then, "I

guess there was Nancy. She had—what's the name of that thing where the new mother is real depressed?"

"Postpartum depression."

"Yeah, that one. That baby didn't live here, but they used to bring it in to see her. And then she got better and left."

Yes, she says, Ann Warner was around then; maybe she was interested in Nancy's case. She liked peculiar stuff. "Hey, about Ann. She stayed at Crystal only a couple more months after the insurance thing . . . Yeah. I always thought that was interesting. Maybe she got out in a hurry and maybe a whole lot richer. She was the kind."

☂ Chapter 14

I am so pleased with myself over the success of the Anneliese Wertiger expedition that I schedule an immediate invasion of Stanton's Mill and another interview with that lady.

I will continue to think of her as Anneliese Wertiger. Ann Warner is less interesting, romantic, and sinister. And there is no Google history on Ann Warner. Maybe she was Anita Wallace or Angela West before she was Ann Warner or maybe she really didn't have any Internet history before that. Maybe she worked at Wal-Mart and was an expert vendor of Mickey Mouse T-shirts.

I leave the Manor early—that is, before four—and am descending the rocky incline into the Mill with enough light to see all the weeds and stones and blind byways and small defiles. Of course, I have to visit Susie and confer with my dad, but I'll tackle Anneliese first.

After I park, I notice that something is happening at the Rock, but I decide not to go. Most of those gatherings have to do with red-hot issues like nude creek bathing or picking blackberries. I take a minute to stick my face into the store.

"Hello, Beau." I'm still feeling good about Anneliese Wertiger/Warner, and I guess this sounds in my voice, because Beau says, "Snoop Lady, what in hell makes you act so human this afternoon? Hormones? Save me some."

"I've been digging into the past, Beau. People around here have pasts."

"Yeah. You betcha. It's futures we don't got much of. You find something interesting about my past?"

"Not yet, Beau. I haven't really tried."

"Don't try too hard. It might bite."

"I'm doing research on names," I say. The minute I say this, I wonder if the statement is a mistake; there's a pause in the badinage. Then Beau says, "Names. Yes, bad. Somebody with a phony-sounding name will be trouble.

"Like, for example," he adds, "Beau La Roche. Was there ever a more invented-sounding name than that?"

I look at him, not answering and thinking, *Yeah. I sort of thought of that, too.* "Has my dad been in here?" I ask.

"Every day, Snoop Lady. We love him; he's one of the good ones. How did that ever happen?"

I ignore the dig, "He's okay? Really okay?"

"Listen, dear, he forgets a bit. But this place is okay for him. We're big on forgetting."

I'm quiet, not asking, "So, no one threw any more rocks at him?" and Beau changes the subject. "Our bakery special today, Snoop Person, is chocolate muffins. Would you like a chocolate muffin?"

My criticism of Mill cookery in general is that it's too

sweet, and this certainly will be true of a chocolate muffin, but I accept one anyway. "I'm on my way over to see Anneliese," I say, to offer a subject to Beau, who has been looking wary ever since I said that about researching names.

And he gestures, seeming comforted. "Go with God, babe. You'll need some kinda god if you're interviewing that bitch. Don't get chocolate on your shirt."

"You don't like her, do you?" I ask. He says, "I hate her, if you need to know. Slippery, opportunistic bitch. Tammy didn't have a chance.

"Hey," he adds, "I'm sending you some papers. Records. Use your snoop talents on them. Minor Tammy stuff.

"And stay away from the Rock. They're talking about stop signs."

Stop signs are another continuing topic in the Mill. There are no stop signs anywhere at any of the four corners of the single intersection, and there are people who will lie down in the road to keep stop signs from ever existing.

I make a mental note to try to keep Daddy away from the Rock. He would love observing those meetings.

All the indications are that Anneliese will be home and able to talk. Not, of course, anxious to talk to Carla, to *me*, but interested in talking generally, say to prospective indigo clients. The outside lights of her spiritualist tourist trap are on and flickering invitingly. I push open the front door, which is unfastened and clangs to announce my arrival.

"Good afternoon, Anneliese," I say, grabbing the incentive before she gets her mouth open.

She has emerged from the back of the spread through a clacking bamboo curtain. She looks appropriately regal and indigo, wearing an ankle-length dark purple dress that sig-nals *couture*, as does the rest of her.

I am feeling empowered by my successful invasion of her past and possession of her former name, but I don't plan to reveal that now. "Anneliese, I need to talk to you."

"And I do not need to talk to you and don't want to." She has started backing firmly away into her bamboo barrier.

"Listen," I call toward her exiting form, "what do you know about the death of Arby Cronkeit?"

Actually I don't expect Anneliese to know much about Arby's death. I just want to unsettle her. Which I've done. "Arby?" She stops. "That little field mouse?"

"He was a good friend of Tamina's, probably the father of her baby. You should be up on that. And he knew a lot about Tamina. She confided in him. That's why he was killed; he had facts about her that weren't supposed to get out."

She has started again to back off but I follow her, mostly by yelling loud. "You know too much about Tamina. You know how she died."

Anneliese reverses; she comes forward again. "Everyone knows how Tamina died."

"Are you saying *you* know? You understand? You're on to what happened to her? Then you're the first person in town to admit it. But I always thought you knew."

"Stop that." But she doesn't retreat again into her hidey-hole.

"Someone pushed her, Anneliese. You're an expert on crime, aren't you? Big crimes, little ones. On things that happen in crimes. You have a history, don't you?"

"Cut it out." She tries to sound scornful and partly suc-ceeds. "You're fishing. You could say that to anybody. We've all got histories." She's partly echoing Beau.

I'm still not ready to reveal how much I know about her. "We've all got histories, but some of our histories are really quiet. And yours isn't. You have that noisy history look, Anneliese. Why did you come to the Mill?"

She's a good fencer. She senses that this isn't my strongest question. "To this beautiful idyllic spot? Why did I come here? Are you kidding; it's been great being here."

"Sure," I agree. "Better than that elegant private hospital. Where you did so well and discovered indigo. Am I right?"

Anneliese and I are standing in her reception room. Around us are the tools of her trade: purple painted walls, purple hangings, racks of indigo literature, the big photo of the guru against the seascape. I'm at one end of her reception room, by the door; she's at the other, by the bamboo curtain.

I want Anneliese to feel threatened. I want her to know I have extra information I'm not telling yet. Hidden stuff. And maybe she's beginning to get that idea.

"Why did you tell the hospital here you were Tamina's aunt?"

She doesn't like this. She flexes visibly.

"You wormed your way into Tamina's life and got her to go to the hospital and got her to drag her baby in. Because it fell; it was supposed to have fallen. You engineered all that. Why?"

"For God's sake. She needed a friend. Just fifteen; they were going to say she was an inadequate mother. I stepped in. I helped her." She sounds pious, a maternal type, outraged.

"And," I say, getting enthused; this questioning is turning out to be all right; maybe there's a bit of the bully in my makeup. "And listen, tell me, the baby was supposed to have rolled off the bed. Did it get some help, maybe?" This is the first time I've had this nasty but attractive idea.

She pulls in a breath. "You bitch. You total bitch. Get out of my house." She points dramatically. Her small upright bosom moves. The hand she's pointing with shakes slightly.

I feel like reminding her that it isn't her house; it's Scope's house. And I'm not ready to stop questioning. "You persuaded her there was something wrong with her, didn't you? Some mysterious something so she didn't notice her baby falling? She thought she slept through that, didn't she, and you encouraged her, right? So she would think she was an inadequate mother and shouldn't keep her baby. That was your idea, wasn't it?

"Listen, lady," I say, getting enthused. "I know a lot about you. I know all about the refined, elegant hospital where you worked and got the idea of indigo. That was Crystal, that's right, isn't it, Crystal? And how you got into trouble there. They still remember you. Important people still remember you; that might be big trouble, don't you think . . ."

I'm not sure what I'm talking about here, but it must be good. I seem to have hit a nerve. Anneliese pulls in a sharp breath. She has moved back so that she's holding on to two hunks of bamboo curtain, and her hands contract. "You'll pay for that."

I grin. "Start planning for it, lady." I'm feeling good.

But I guess I've lost my audience; Anneliese has clacked herself entirely back behind her bamboo protection. In a minute I hear her footsteps retreating into the back of the house.

* * *

Scope intercepts me on the walk outside. "Hi," he says.

I stare at him. I haven't thought of Scope as the *hi* type. More as someone who grunts to show he's there.

He looks a little better than the last time I saw him. Shirt inside of pants, belly tucked in, maybe smaller. He has cut his pigtail. "So you been seeing Anneliese."

Perceptive of you, Scope. I don't answer.

We proceed a few paces. "Good conversation?"

"All right." Actually, not really good, but about what I expected. And why is it any of your business?

"Anneliese is an excitable lady," he volunteers.

"We don't get along very well," he suggests after a few more feet.

Yes, Scope, you told me that before.

We go a couple of paces farther. "You know, it's almost accidental that she's here." Scope is flaccid and doughy and irritating. He gives the impression of wanting something.

"Then why don't you make her leave?" I didn't intend to get that specific with him. He riled me into it. Whatever his personal life with Anneliese, I figure it's none of my business. But then, no, after a minute I decide maybe it matters. "Boot her out," I say.

He looks at me with his eyes half-closed in the *oh yeah* look.

"What do you think happened to Tamina Kerry?" I ask. I didn't exactly intend to ask that, but I'm fueled by frustration. I add quickly, "Before you say what everybody else in town says, that she fell off the edge of a cliff, I'll announce I think she was pushed. I'm investigating things that way. She was pushed."

We've arrived at the place where their front path joins the main road. Scope looks a little rattled by my question, but not very. "Well, Deputy Sheriff, time to regroup. Part-time deputy sheriff, are you? What does that mean?"

I guess it means something, because you're acting wary of me. And I haven't been thinking of you as being wary, or sensitive in any other way. I thought of you as a clod, Scope.

From Anneliese's, I go back along the road to Susie's and to my dad.

Here he is, sitting on the edge of the front porch with his feet resting on a mildewed green support. He gives me the crystalline look I remember from my childhood. "I love you," he says.

I subside onto the edge of the porch beside him. There's silence while he smiles at me and I caress his shoulder. I ask, "How are you?"

"Why, fine, darling."

"No . . . problems . . ." I pause for the wording. "Nothing to worry about?"

"Susie has mice. We don't know how to handle it. Where have you been?"

"I was talking to someone. Do you know Anneliese?"

"Anna? Anna Lisa? Yes, I think I must." He pauses, looking down. "You know, there is someone I know and I am not supposed to. Who is not supposed to be here. I should not tell people. It would make someone else very surprised. Or sad. I do not like to make my friends sad."

I massage his shoulder.

"Darling, I'm not certain about it. I think of telling someone and it starts to go. When I want to do it, that's when it starts to go."

"Yes," I say. *Accept him,* the books tell you. *Just as he is.* "Relax, dear."

"You know," he says, "there was a lady named Molly."

"Molly Littlefeather?" I know I sound surprised and my voice rises. I haven't been thinking about Molly. I guess I resisted adding her to my list of Persons of Interest.

The front screen door squawks open and Susie emerges, exclaiming, "Carla dear! Why didn't you say you were here?

"We miss you so much. What don't you come live here? I am entirely living here this spring; I have this wonderful Rosa who runs the Berkeley store, and I get to stay in the Mill and see the birds, and did you know we have a blue heron?

"Well, come on in and we'll talk about something better than those awful murders you want to talk about."

So of course, that's the end of my questioning my dad.

⌐ Chapter 15

"What are you doing, Carla?" Mrs. La Salle asks. "You look distracted."

I've chosen a corner of the Manor library to wrestle with my e-mail and today's Complaints. The dark redwood walls and rows of green-bound books seem to promise a life beyond all that.

"Good morning, Daphne." Mrs. La Salle still scares me some. But I'm grateful to her for tracking down the Crystal Facility on the Internet. And I continue to love the way she looks, especially the jewelry, which today is some asymmetrically shaped aquamarines.

She smooths a seam of her white pants and subsides gracefully into an easy chair. "Are you all right? Such trouble for you in that Stanton's Mill community. What a shame. Enclosed societies have an allure. Did you follow up on the psychiatric hospital? Did Anneliese Wertiger really work there?"

"It was nice of you to help me so much," I say, eluding questions.

"I've been curious about them," she continues. "I mean, the Stanton's Mill settlement. An artificial pocket of an extinct society. Holdouts.

"And of course I wondered about that beautiful Tamina child. I got to know her slightly.

"So lovely," she adds thoughtfully. "What a shame. That one should be more sympathetic when the person is appealing."

I'm touched by the most peculiar emotion. I'm jealous that Mrs. La Salle knew the living Tamina, while I can know only a dead one. "I didn't realize you knew her."

Mrs. La Salle watches me. "Ah."

In a minute she adds, "I was researching a story about hippie art . . . which is why I went to Stanton's Mill. I wanted Flower Child stuff. The remnants of the sixties. What has happened to them, and how does it look now, and in retrospect, how do we feel about them and then about their art? But the story refused to jell. Perhaps not enough time has elapsed. What art I could find didn't seem right. Not exotic and witty. Just labored. Not enough lush curving lines."

It's my turn to say, "Ah." At first I can't remember any art at all in Stanton's Mill, and then I recall rococo fences and house signs and some of the houses themselves with their carvings and eccentric colors. To say nothing of lopsided clay pots.

"Did you talk to Anneliese Wertiger?"

"Our friend Anneliese? She wasn't interested; art isn't her thing. She watches you carefully all the time she talks. You can see her planning the best way to use this moment. Do you know what I mean?"

"I think so."

"I regretted talking to Anneliese. You meet a lot of people like that in publishing.

"But," she adds after a minute, "I did talk to Tamina."

I wait. I'll be damned if I'll say "Ah" again.

Mrs. La Salle frowns. There is only one aquamarine earring today plus a lopsided ring; apparently imbalance is the current fashion. She fingers the earring. "I had hoped she'd be a source of art. Did you know she painted?"

I say yes, people have mentioned something.

"Little paintings," Mrs. La Salle clarifies. She indicates with her hands a six-by-six-inch space. "Such an interesting genre. A multigifted child. But of course her art wasn't hippie; she was the wrong generation. It was neorealist. Bright miniatures. Watercolors of somebody's motorcycle."

"Arby's."

"Perhaps. And the large refrigerator in the store? Isn't that a strange choice?"

I'm still thinking about Tamina as a neorealist painter. And no work exhibited at the memorial. Maybe she painted mostly for herself. "Did she talk to you about indigo babies? About her own baby? About maybe losing it?"

"Lose it? Why would she lose it? She talked a lot about the baby and how wonderful it was and all that new-mother emoting. And this was strange, a lot about duty. As if that were a new idea.

"Duty, duty. Was love enough in a parent—suppose you were lacking in some way? Maybe she wasn't doing right by her daughter. I got the feeling someone had been lecturing her. Do you think that's possible?"

"Yes."

"I guess Stanton's Mill isn't much interested in duty.

And guess what—this is strange—she was planning to make some money. I guess to sell her art. In the big outside world. She asked me about Tirza's List. Do you know about Tirza's List?"

"I've heard of *Emily's* List."

"Emily's List is political. This one is commercial. Like eBay, but very exclusive and high-priced and secret. Could you get into that list, she wanted to know, if you had something very valuable to sell? Were the Tirza people honest? Would they guard your valuable possession? I thought that was odd. That she would think her art was that valuable. Commercially so. It's not a Stanton's Mill approach, now is it?"

I agree with Mrs. La Salle, but only sort of.

Not a Stanton's Mill way, to plan to sell your own art through a high-priced Internet auction house. Also, it's not Stanton's Mill to think of selling anything that way. But maybe—I don't want to think about it, but maybe—

Maybe there was something else valuable that Tamina owned. An uncomfortable thought invades the back of my mind, waving a sign. It has happened before in the world's history. It takes some getting used to.

Baby selling? Oh, God, no.

Hey, the uncomfortable thought tells me, you've been looking for an answer. There it is. Baby selling.

But how in hell do you advertise on the Internet?

I say weakly that this is interesting.

"I certainly thought so," says Mrs. La Salle. "I've thought about her a lot, as if there was something in the situation I wasn't getting. Do you know that feeling?"

Oh, Mrs. La Salle, do I ever.

"And then she died. And I certainly wasn't expecting that."

Mrs. La Salle says she ha~
and that she'll show them tc
goes off to get her wires and

So in a minute we are lo
that might be sold on eBa~
elegant miniature, is the n
railings, a light standard.

Even though my mind
of Tamina with baby. But no, ~~~ ~
Salle points out, resolutely of inanimate objects.

"You know," she says thoughtfully as she packs up her gear, "that Tirza is a puzzle. Because I do an awful lot of Internet research. I know most of the tricks, and I got curious about this list because the honchos around publishing talk about it. A lot of my old colleagues—well, I worked for an antiques magazine once, did I tell you that?—well, those people gossiped about Tirza's List and planned to buy goodies from it. Cellini salt shakers and Babylonian fertility goddesses and Tanagra figures. Million-dollar goods. Undercover. Stolen, probably. And loads of secrecy, even about the fact that the site exists at all. You have to get referred by someone and there's a private access address. Just like an old speakeasy. I was surprised Tamina had even heard of it."

Yes, I tell Mrs. La Salle, that is peculiar. I don't put it this way to her, but I am really, really interested.

"And I couldn't find it. I tried every Internet trick I know and I couldn't find it.

"I guess it had to be her art she was selling," she adds. "She never actually said so. But there wouldn't be anything else she owned that she thought was that valuable. Couldn't possibly be."

I tell her it
this Tirza's
puter pro
assured

would be wonderful if she kept on chasing
ust question. "You're so good with these com-
blems," I say. Mrs. La Salle is staid and self-
, but she pinks up at my compliment.

🦅 Chapter 16

I am descending on Stanton's Mill determined to ask some questions.

Meaningful ones. Questions that might lead to Tirza, although I don't know exactly what that is.

I'm going to interview Susie. My dad. Beau. Sunshine. All the people who haven't really talked.

I pull up in the co-op parking lot full of this agenda and am stopped by meeting Rob. He is on his way to his car; he's leaving his mother's house.

I remember that I'm mad at him. I haven't heard from him since that night on the Manor oriental rug.

"Carla!" he says, sounding enthusiastic, and I respond, "Rob," sounding repressive.

"Listen. The hospital had an epidemic of dysentery. All-night stuff." Rob's specialty is tropical medicine, which seems like a peculiar specialty for northern California, but he gets his clients from the big Latino population in the growing fields.

"God, have I missed you," he adds. "But," he continues, not stopped by the chill I'm radiating, "but I did some research on your stuff and looked at Tamina's records. She'd had a brain scan."

I repeat, "Brain scan," and then say, "Oh, the headaches." To which Rob says, "Yes, and it was negative, and guess what, the nurse reports that Tamina said, 'That woman is a bitch.' After she heard it was negative. And the nurse thought that was weird because, I quote, 'She looked like an angel.'"

I say, "Right," and fall into step beside him. This information doesn't add anything, but it shows Rob cares.

Tamina had it rough. Baby, alcoholic mother, Anneliese. Tirza. What's Tirza?

For sure Anneliese pushed her. Anneleise had a baby scheme. Tamina knew too much about it.

I move closer to Rob. It's a chilly night and he lets off steam and warmth. "Thanks," I say.

He tells me, "Right," and we walk for a minute or so across a dark and rutted parking lot. He sticks out an elbow for me to hold on to. He says, "Jesus, I did miss you."

Rob has to get back to his hospital; he is scheduled for an evening in Emergency.

We take our time making our way down to his car, which is at the far end of the co-op parking lot. "I wish I could stay," he says, and I'm neutral toward him. Almost friendly. I hang on to his arm and murmur stuff about how pressured Emergency must be. He says, "Nada. Zilch. All the dysentery cleared up; just sprained fingers. You've got more pressure here," and we hang on to each other some more (it is pitch dark at this end of the lot) and talk about the people that I suspect in general. "Anneliese, of course," I tell him. "And Beau, because he's too smooth and polished for here. Why doesn't he go off and live in San Francisco?"

"Here he can feel superior."

"And I think we have to listen to poor little Arby—to what he told us—after all, he did confess."

At this point my monologue is interrupted by Rob, who moves his arm up and around and his hand along my shoulder until he encloses my sharp shoulder bone. Then he gets his face close to mine, which, in the dark, I know more by breath against my eyelids than by sight. I could pull away, but I don't. I tell myself that I've really been giving Rob a hard time. I tell myself that the cedar chip surface we're standing on is wobbly, but that's not the reason I don't pull away. Actually, I lean against him. Once again I think, half self-satisfiedly, about poor-little-Carla; at last somebody is comforting Little Carla's Inner Child, whoever that is.

We kiss. A good kiss. Maybe being unstable and insecure and partly blind makes it better. Focuses your perceptions. It's the kind of kiss that you feel across your chest cavity and branching down and forking out, as if all the important channels in your body got outlined in red.

It has been a long time since I was kissed like this. Well, at least two weeks, or whenever it was that I fell asleep on the Manor Oriental rug.

It feels fine. It wakes up the orgones in the front of the body. I let a hand go around Rob's waist and push myself against him.

It takes us a half hour to get the seventy-five feet to his car. We have to stop along the way to admire a raccoon and we stop because I say we have to. We stop while I tell him that of course he doesn't really need to go in, for sure he can get someone to trade shifts with him. And he points out, with his nose buried in my neck, that he is already late. He says, "Oh, God, have I missed you."

I decide that this is something like coming down with the flu, and it grabs me in the same places—throat, chest, belt line. Of course, I really believe love depends on mutual respect and honesty and all that stuff. Just not right now.

"Oh, my *God*," I say.

Rob says, "Darling, darling," and a few other meaningless mutters. We stumble back and forth. We hold on to each other. The atmosphere is pitch-dark and enveloping and the terrain is unstable and everything is great.

We finally stumble against the hood of his car, where we lean for a while. Then we separate and he gets in and starts the motor and leans out the window and says, "Stay here tonight. I'll be back in the morning," and I say, "Sure," and he says, "God, Carla, have I missed you," and then he backs off into the darkness.

Now I have to make my way out of the parking lot and up the path to Susie's house. I seem to accomplish this okay. I suppose I'm feeling good, but it seems more peculiar than that.

Susie's house is brightly lighted. That shouldn't surprise me; Susie's house is usually brightly lighted. Although somehow I'd expected it to have gotten darker, to go with my confused emotions.

It is, however, quiet, which doesn't accord with bright lighting nor with Susie. A silent house seems unnatural. It's so quiet that I think something odd must be happening. I am wired and feeling peculiar from my long romantic session with Rob and that seems to make me especially jumpy. I sneak up the path and station myself behind the porch swing.

From there I can see most of the main room, which is part living room and part kitchen. It is looking strange. It contains four people who are sitting on a row of chairs lined up neatly facing the kitchen. Susie and Sunshine and Sunshine's mom and my dad are sitting on these chairs with their knees together, Susie has her arms straight at her sides, Sunshine's mom is crying silently. Everyone is watching the inside of the kitchen.

I can't see the inside of the kitchen from where I am. I move, and still can't see. And move again, and realize that I've made a noise, because everyone reacts, surreptitiously, as if they're trying not to let on they're reacting. Even Sunshine's mom restrains herself some.

But I decide this is it, the time is now, and I cross the porch and rasp open the screen door and stride into the room.

Susie turns her head. She opens her mouth and then closes it. She says very forcefully, "Run, darling Carla."

My dad readjusts his chair. He proclaims in a pleased voice, "Why, that is my daughter. My daughter, Carla. Come in, my dear."

Sunshine's mom cries harder.

A voice from the kitchen commands, "Shut up, all of you."

The kitchen entrance more or less frames the stove. This stove is a nice old cream and green enamel one, and seated on top of it, her legs braced against the closed oven door, is Anneliese Wertiger.

Susie uses her stove a lot, but I guess it's been turned off long enough to be okay to sit on. Because Anneliese would not rest her butt on a hot stove.

She holds something in her hand that I take to be a gun.

This object is shinier and more ornate than the gun Cherie gave me. But yes, it certainly is a gun. I am sorry I don't have my own gun. I agree with my inner voice, which is now lecturing me about wearing it and reminding me that Cherie cautioned, "all the time."

Anneliese spots me and she reacts. All of Anneliese reacts. The legs, braced against the closed oven door, flex. Her shoulders brace. Her head inclines forcefully. She grins; I guess you could call it a grin. She speaks. "Well, hi. Here she is. Here she finally is. Greetings, oh, bitch."

You don't have to answer a remark like that, so I don't.

"I flushed you out, babe, didn't I? I got your little know-everything dad and he pulled you in. That was real smart of me. So now, little part-time sheriff, what do you do?"

Again I just stare. Anneliese is holding that piece pretty firmly.

"You couldn't leave it alone, could you? Had to go fussing around, trying to figure it out. And now I bet you're sorry. That wasn't such a hot move. Up to your chin in it now, aren't you? Well, little Miss Detective . . ."

Here she starts getting creative, wobbling the gun around in an alarming way, pointing it at people other than me, my dad primarily.

He says, "You know, that weapon could be dangerous."

She says, "Shut up, you old fraud. You're the principal one." She puts a lot of venom in that.

I, Carla, am supposed to react. Do something.

"What do you want with me?" I ask reasonably.

I guess Anneliese can't see my hands, which are fiercely clenched, nor my toes, curled entirely under inside my boots. She can't see that I'm biting my lip and cursing myself for not having my gun. My perfectly good gun, property of the Del Oro Sheriff's Office, with perfectly good instructions from my superior officer, Sheriff Cherie Ghent.

"What do I want?" Anneliese echoes, amping her lungpower up to a screech. "Guess what, bitch . . . Hey, cut it out there, you little old fake Daddy Alzheimer's."

My father is making small motions. He says, "Anneliese—that's your name, isn't it?—this seems quite pointless. What are you talking about?"

Daddy has had experience in Egypt with hysterical people holding guns. Maybe that's why he doesn't sound upset enough.

Or maybe he simply doesn't get it.

"Investigated, right?" Anneliese asks. The gun swivels my way again. "Looked into everything, figured it out. And now do you know it all, bitch? Can you tell me, Miss Deputy Sheriff, what's gonna happen next? And tell me, what do you know now? Who's gonna get arrested now?"

Even though I'm facing a crazy lady, my face must still register that I'm baffled. I don't know exactly what's bothering her. She waves her piece around. "Okay, okay.

"What I want you to do"—she turns full attention on me—"Miz Part-Time Deputy Sheriff, I want you to erase all this stuff that has happened and forget it all and wipe it off the official records. Say good-bye to Crystal. You never ever heard of such a thing."

"Good-bye to what?" My father asks pleasantly. "Crystal? Crystals have special powers."

Anneliese's irritation meter is on high. "Will you for crap sake shut up?"

Daddy says, "Oh."

Sunshine's mom makes noises.

Anneliese focuses on me. "Just forget the whole goddamn mess. Forget you ever heard of or thought about me or my history. There is no such thing as indigo. There are no indigo auras, no indigo babies, shut up about all that stuff, nothing. And you don't know anything about the Crystal Facility. No story there about any insurance agencies, no history. If you want to get this gang of idiots out of here or get your little know-everything dad back in one piece."

"Anneliese, that's . . ." I want to say ridiculous, but I don't.

I'm armed with comments on how amazingly childish this idea is. What does she think we're doing, playing a game? Retract this move, go back to Go. Law enforcement already knows about indigo and indigo auras because I *am* law enforcement. And I've talked to Cherie, who is double law enforcement. And the story about the insurance agencies at Crystal is history. It got written up in the newspapers.

Anneliese breaks in. "And who in the hell gave you permission to call me by my first name?"

This question is so idiotic, especially delivered in the middle of everything else, that it stops me cold.

She squats forward. It's hard to sit gracefully on top of a stove; she leans, looking ready and mean. Her heels grip the closed oven door; ropy tendons show in her legs. She is wearing an Anneliese-type dress, black and probably well cut, if it weren't rucked up over her knees.

"Your name isn't Anneliese." Maybe I'm fired by the

recklessness of desperation. Actually, I feel a little drunk. "You're Ann Warner. That's one of your names."

Anneliese says, "Oh, God." After a minute she adds, "Quit showing off, what I want to know is, who turned me in . . . which insurance company was it? There were two of them, right? Okay, which one?"

I say, "Oh." And suddenly I more or less understand. Anneliese has been swatted with two problems at once. Number one is the indigo situation; her wonderful scam and her customers here. She's worried about that; she sounds as if it has begun to get shaky in some way I don't know about. And the other problem is her own personal situation. The one from her Crystal history. Her former insurance buddies may be after her. They may be murderous. She blames me because I investigated that.

And she blames my dad. Because he's with me. Because he sounds as if he knows something.

And so she is baffled and angry and is threatening to shoot me and my father.

Or all of us.

I am trying to figure out how far away I am from Anneliese. I think I know a couple of ways of disarming someone. These methods are not from lessons with Cherie, who doesn't do things like give lessons; these methods are left over from when Rob took aikido classes and practiced his moves on me.

It's hard to remember those moves while figuring out what else is happening.

Next to me my dad has started making get-ready-for-something noises.

"Oh, cut it out," Anneliese says. And she raises her piece and aims it full on me. She does it all wrong, squinting and using only one hand. You're supposed to use two; anybody who has ever watched TV knows that.

"Get ready, bitch," she says.

There's a ferocious commotion behind me. It's my father.

My dad is eighty-seven years old but he is astonishingly wiry and fit; he has had all those years of climbing up pyramids and down excavations and dodging falling rock and squashing poisonous snakes and jumping over fissures in excavations.

He does one of those gully-spanning leaps now.

He springs from my right rear side like a rocket and is across the kitchen in a superninja move. There's a scuffle and commotion when he bangs against Anneliese and they both go down, the details lost in flailing arms and legs. And a moment later, in the noise of the gun explosion.

Anneliese lies on the floor, her black lace underwear exposed. My father is on top of her. Smoke or dust hovers above them. The oven door has clanged open and partly obscures the view.

"*Merde, scheisse*, shit," Anneliese says. "Oh, God, why was I ever born? All I wanted was to do good."

After which amazing remark she wiggles loose from my dad and pushes herself out from under the oven door and into a sitting position. "So now you've got to arrest me," she says in my direction. "Or else kill me. Choose."

She is, however, still holding the gun, which she aims drunkenly toward me.

Daddy lies motionless where he fell. He's on his stomach, his white hair fanned out in a halo; his arms extended, hands limp. I get the horrible idea that maybe the gunshot didn't go harmlessly off into space but found a home in him.

The same thought has apparently occurred to Anneliese. "Shit in the third degree," she says, shaking him by the shoulder. "Don't do that. I didn't mean it. Wake up. Quit. You can't do this to me."

In a minute she apparently sees something partly reassuring; she says, "Okay. The old fart is okay." Then she brings her gun up to her nose and examines it critically. "Five more shots. No, he isn't dead. He just looks dead. So you can't accuse me of killing him. Oh, God."

She starts once more trying to aim at me, but not very precisely.

"I'm coming to look at him," I say, and she says, "No," and positions the gun better.

"I am," and I move one foot. She says, "No." We do that a couple of times until Daddy groans and swipes one hand along the floor and I settle the debate by flinging myself along the linoleum pretty much the way he did.

I'm lots younger than he is but I'm not athletic and I make an apprehensive, ungraceful mess of it. It takes me maybe five seconds, and that whole time I'm braced for a gunshot. Not knowing what that might feel like. Maybe a smashing knockout pain. Maybe oblivion, the total end.

"Daddy, darling," I say. Nothing has happened to me on my way here.

I push myself into a sitting position and tug him partway onto my lap. "Are you all right, honey? Let's see, turn over now; can you move this arm? Sweetheart, now try for the other arm . . ."

He lies flaccid, hair spread out like an electrified saint.

"So." Anneliese climbs to her feet. "They told you my name?"

Her gun is again wobbling toward me.

"No." After a minute I add, "I found it out for myself.

"Don't move Daddy," I say.

Anneliese says, "Oh, shit. So you don't really know anything. Only what Jenny . . . Which is too much. Everybody knows everything. But I guess you're not connected . . ."

"No," I say. "Not connected." Whatever *connected* means. Obviously something bad.

She clicks the gun; it sounds to me as if she's manipulating the safety. "You learned all that from Jenny?" she inquires meditatively.

"Well," she continues, "I guess you got to arrest me now, right? Because I pulled a gun on a deputy sheriff? I guess the fact that I was being followed and threatened and that I didn't really mean to shoot doesn't make any difference, right?" She assesses my face and agrees, "Right.

"So then . . ." The gun is out again, trained on the seated crowd, but mostly on my dad, still spread out on the floor. "Okay, then, it's good-bye to all of you for a while. Think of me."

Susie has a tall kitchen window to the right of her stove. Anneliese retreats to this; I notice with surprise that half of it is already pulled all the way up. Maybe she came in that way.

She bows her head in order to go out backward. She pauses for a minute with one foot on the outside and the other one still in the house. "If you want to know who pushed your little Tamina-cutie, it was that slimy bastard Beau. I saw him. He was right beside her."

Then she gets herself entirely on the other side of the

window and disappears into the native scrub pine, eucalyptus shoots, blackberry bushes, and poison oak.

Sunshine's mother fans her face and says, "Oh, hey, wow, I mean!"

Susie says, "My dear, how is darling Edward? I think he was hurt."

Chapter 17

When I am able to pull my dad's jacket off and unbutton his shirt and look at his shoulder, I find that Susie is right and he has been hurt. Blood has soaked his shirt; there is a ragged crease in his bare shoulder.

But he can talk. He's a little cockeyed and groggy, but verbal. "Sweetheart, it doesn't hurt. It feels peculiar. As if someone has hit me. I think someone did hit me. That happened once in Tell el-Amarna."

Yes, that's how I thought it would feel. Very hard. I reach for my cell phone.

But Susie has grabbed Daddy's phone; she's also calling 911.

The ambulance arrives fast, and it usually takes a long time to get to Stanton's Mill. Maybe our double call speeds them up.

At North Coast Hospital, people start clustering around the gurney in the emergency room.

At first there is Tallulah, the doctor whom we know, and then there is Rob, and after that Belle from the Manor. And finally Cherie.

They are cross, especially with me. They are noisy about it. They use words like *care* and *caution*.

They are mad at me for not having guarded my father better. And then each one is angry with some other person whom they can hold responsible. Rob thinks his mom could have done *something*; Cherie is furious with her deputy who was supposed to be guarding us ("I never told that idiot jerk Delray he could leave so early"); Belle is mad at Cherie ("What's a sheriff supposed to be for, anyway?").

Tallulah wonders loudly what on earth is wrong with all of us.

Meanwhile my father is examined, exclaimed over, listened to, photographed, fed oxygen, bandaged, cuddled. "Really, it was just a scrape," Tallulah finally admits. "An inch more to the right and it could have mattered. But this little friend of mine is Mr. Luck, aren't you, soldier?"

"That is my darling buddy, Crocodile Dundee," Cherie says from the foot of the examining table, where she has wrangled herself a position. "But, darling Croc, we got to get you out of there. No more Stanton's Mill. You've done your job now; I heard you were real, real brave . . ."

"Was I?" my dad asks around the oxygen support cannula in his nose. "How nice."

"Totally brave and saved your daughter. Wonderful thing to do. And now we have to get you back to that Manor, where Miz Belle will keep an eye on you."

"Better than some did," Belle says darkly.

Tallulah remarks that there are too many people in this emergency room.

My dad is given a private room, which shortly is full of pots of flowers, bunches of the same, boxes of candy, stacks of books, and a stuffed crocodile. He sits up against three pillows, still getting oxygen. "Was I really brave? I am so happy to hear it."

And he says that he hopes all the flowers in pots can go back to the Manor with him. He thinks the potted plants will look nice in his apartment.

So I guess the question of whether he will return to the Manor and give up the Mill has been settled. A bullet wound is a surprising experience, even for someone as seasoned as my dad.

Dr. Tallulah says, "He's okay but I did five stitches and I'll keep him a couple of nights. He's having fun."

Tallulah is an appealing woman with short brown hair and a straightforward gaze. One trusts her.

Rob and Susie and I go back to the Mill.

"Oh, dear," Susie says. "I don't feel quite the same about it." She seems to mean the Mill and its atmosphere.

"You have to lock your windows tonight," I tell her, and she is appalled, murmuring things about fresh air and miasmas and feeling enclosed, until I remind her that there is a crazy lady with a gun out in her bushes.

Susie gives in, rather sadly.

"Do you know," she says as we are turning the catches on the floor-to-ceiling windows (and I wonder how much good they will do, but decide they're worth trying anyway), "do you know, the other day I thought I saw darling Squeegee. On the walk going away from here."

I say that you often think you see a person that reminds you of someone dead and she says, "Oh, no. I mean there was something special about him. How he held his head and all. It was Squeegee. But of course it could have been his spirit."

"No, it couldn't." I itch when people talk like that.

"Molly Littlefeather told me the same thing," Susie says. "But of course, Molly only met him twice. In this life, that is. Sometimes that makes it easier."

I decide to bolt the door out to the porch where Daddy usually sleeps. He won't be back here for a while.

So Susie distributes Long Jan tea and says it is wonderful for trauma and she is certain that we have all had trauma but not the serious kind. She then retreats toward her bedroom.

She is very gentle and diplomatic about arranging this. "Oh, I am so tired. I need my bed. And I do feel quite calm in my soul. That tea is so good for the hopeful part of the spirit.

"And," she adds before she exits, "it is so good to have my two darlings together again." Susie always needs to do that.

Once alone, we do not have an easy time of it. The marijuana couch is narrow. There are not enough blankets. I have begun to ache in some of the places that I overused in my skate across the floor.

Rob is concerned about this. "How did you do that

move?" he asks. "You just stretched yourself out? Don't you remember that you're supposed to . . ." And he starts a description of a successful aikido body projection across space, and then stops midway to kiss me and say, "Oh, God, how stupid I am."

We're not in a good position for cuddling. But we manage some. And I say, "Hey, bro, darling, I thought about you." Which is pretty much true. During that slide across the floor I thought about two subjects: (1) was I going to be shot, and (2) sex. Save me for more sex. "I'm glad it came out okay," I say.

Rob says, "Oh my God, my God." And he kisses and smooths and kisses and feels and kisses and unbuttons buttons. And starts removing articles of clothing. And saying occasionally, "Does this hurt?" but then forgetting all about that.

It takes a while, because I am thinking about my dad and being grateful that he is not really hurt and also thinking about Anneliese, out there in the bushes and also remembering that my head is still reeling. But eventually it happens: I get electrified down to my toes, that great feeling that makes everything curl under and then curl up. And I am saying, "Oh, Rob, oh my God, oh, darling."

And he is not saying much, except that at the end he says, "God almighty, I've missed you."

He kisses me a lot.

Then we try to get to sleep, which is another story.

The couch is too small. There aren't enough blankets. I have a crick in my neck.

Rob says he knows just the answer for that.

And he does.

I am so out of practice that I would never have thought of that as the remedy.

He sleeps on the edge and does not complain about falling off. He kisses and gets into the moment. He says, "You skin is so soft. You feel so great. Carla, I do love you."

I tell him, "Don't talk," and try not to think, which is my big problem.

In the middle of the night I get up and check all the windows.

Susie is prowling around. She has been careful to prowl only as far as the kitchen, not into the living room, where we are.

"You aren't supposed to worry," she tells me, although she obviously has been doing that. "Maybe we should check up on dear Edward in the hospital?"

I persuade her that dear Edward is better off than we are and I go back to the marijuana couch carrying a full complement of blankets and sheets and somehow manage to make the bed around and under Rob and then to squeeze myself into it. Rob wakes up as I get back in. He is very affectionate. He says things about missing me and learning at last what I am really like and after all we have known each other almost all our lives. He squeezes and I say, "Ouch," and then he does it again.

He says that it is fine that the couch is small. It is exactly what he wants. He gets me encircled, in order to prove how enthusiastic he is, and asks if I want to try again. Maybe tonight will be the night for the trifecta, he suggests.

He doesn't want to give up this idea until I announce that I'm going to sleep on the floor.

Then he is apologetic. It takes a while, but eventually both of us, wrapped around each other like cuddling hamsters, fall asleep.

Rob is somewhat bleary in the morning. I have trouble determining this, since I also am bleary. And sleepy. "Do you ache?" I ask him. I ache.

In the kitchen, about fourteen feet away, Susie is cooking eggs and some kind of tofu and oregano sausage. It smells wonderful. "Let us arise and go now," I tell Rob, and roll off the couch after him.

"Well, good, good morning," Susie says. "And a beautiful morning it is. And both of my beautiful children together again, what could be more wonderful?"

If it weren't for the seductive smells of eggs and sausage, I think I would deeply resent Susie being so interested in my affairs. I search around for a bathrobe, of which Susie has several, and wrap one around me and go off into the kitchen, where the windows are again open and bird song from outside contends with the noise of coffee bubble inside. Tofu sausage snaps and crackles, sounding like ordinary sausage. "Susie, I love you," I tell her.

She pays no attention. "You've lost weight. You're going to turn into a skeleton. Sit down."

Rob joins me. He eats five sausages and I eat three. There are two kinds of toast and three kinds of jam. "Yes, it's Happy Dawn's jam," Susie says. "I've thought, after all this started, that her jam is infused with dear Tamina's spirit."

I pick up a round-bellied jar filled with sparkling amber jelly. It's easy to think of it as a crystal ball with some of the essence of Tamina balleting inside.

After breakfast, Rob pretends to have some ideas about hiking. I tell him no way. I say there are wild animals out in this woods. I say we both should rest and that I haven't read my latest Tamina document, a Letter to God. The letter has been in my pile of stuff since last night.

Beau dropped the Letter to God off, saying that it's from Tamina and he thinks I will be interested. I guess Beau was sympathizing about my tussle with Anneliese.

So I settle down on the couch and rip open Beau's envelope and extract the Letter to God.

It's labeled, in pink marker, "For God."

And it wasn't mailed. Tamina just left it with Beau, I guess.

It begins, *Oh, God*. But after that it gets harder to track.

Rob has established himself in the leather chair opposite. He seems to be reading. Susie's library is a collection of books about raw and waterless and sun-powered cookery plus some books or pamphlets that probably belonged to Squeegee and discuss philosophy, history, and Marxist protest plus the ideas of *Mad* magazine. Rob is immersed in one of the *Mad*s.

I tell him, "Hey, she's not sure God exists," and he doesn't answer.

I'm ready for a whole range of expressions and emotions by Tamina but mostly for mention of her illness and queries as to why, oh why. But there's none of this in the first two pages. Tamina apostrophizes God (*if You are really there*) for a couple of paragraphs about how beautiful her baby is, and spends what I think is some useless time admiring the baby's hair and intelligence. (*She really looked at my painting. Really focused her eyes on it. She loved it!*) After which she diverges. (*Oh, God again, if You are really there, tell me what to do.*)

Okay, I think. But then it appears that Tamina can't be forthright, even with God. *Indigo consciousness,* she begins. *How fortunate I am. To recognize that I have this wonderful baby, with her brilliant aura—and last night I truly almost saw it—I was looking at her, sort of out of the side of my eye—*

Tamina, it seems, saw the indigo aura. Arby, who was present, did not. But Arby, Tamina disloyally says, has not yet worked his way into a higher level of consciousness. He's not arrived yet. Tamina apparently has almost arrived. She almost saw the indigo. She understands the value and power of indigo. That she has special responsibilities to it, yes, she gets that. She knows that she has a DUTY. She uses this word several times. *Yes, Oh God I understand about my DUTY, I want to follow what is called the dictates of DUTY; I simply count on You to reveal these to me; I am perceptive but not awfully so . . . If the course of action is the true course of action, ordained by our forefathers and mothers back into the fifth and sixth generations?* Help. Tamina darling, you're supposed be more original than this. You've been dipping into the Book of Leviticus for inspiration.

In a minute I ask Rob, "What does *out of the portals of the children of Baal* mean?"

"What the hell?" he bleats, and grabs the Tamina letter from me. After perusing it for a minute, he's mournful. "Oh, Jesus, that poor kid. Is that what they were doing? Drowning her in this stuff?"

I tell him I don't know, Tamina was too inventive for her own good; maybe she dipped into an old stack of hymn books all by herself. "She even has some of my dad's Egyptian poetry in there. *Guide my footsteps toward your daylight, oh, Ra.*

"But, Rob, listen to this: *The way up and the way down are totally different; I will give her to the perfect setting from which she will blossom a queen indeed. And how it rakes my soul to lose you and how I will follow you all these many years . . ."*

"So she's deciding to give the baby away," I summarize. I read a little further. "Oh, and now—and now she mentions her sickness. 'A sort of sickness,' she calls it. She says, *Oh god of my fathers and mothers, you have told me this is right. And now that I understand that I have a sickness—that I have a sort of sickness that may be with me. I understand this now. Because that time that she fell. I did not really understand that I was there and didn't see it.*

"It's not fair," I tell Rob. "I hate those bastards. They leaned on her until she broke.

"But here"—I have arrived at the back pages of the letter—"here is something again about her illness, maybe. She says, *That wonderful seeress Anneliese has explained to me, actually I do understand; I think I have no memory of my darling Penny falling but she obviously did fall. And Anneliese, who knows so much about it, says I am part indigo because of being the mother of an indigo child, and indigos have these out-of-body times when they just blank out. And that is okay, it's part of the indigo process, but it means you can be a faulty caretaker. Just for a while. And that's another reason why it is my DUTY—yes, I understand that now. Just the way God said it to Abraham. And I understood all about that in that wonderful, strange, transporting session with the guru. Anneliese explained all that to me; I didn't know about it.*"

"That Anneliese really surrounded her, didn't she?" Rob says.

"The last thing she says," I tell Rob, "is something about Lana. The Lana that went away to Placer County. *I talked to*

Lana and maybe she isn't as much Indigo as I am, because she is not thinking about DUTY the way I am. She is resisting the idea of her DUTY."

"I guess we have to go and see that Lana," I tell Rob.

☂ Chapter 18

But before we can see Lana, Rob has to do another hospital shift, and before that, I tell him, we had better go visit Scope. Right away, like today. "Because Scope's is where Anneliese usually lives.

"And she can't stay out in the woods all the time, can she?" I ask rhetorically. "I mean she has to come in sometime. At least to collect her camping gear." I stop to contemplate the prospect of Anneliese as a permanent camper. She doesn't give off any outdoor-enthusiast vibes. She's not the sort to perch in a tree for a year or ascend Everest all by herself. Anneliese is more of an indoor darkened-room type.

"Scope said he hated her," Rob remarks critically.

He has absorbed a lot of facts about our situation. I guess he really has been listening to me.

I tell him, yes, right, but Scope's house still is where her clothes are, and furthermore, yes, Scope *said* he hated her,

but he went right on living with her and letting her give indigo consultations in his living room and shining indigo
neon signs out front. "And I'll bet," I say, "he continued letting her buy groceries with the money the consultations
brought in."

At this point Susie, who has been listening while she
shovels *huevos rancheros* onto our plates, gets interested.
"Scope," she says. "Yes. Scope Fugasi. He was a good friend
of Squeegee's."

I am amazed and ask the pertinent questions. *Susie, that's
interesting. Why didn't you ever say this before? But you weren't
living here then, you and Squeegee lived in Berkeley, didn't you?
And what do you mean by good friend? Say more.*

Susie says, "Oh, my goodness, why should I have mentioned it; nobody asked. And of course we didn't live here,
but of course we visited often; that's how Squeegee got this
house; Stanton's Mill was the place to visit then, such an atmosphere of freedom and love; I have this wonderful video
of all of us on the beach and cooking mussels and making
faces at the camera . . ." Susie sighs and says, "It is so wrong
to think about the old days and tell yourself today isn't as
good as then, of course it is just as wonderful today if we
choose to make it so."

"Susie, darling, tell me about Scope."

"He was quite visionary then; it was lovely."

I am stopped cold at this picture of Scope being visionary
and lovely. I think of him as fat and sloppy. Exhortations to
be more specific do not get far. "I don't know, perhaps it was
mushrooms but I don't think so; I think it came from
within; there was an amazing prescience, do you know what
I mean? Scope was quite astonishing. We all listened to
him. He was a poet then, he talked poetically." Susie isn't

looking at me, so she must, in an un-Susie-like way, intuit that I don't believe her. Scope, I am thinking, is and probably always was, a silent clod. "He was thinner then, too," she adds in a non sequitur.

"And he was sensitive. In touch with higher powers," I say, trying some irony.

She sounds puzzled. "Oh, not exactly, darling; he just had this gift; he would start to talk and it was, well . . . lyrical . . . Squeegee in particular was captivated."

"Scope doesn't do that anymore."

"Isn't it a shame? I think not. I think perhaps he has lost the gift. But for a while he had an enormous influence. For a while I thought he had influenced Squeegee to leave me. Because at first, when Squeegee left, Scope also wasn't around. But that was just at first. Then Squeegee was around here, in the Mill, for a while. And then he was gone."

Susie sighs. "Squeegee was so different then. At least I thought he was. Your dear father said I was misled.

"Squeegee's fierce side developed slowly.

"It only came out toward the end.

"I worry sometimes. I never wanted to talk to you about it. But I worry that Squeegee died as a result of his fierce side."

I have no memory of Squeegee and am amazed that Susie would like someone with a fierce side.

"Oh, but so masculine," she says vaguely when I start questioning her about that now. "And Scope. I think he had a fierce side, too."

"No, he didn't," I say. "And did Scope come back after Squeegee left?"

"Oh yes, he was back, just as you see him.

"Only," she adds, "of course, not with Anneliese. She came much later."

"Does Scope have a job of any kind?" I ask. Many residents of Stanton's Mill exist on dwindling trust funds. Others have disability payments.

"Why, darling, of course he does. He works for the water company. You know we have our very own water company here at the Mill.

"That's an important job when you live here," Susie adds, assessing my surprised expression. "Septic tanks, you know. And the drip from the trees, and all. They have to bring the water down from the ridge."

I am imagining Scope in overalls, driving a truck. Nothing about Scope computes too well.

"Why, you've lost weight," I tell him. Which is not at all the way I've planned to greet Scope, whom I want to question about Anneliese. I was planning to smash him with an accusation and get him suspicious and on the defensive.

He must have been dieting and it has begun to show. He looks twenty pounds lighter. His pants hang, but somehow he's rustled up a perfectly presentable shirt, which looks okay. His arms exhibit muscle. He holds on to one side of the door frame and stares with dark-circled eyes.

People usually like hearing that they've lost weight. Not Scope. He watches me glumly. He's still a beefy man, big enough to block the path into his house. Above our heads the INDIGO SPIRITUAL sign blinks its bright message.

He looks a lot better because of the weight loss. I haven't seen him for a while and all this physical change has happened quickly.

Maybe he's been worrying.

"Scope, why don't you let us in?" Rob asks.

Scope grunts and looks as if he's planning to tell us to get lost. And then moves aside.

The front room seems pretty much the same except that it's dusty, rays of sunlight riding the light cast by the windows and churning the dancing motes.

"I have applied for a warrant for the arrest of Anneliese Wertiger," I say, stretching a point or two. I plant my feet apart and stick out my chest in my new sheriff's jacket. I'm trying to establish the facts here. *Listen up, Scope; I am your enemy. I regard this household with suspicion. I want to get you apprehensive.*

So far the guy just looks bored.

Rob and I sit down, side by side, on the leather couch with the Peruvian blanket.

"She corporeally threatened an officer of the law." It's funny how you start framing pretentious sentences like that once you have put on a sheriff's jacket. "I mean, she pulled out her gun."

Scope stares. He is either chewing gum or munching on his dentures.

I decide not to fill in the rest of the story, which I'm sure he knows. Of course Anneliese came back here last night for something. To get her toothbrush. "Tell me, have you seen her?"

"Nope." He offers this in the laconic tone of somebody who's lying and couldn't care less about being found out.

"I need to be informed when she comes back."

Scope stares. So far he's not sitting down. He is standing near the front door, scanning us; we are seated; he is erect. Which seems to me not the best arrangement.

"Scope," I say, "you are a coworker of Anneliese's; you've

shared the things she's done here; we aren't certain what all her actions in Stanton's Mill have been but a lot of them are questionable, and now there is—"

"Oh, shit," Scope says, and thumps into a leather chair, which squeaks. Despite his weight loss, he still sits heavily. "I didn't cowork with that bitch on anything."

"Sure you did. She lived here in your house and gave consultations and sold literature; all her work on the indigo aura came out of this . . ." For some reason I want to use the word *venue*. "She worked here. She did lots."

"Damn right. Took over my house."

"And you let her."

"Encouraged her. Sure. La Belle Dame Sans Merci. You know what that means? 'Oh, what can ail thee, knight-at-arms,/Alone and palely loitering . . .' Sure. Came up out of the creek dripping wet, holding up some damn sword . . ."

Rob says, "Hey, for God's sake," while I forge ahead. Susie, with her little speech about how much Squeegee had loved Scope, prepared me for something or other weird in his personality, although not this exactly.

"The first time I saw you," I say, "you told me she latched on to you at the bus station."

"That, too. The Loathly Lady. From prehistory. The archetypal figure. Did you know that I wrote poetry?"

"So you knew her from before?"

"Oh, fuck," Scope says. "Why don't you say what you want and get out of here. You got nothing on me. Not a damn thing. Why did I let you in? I guess I'm worried about the bitch."

"And you have known her before?"

"Cut it out. If you want to question me, come back with a warrant for that."

"Where would she go?" I persist. "She doesn't look like the kind to camp in the woods."

"Unpredictable. Unreliable. Oh, variety, thy name is Anneliese. If you think I know where she is, you got another think coming. Behind her lie the great Azores, before her only shoreless seas."

"Are you drunk, Scope?"

"I don't do that, dear. Nor Percocet. Nor meth. None of the backwoods entertainments of this area. This is just my normal abnormal personality.

"So"—he stands up and adjusts his belly to fit under his belt—"you better get out of here now; you got no right to be here; your welcome is real threadbare."

"Listen," I say. "Please call me if you hear from her."

"No."

Of course, I could hang around, but it seems to me that would be counterproductive. Rob and I exit moderately gracefully.

"Wow," Rob says when we are outside.

I am turned around, watching the neon sign go off. Does that happen automatically, or is Scope flipping a switch? "Not exactly what I expected," I say.

Rob is thoughtful. "A place like Stanton's Mill collects weirdos. Pulls them in."

I tell him, "Uh-huh." We are walking along the path on our way to Susie's, but I don't want to go in right yet. I want to stand around for a minute and think about Scope, who doesn't seem to fit into things. Not that any of the rest of it fits together either.

I also want to stand around with Rob for a while. Last night was really good. I'm still thinking about it. I lean against him.

♟ Chapter 19

My dad is separated from North Coast Hospital with a good deal of difficulty on both sides. That is, North Coast is reluctant to let go of him. Several nurses have to come and enthuse over him. I am told what a darling he is and how lucky I am and how handsome he looks now that he is dressed in his tweed suit and vest and dark blue shirt and red-striped tie.

Tallulah comes in and says she has never seen recuperative powers like that in a person his age. She says, "Now, soldier, you will watch it, won't you? Don't stop any more bullets?" She makes faces at me about taking better care of him.

I am perfectly capable of driving us home, but Rob insists on doing that. Twenty-five miles later, when we arrive at the Manor, Belle has to greet him and say, well, he doesn't look too bad. Of course, she doesn't understand how his daughter could have been so lax. But it is good to have him back.

Belle doesn't usually say things like that. She doesn't usually admit to being fond of her clients. So this is a red-letter day.

A whole lot of residents of the Manor are lined up to greet him and kiss him. Foremost is the elegant Mrs. La Salle, for whom he is a special pet.

But Mrs. La Salle is too sophisticated not to understand the limitations of their relationship. "There is this little person here now," she says. "Her name is Happy Dawn. Do you remember her?"

Daddy says perhaps.

"I have taught her to play dominoes," Mrs. La Salle says. "She is pretty good at it."

Dominoes is a challenge for Daddy, which makes it fun. "Aha," he says.

I am pleased to hear that Happy Dawn also is okay. The Manor is a distance from Stanton's Mill, and inhabits another world, but you never know, with a big crime like murder, how far it may choose to reach out.

Daddy seems to welcome his Manor apartment, which Happy Dawn has left patted down and dusted. She is giving him a Victorian doll and a picture of Tamina. "It is quite a nice room," Daddy says appraisingly.

I call Rob and say that he should pack his kit, we are ready to go to Placer County. Yes, I say, there is a place to stay up there. I know a little motel in Gold Run. I've made plans to stay overnight. We can have a good time. That is beautiful country and—

"And," Rob interrupts, "we can have a good time."

I say, "Sure." I feel slightly guilty about making a holiday in connection with this case, which involves two unsolved murders and some disappeared babies.

Rob seems to have a mental picture of Placer County as a forested wilderness where you go from tree to tree and yell out whether anybody knows Lana, and he acts deflated when I say that I have, via Beau, the name of an actual town where Lana can be found.

Placer County is civilized; it is more or less a suburb of Sacramento. But there are still some pockets of the original Gold Country remaining, and I assume that Blue Dog, where Lana is to be found, is one of these.

Rob likes the idea of Blue Dog, and says that this trip is going to be fun.

And he is glad Ed is doing so well.

He is glad we are staying overnight. Gold Run Motel sounds just fine.

We go first to Gold Run, which is seven houses and a few pine trees. We leave our bags and do some kissing and I say that we have to get going.

Which we do, back to the freeway, where there is a lot of traffic but the sky is blue and the air, in spite of gasoline pollution, is blue, and the soil is beginning to show the distinctive red. I love that red soil. My dad and I once spent a couple of pleasant weekends in the town of Deepmine, breathing pine smell and forgetting my mother.

We turn north off the freeway toward Blue Dog, and in a minute the overlay of laboring trucks is behind us. Sun dazzles and pine trees sparkle. It begins to be really hot.

Blue Dog seems to be ten houses and a small store. The store is fronted with asbestos shingles and has a Coca-Cola sign and a self-service gas pump. The man inside looks Near Eastern but he greets us in precise English.

Beau has supplied me with a description of Lana: "Tall, skinny, short dark hair, meek looking. A surprise to be an indigo baby mom. You'd never spot her for any kind of a mom. Kind of beaten-down. She was here for maybe ten years but I never got to know her."

I boil this down for the store man, who looks thoughtful and attentive and finally nods. He wears a white butcher's apron with a ballpoint stuck in the top pocket; he pulls this out and begins drawing on a piece of butcher paper. *Up here and then left here.* Et cetera.

Each of us buys a Diet Coke and we go out again into the hot, dry, sweet-smelling dusty road with no traffic at all. Rob says, "Jeez, it's wonderful to be here with you at last." I squelch some remarks about how he could have been going places with me for a long time if he'd felt like it. Which is not entirely accurate.

Lana's house is pale yellow, very sun-baked, looking sweet and rustic. She has a lopsided front porch and a rusty couch swing with oozing cushions. Inside there are signs that Lana and the indigo baby are at home. The baby is making the whooping noises that babies use to assert their presence.

I try, "Hi, Lana," and "Hey," and "Coo-ee," and various other I-am-here noises, to no avail, and finally just walk in.

The house seems to be two rooms: a front room devoted to baby furniture, baby toys, baby mat, rug, pen, plus a couch where, maybe, Mama sleeps. And at the back, the kitchen, where baby is being fed.

Lana is spooning mashed orange food into the baby, who

has gotten a lot of it on his/her face and torso. Lana looks interested when we appear. Not startled.

After I say that we are from Stanton's Mill, she does act
startled and withholds food long enough that baby protests.
Lana says, "Jesus." Then she says, "Why?"

I ask if I can help feed the baby while I talk to her. I don't
know anything about babies, but it looks easy enough.

She doesn't say no, so I pull a chair up beside her chair
and Rob settles into the background. The orange food appears to be carrots. The baby is perfectly cooperative, so
Lana lets me take over for a minute; she settles back in her
chair and scoops her body over into a U and says, "Hell."

"You wanted to get away from Stanton's Mill," I suggest,
sounding like a cut-rate psychiatrist.

Lana says, "Yep."

I don't say, "Why?" I suggest, "The indigo baby atmosphere got too much?"

"They said I wasn't fit to have her," Lana bursts out.
"And I knew I wasn't fit to have her. Because she was illegitimate. She was a little bastard."

I'm stopped for a minute. It always surprises me to meet
this censorious idiocy, but there's a lot of it around, even in
a hippie center like Stanton's Mill. It's prevalent in rural
California. In everywhere.

"She's a love child," I say firmly, trying to remember
what Susie would say. Except Susie would put it more
firmly, offering stuff about a "wonderful demonstration of
the life principle."

"A beautiful, radiant love child," I add, getting carried
away in my Susie impersonation.

Lana says, "Oh," in a despairing voice and reaches for her
carrot spoon.

Baby pushes the spoon away. She has had enough carrots.

I suggest to Lana that we wipe the baby's face and go out to the porch swing, where we can talk.

Outside, I get a good look at Lana. She is stoop-shouldered and defeated-looking, as Beau suggested. But not when she holds baby. She brightens up then. She holds her in that kind of encircling way common to Renaissance Madonnas. And she looks so good that way that I start being afraid for her.

"Did you think you were in danger in Stanton's Mill?" I ask.

"I thought they were going to take her away from me. And maybe there was something else. Maybe some other kind of danger."

"How could they take her away? If you didn't want it? And what other sort of danger?"

She cradles baby, her chin against the baby's head. "I dunno. I don't have such a strong will. And they had some real good arguments. And they talked about the Social Services and whether or not I was fit. About her welfare, that was it. And then . . ." She looks out over baby's head. "Then Anneliese said I was getting to know an awful lot. I got scared. They started getting fierce."

"Who's they?"

"Well, Anneliese, of course. She was real interested. She discovered that Chelsea was indigo. Of course I knew she was special, but indigo! That was real special. And Anneliese was great at first. Just great, really helpful and exciting. But then she got scary. After the guru came into it."

No, Lana says. She doesn't know who the guru was. He was a guru. He wore a white robe and a hat. And he had big scary eyes. And the purple curtains were shut. And maybe

there were two of them. She's not sure. There was a lot of
smoke, and funny lights, and they gave her something to
drink . . .

"And they told me, there was this special way I could
use. This way that I could keep my baby safe. Because there
were all kinds of dangers. The state might come and take
her, because she was a bastard. They told me that."

"That's absolutely, totally untrue," I say, angry. But Lana
just shakes her head and looks out onto the road.

"They were going to send her somewhere," she says.
"They knew. They were sure the state would come in. Because she wasn't legal. That's what *illegitimate* means. Not
legal. But they had a place to send her. A wonderful place.
Where she would be safe, and have every advantage. That's
what the man said. Every advantage."

"What man? The guru?"

"Yeah, the guru. He did a lot of talking. He was good at
it."

"So you got afraid?"

"If I stayed any longer, I would of done it. I would of sent
her away. And I didn't want to. Maybe I should of wanted
to, because she would have a better life, but I didn't want to.
She was mine. I was her mother.

"I had some money saved," she says, answering a question I've been harboring. "Just a little. This guy Graham.
He was my baby's dad. He went to Mexico, but before he
went . . . Anyway, I had a little money, and I figured it was
cheap up here. And I sent Beau my address in case Graham
came back. Which I guess he didn't."

I am wondering whether to tell her about Tamina's
death. Finally I do. She says, "Oh, Jesus."

She leans over her baby and says, "Jesus. Jesus.

"Do they know where I am? Here?" She is clutching baby too hard; baby lets out a squawk.

I tell her, "No. Absolutely not."

Actually that is a kind of promise. I haven't been thinking until now about keeping Lana's setting a secret.

She says, "That Tammy really loved her Penelope. Really loved her."

I agree, "Yes."

"And she sent her off. But because she really loved her." She is half crying. But in a moment she offers an amendment: "She was way, way smarter than me, but I was the one that was right. Not to do it."

"Lana," I say, "please tell me about the guru. Try to describe him."

I think Lana understands that I want this for a good purpose. And she really tries. The problem is that her powers of description are severely limited. "Well, like I said, maybe there were two of them; I'm not sure. He was real tall, and he wore this hat. And he had this deep, like, voice. And there was something wrong with his face. Like a big scar. You know. Scary. There were candles and purple curtains."

At this point Chelsea starts to cry, and Lana says, "Y'know, I got to change her? Are we about finished?" She has begun acting nervous.

"A scar?" I asks. "I wish you could remember more about that."

And Lana says, "Oh, hey, I don't think I should have talked this much. I mean, I got to shut up. Listen, don't tell anyone where I am."

"I won't," I say, rising to collect Rob. "Really I won't. I'll tell Beau to be really careful."

Lana says, "Okay," muffling her response in Chelsea's skull.

But I can see that she doesn't believe me, and I reinforce, "I'll be extra careful, Lana. You can count on me."

The look Lana gives me seems to say that she has counted on people before this, and it didn't work out.

Rob and I buy a six-pack of beer and four ham-and-cheese sandwiches and repair to the Gold Run Motel, where we eat and drink and make love. In reverse order. That is, we make love first.

The pillows at the Gold Run Motel smell of pine tree. I tell Rob I hope whoever told Lana her baby was illegal fries in hell.

⌐ Chapter 20

"Hello, darlin'. How are you, darlin'? I have missed you so much. I think about you all the time. I mean, baby, I have been unbearably, stupidly busy—you just couldn't believe the degree of garbage piled up in my life and my little jail is full again. But still. Right. It just isn't right, if you know what I mean. Darlin', how are you?"

Believe it or not, I am glad to hear from Cherie. I have missed her. "Things are weird, Cherie. But maybe we're finally getting someplace."

"Well, sweetcakes, if you are getting someplace, that is a whole bundle more than me. Can you trundle over to the Best Western tomorrow for lunch?"

I get to the Best Western feeling peculiar. About me, Cherie, and Rob.

For a long time I was totally righteous about all that. Cherie stole my boyfriend. I hated her and that was justified and normal and I was right to do so. But now that Rob is more or less back with me and I am more or less the victor, I feel different. Maybe slightly guilty. After all, I'm a lot younger than Cherie. Not any prettier, but younger. And Rob also is young. And he and I have known each other forever. Maybe I had unfair advantages.

I sneak into the dark green lounge feeling uneasy.

But you do not get to be the sheriff of Del Oro County and one of the few female sheriffs in the state by being slow on the uptake. Cherie, replete in her new tight-fitting uniform and four-inch-heeled gold sandals, trips across the lobby to plant a kiss on my cheek. "Darlin', I heard about you and Rob being together again; I am so pleased. You know, that business of me latching on to him was one of the big stupid mistakes of my life. How could I possibly believe that wonderful, vital young man would ever want to stick around with old me? He didn't, you know, and it was the right thing for him to break it off." By this time Cherie has me by the hand and is leading me to a table in the dining room.

Of course, I'll go along with the fantasy that Rob found her insufficient and therefore left her. I think it was the other way around.

"Lover girl," she says, settling into a striped chair, "I need a drink. I am so glad I got you that jacket. It looks marvelous on you."

I don't, the way Cherie does, have a leather belt with handmade silver studs to go with my official sheriff's jacket. I must shop for one.

She dazzles a smile at the Western-booted waiter and asks him for something strong.

"Now," she says, "we have got to talk, and the first thing we are going to talk about is, let's see, Anneliese. Nobody has heard from her since. At least, nobody admits to it. Maybe she's still out there in the woods. Maybe she's decamped to Back-of-Beyond, Saskatchewan. Maybe she's killed herself."

I say, "Nope."

"Well, I agree. She's not a suicide type.

"Incidentally, I fired that Klingon, my so-called deputy that was supposed to guard your darling father and went off and left you all by yourselves that night. And I hired a new sincere one with glasses and he's been doing research. Do you want this olive?"

She is offering me her martini olive. I decline.

"Well," she goes on, "this new sincere idiot has been doing research and it's interesting. Incidentally, is darling Crocodile okay?"

I tell her Daddy is fine, and she goes on to say that the new deputy is looking into the backgrounds of individual people in Stanton's Mill. "I got the idea to do it from the great way you checked on Anneliese. And everybody seems to try to slide into the Mill pretending they got no past history, as if they came off a star or just got hatched . . . where was I?"

We stop to order lunch, and Cherie picks up about how she was researching Beau. "I mean, baby, assuming he was a different person once with a name sort of like Beau La Roche, which is a ridiculous name. And my new Klingon, who is really bright, started with that name, Beau, and how it means handsome or belle, and then took Roche or rock and from that got Peter and then to Peter Bell for a name. Are you following?"

"Not at all."

"Well, it's all association and similar initials, which is the way people choose new names and I was assuming Beau did that—God, is that what we ordered?"

The lunch, which has just arrived, appears to be shrimp in some kind of pink sauce. "Oh, well, punishment for sins in a past life, I guess." She spoons shrimp onto both our plates. "So for Roche, he sort of translated and got *rock* and tried for lots of associations with that and finally got the one in the Bible . . ."

I say, "Oh, yes, Jesus said to Peter, 'On this rock I will build my . . . '"

I wind down here. I spent a lot of time in archaeology settings, where people were always chasing these kinds of coded associations, and I really don't want to hear the ones that Cherie's deputy made. "So," I say, "he came up with Peter for rock and Bell for beautiful. So who's Peter Bell?"

Cherie is dramatic. She waves her hands with a flourish when she gives me a couple of printouts.

The first one is dated April 1988, Des Moines, Iowa, and is about a fire in a school. Where Vice Principal Peter Bell, "although badly burned about the hands and chest, distinguished himself by leading students out of the crowded assembly hall and into the street . . . He was the hero of the event, says Principal Eileen Walter."

"Wow," I say.

Cherie says, "Yep, but there are questions. That came up later. About delay in calling the fire department. And about whether Vice Principal Bell and Principal Eileen Walter had left the school during the program. Translation, baby, it was an assembly and both teachers went away in the middle of it—maybe to go canoodle someplace—and that's why they didn't call the fire department."

Cherie watches me. "And take note of that name, Eileen Walter. I mean, note the assonance."

I tell her that I am taking note of it. Eileen Walter—E.W. Ann Warner—A.W. Anneliese Wertiger—again A. W.

"Vice Principal Bell retired from the school system," Cherie says. "He said that nothing could make up for that loss of one life. Because one student died. He retired and then he disappeared."

"What happened to Principal Walter?"

"She didn't apologize, but she disappeared, too.

"For what it's worth," Cherie winds up. And then, "My God. They've got Baked Alaska for dessert. I would almost kill for a Baked Alaska."

"You think maybe Beau and Anneliese knew each other. Before Stanton's Mill. In another life."

"Baby, I think it's possible."

I say that he really dislikes her now, and Cherie says, "Yep."

And then I also order Baked Alaska.

"Hi, Beau, how are you?" I call up as I enter the store. He's just a dark shape on his raised dais.

"The snoops have landed," he announces in an unfriendly voice. "What are you poking into now, Snoop Lady?"

The store smells good tonight, lots of cinnamon in the mix. The co-op is a pretend country store. People move to Stanton's Mill to escape the world; they want a pretend small town with lanes and leafy roads and no sidewalks;

they want a Grandma Moses store with wooden floor, smudged grocery cases, varnished wood beams, pots, hams, and printed dishcloths hanging from the ceiling.

The store often smells gently of mice, so cinnamon helps.

I don't really know what I'm poking into in visiting Beau now. I simply want to look at him and try to judge him after the possibilities that Cherie has raised.

"I keep thinking about Tamina," I say.

He stares.

"Something about her," I say. "Not just that she was beautiful and talented, it's that—"

"That there were lots of facets. Varieties. Many different kinds of ability. Varied interests," he finishes for me. "And you don't get it how she could have flourished here." He sounds tired.

"Maybe."

"The flower on the dung heap."

Why do I want to talk to this man? He's a little bit like my dad, I suppose. But much younger. And meaner. "Don't be silly; I know perfectly well that Stanton's Mill has educational opportunities: schools, libraries, educated people, doctors, lawyers . . ."

"Oh, for God's sake, climb up here and relax. There's no library closer than Conestoga and the school isn't very good and her mother is borderline retarded. And yes, how did Tamina happen? People like that occur sometimes. She was out of synch and knew it." He is pushing a chair in my direction.

I want to ask if he's her father, but decide to let that wait.

"I wish to hell she hadn't died," he says.

"Was she pushed?"

"Sure she was pushed."

"Who pushed her?"

"If I knew that, there'd be another murder in this idyllic town. And there will be. I'll do it. Kill the summabitch. When I find out. Just wait."

I haven't seen Beau look like this. He's jittery and his hands are shaking. I say, "Hey, Beau, I'm a deputy sheriff, you shouldn't be telling me that stuff," and he says, "I wanted to."

"Has something else happened?" I ask.

He's closing and unclosing one hand. "After a while it piles up. Know what I mean? No, how could you. But I go along, not thinking too much . . . oh, what the hell. That kid was a ray of light. Not too many rays of light in this quagmire.

"Know what? In all this stupid place, maybe you're the one showing some real concern. As if you really cared. And you didn't even know her."

I wait. I could say that I care especially because I'm pretending Tamina is a younger version of myself. But that's just the way it started, not the way it is now.

Beau is getting up. He's going to walk away and leave me. I understand.

"Beau," I say. And the sentence I come up with is one about my father. "My dad loved her," I say. "He really loved her; he remembers her still. And his memory usually has a life span of seven minutes. But he still talks about Ta-Ent. He's approaching a point where he won't remember anything. She made him feel . . ."

"She talked to everybody as if they mattered," Beau says, sitting back down again. "But she really liked your dad."

"She was still at that age when it's all new. When she thinks maybe everything matters. Do you remember that?

Remember it in your own life? When you went around looking at the world, thinking, oh, maybe I can learn from this, learn what life is really like; so this is the way it is?"

He examines me and picks up my slight affirmative gesture. "Sure, you remember. Lotta people, they try real hard to forget. Or they never were open like that. But Tamina had it, in spades, the primal curiosity—what's it all about, will it add up, why am I here, that curiosity, there has got to be a purpose; I'm going to find out. Maybe I'll find out today.

"That's why I hate that bitch. That shiny, slippery, smooth Anneliese bitch.

"Because she came along and saw all that bright curiosity and fed off it. Just like a shark on a bright pulsing body. And that's what she was, a shark. Smooth, organized, motor-driven. And with those beady, watching eyes. God, I hated that woman."

"You knew her."

"Sure, I knew her, I watched her. I watched her circling Tamina. Her juicy, fresh prey."

"You knew Anneliese from before, Beau."

He shrugs. "A type like that. You see it around. How can you miss it?"

For a minute I want to chase this and pin it down. And then I figure, oh, what the hell. What's the point?

Beau fiddles with his ballpoint pen. "You asked, was there something more. Well, only sort of. Not really something new.

"You know, she kept doing paintings of our refrigerator? As if it was important, or she thought about it a lot. Or something.

"Anyway, I turned up Tamina's medicine in the fridge

today. We aren't as systematic about keeping track of that fridge as we ought to be. System's not the Stanton's Mill way, and living here, even if you used to be systematic, you fall into that laissez-faire. Not really my approach to things, but hell . . . Well, anyway, today I dug into the back of that big old monster and along with the old acidopholus and other stuff was Tammy's medicine. Stuff that Anneliese prescribed. Anneliese pretended to be a natural health doctor. She invented this medicine for Tammy. But first she invented the disease. It was all part of her plan to get the baby."

"Oh," I say. "The headaches."

"Right. Headaches. *'Something like epilepsy,'* " Anneliese told her. "How would you feel if you were fifteen and somebody said you had epilepsy?"

I can feel myself looking at Beau bleakly.

"Yeah," he says. "God damn it to hell."

"So she sent her baby off."

"I guess."

But when I ask where did she send the baby to, Beau gets defensive. "How the hell do I know? Lana now, for instance, she just took off."

"I know about Lana. You never heard where Tamina's baby went?"

"All I know is, she was really sorry after. About three weeks after that baby kind of wasn't there anymore, she came around and said, 'Beau, I was ashamed to tell you. I made this awful mistake. I sent Penny away. I shouldn't have done that. I realize now, how much of an arrant error'—a funny term she used—'how much of an arrant error it was.

" 'But,' she said, 'I'll make up for it.' She stood beside my desk, feet planted like Joan of Arc, and said, 'I'm going to put a stop to all that. I'm going to get her back.' "

"Yeah," Beau says. "That's what she said. She signed her death warrant then."

Chapter 21

I feel that I'm clutching a collection of high-powered wires; there's the chance of plugging one into the right place and getting a bright illumination; there's the chance of doing it wrong and frying the whole mess. And of course, I could make a really bad move, and—light myself up terminally.

And then help arrives the way it sometimes does. From that corner of the world you've completely forgotten. Help is supplied by Mrs. Daphne La Salle.

Daphne arrives in my Manor office and leans over my desk. "I have something serious to talk to you about."

She is a smart woman and she's being solemn about this, which makes me decide I should take her seriously. After a minute I stack my Complaints neatly and abandon them. I haven't done much Complaint reading today and I won't do much tomorrow and my boss, Belle, is unlikely to come by and read my stack and recognize that I have been neglecting it. My other duties take place in the early morning; they are over for the day.

Daphne and I form a little parade down the hall to her apartment.

"Now," she says, settling into a structured modern chair, "no one has ever tried to be coherent with me about this. Talk about those babies in Stanton's Mill."

I suppose I look puzzled; I think I've talked nonstop about the purple babies. "Oh, of course," she says, "I've heard some of it. But I wasn't really listening."

She sits back, looking glamorous, which is one of the advantages of being well groomed and having white, form-fitting hair. Yes, she is glamorous; her apartment is, too. The apartment has three modern, elegant rooms, full of clean-limbed Asian furniture. There are a couple of interesting, blocky Japanese prints. She sits now in a bright red chair, which she claims is comfortable although it doesn't look as if it could possibly be. I have a leather basket-type chair.

"Just start talking," she says.

I do. I spout for ten minutes or so, about indigo babies in general, and then about the rumors in Stanton's Mill: the babies that have been indigo-identified, the babies that maybe disappeared, the people who say yes, they have, and no, they didn't. About my visit to Lana.

After which she comments, "Well, my God."

"And in the middle of all this," she clarifies, "someone killed poor little Tamina."

I don't try to clean that up. I just say yes.

"Well, I must say," she announces, "on those disappearing babies, I think it possible I can help you."

She's usually very concise, so I just wait for her to explain.

"You know, I got intrigued with Tirza's List—what it is and how you get onto it. Frankly, I thought there might be an investigative article somewhere in there. So I began digging around, following leads. And I met this awfully attractive woman—depressingly good-looking, and rich and well dressed and probably not very nice, but fun to observe, and she suddenly, unexpectedly says to me, 'To this day,' she remarks, 'I'm not sure that it was really connected with Tirza's List—all I wanted was some interesting, you know the kind I mean, jewelry—but suddenly I was in the middle of this discussion about babies. This was all about three months ago.'"

"Yes?" I say. This sounds promising. In fact, it sounds very promising.

"And she said that before this, she had been shopping babies. Trying to adopt one. She didn't look the type, to say nothing of being too old. But her husband, who is a lot older, is apparently nuts on the subject of babies. It's an ego thing, the way it is for some men; he's determined to find a baby; he and she had been shopping kids for two years. And he is ridiculously rich, with a house in Monaco and one in Acapulco and one in three or four other places, Saudi ones or Dubai ones or whatever. He had been very, very choosy about the babies.

"They aren't together anymore," Mrs. La Salle adds. "She was on her way out of the marriage when all this started."

"Please keep on about the babies," I tell her.

"Well, she thought she was just shopping for stolen jewelry, and when they asked her what price, she said, 'Any price,' and waved her hand. And then said, 'One mil, maybe?' meaning a million dollars. So—well, she said it actually took hours; they brought out some inadequate jewelry, and she looked bored. And finally, after this and that and a whole lot of drinks—it was all happening in somebody's Las Vegas apartment, did I say that—this man told her, 'There might be something else of interest, I understand you've been searching another field.' And that was it. Babies. Or rather, a baby.

"A girl, he said. Beautiful. And he went into the indigo baby spiel. But the way she described it sounded as if he didn't really believe all the indigo hype."

"Did she?"

"She was intrigued. She'd never heard about it before. And he gave her literature and said, 'This is a truly remarkable child. She is certified indigo. And she's beautiful. I can give you a photo of the mother. The mother is beautiful. The dad. Everybody. Gorgeous, superior people.' "

"He had a photo of the father?"

"She said no. Just Mom. He said this was the only child of its kind in the whole country right now. Indigo babies, he claimed, come in batches. There had been a batch of three and they were all placed; this was the last one.

"Well, she was taking it all in and at the same time thinking about how she wanted to divorce her husband and would she want a baby if she were by herself and on the third hand beginning to get a disbelieving itch—that indigo stuff is truly weird and she isn't stupid, just selfish and rich and careless."

"Would she be willing . . ." I start to ask, meaning, *Would she be willing to get further into this and do whatever the man suggests, following along until near the end of the deal and also keeping us posted on it,* and then I don't say that, because why would she? Money wouldn't be an incentive, and she doesn't sound altruistic.

"No, she wouldn't," Daphne says, picking up my thought. "Since all this happened, she's started on the divorce. That's what she thinks about now. But she'd be glad to talk to you. Her husband got involved some in this baby deal and of course behaved badly; I don't know just how. And she loves talking about him, and how she hates him.

"Here's her name and here's her phone number. For some reason she liked me and gave me the number."

"She liked your jewelry," I suggest.

"My jewelry is thrift-shop compared with hers. Maybe I remind her of her aunt."

"Oh," I say, because Daphne is showing signs of wanting to finish off this conversation. "The man in Las Vegas. Any idea what he looks like?"

"I asked. Just an ordinary corporate-type man. Lower-level corporate, she said. Tall and substantial. Very groomed, head shaved. She's a pretty good observer.

"But, she said, there was something about his face. I think she said a scar. Like a knife scar.

"And he doesn't sound like somebody from Stanton's Mill," Daphne adds.

"So how do you reach him?"

Daphne turns a searching appraisal on me. Her combination of snow-white hair and shaped dark eyebrows is great for registering disapproval. "Maybe you'd better brief me again on exactly what you want out of this."

I listen to myself talking and it sounds very chaotic.

She doesn't just think it's chaotic. She thinks worse than that. "This is dangerous garbage, Carla. You ask, how do you reach him? I think you don't. And *you* especially, I repeat,

especially you, don't. These are professionals. They're crimi-
nals. They're . . . well, evil. Somebody in that setup has a
photo of you."

"Stop being romantic."

"That's not romantic. These people project *experience*.
They'd be up on everything in connection with Stanton's
Mill." She examines me again. "You look different today.
Did you get back together with Rob?"

We spar some. Maybe I look good today but I always
look younger than I am and people often try to protect me.
I hate that. "Daphne, I have a title. I'm a sheriff. Talk. How
do I reach the Tirza site?"

So finally she outlines one of those ridiculous procedures
where you begin with a site, which in this case is a real estate one. Perfecthome Realty. And then when it asks you to
fill in the blanks of what you want, you put the word *Tirza*
in some of them. Like NUMBER OF BEDROOMS: Tirza. PRICE
OF HOME: Tirza. Et cetera. Not in every blank. Just the
right ones.

"Good," I say unenthusiastically. I hate these information
trees, even when they're part of a detection process.

"Listen," Daphne says. "Be careful. They're smart."

I have to agree. If you're fencing several million dollars'
worth of jewelry and babies, you need to be smart.

The lady's name is Mrs. Avedian, and I salt her telephone
number away for later. But I'm not sure I'll waste time on
Mrs. Avedian. I have other, more direct plans for dealing
with Tirza.

I get on the phone to Rob. He is at the hospital but apparently not terribly busy. I can hear clicks and buzzes and bells

sounding behind him, but no one yelling his name or number.

"Listen," I say. "Hi."

He says, "Oh, am I glad to hear from you; I've been thinking about you all day. Have you been thinking about me?"

My standard picture of Rob is of somebody square, stolid, and reliable. Have I always been wrong about the stolid part?

Our conversation uses up a lot of nonfree minutes on my phone. I have to explain about Tirza and to ask if Rob would like to adopt a baby with me.

In the middle of explaining that option, I hear the loudspeaker claiming that it needs Dr. Ackroyd and we have to break off.

Which turns out to be beneficial because when he comes back again, he says, "At first it seemed like an idiotic plan, but the more I thought about it, the more it made sense. And so, yeah, okay, let's apply for an adoption; what do we do?"

I tell him that we need pictures and histories, all phony and not traceable, and in the middle of trying to explain this, I give up and say, "Can you get over here tonight?" to which he says, "Well, I was supposed to go to this—oh, hell, I'll tell them I have to do this Trop Med thing; sure I'll be there, can't wait really; did I tell you how great our trip to Placer was?" Somewhere in his background the loudspeaker starts squawking again.

I hang up feeling scared, but triumphant. Feeling that we are really getting places. I'm just not sure what those places are.

Chapter 22

Rob and I have a silly time with the photographs and the personal history. I get Rebecca from the front office to be in the picture, posing as the would-be mama, along with someone named Bjorn from the kitchen. Bjorn is a Swedish exchange student, very blond and muscled and suitable-looking, should the Tirza people be racist, which I suspect they are. Also Bjorn, because of his muscles and broad shoulders, looks older than he is. At first, Rob wonders why we can't pose for the picture ourselves, but when I say that this outfit may be folk we know, he says, "Ohmigawd, ouch," and then spends his time encouraging Rebecca with "Chin up, Becky, great," and telling Bjorn not to look lecherous; he's supposed to be a businessman. We pose them on a Manor Victorian couch, then standing on the graceful front entry steps (presumably of the mansion where we'll bring baby), then, with arms linked, looking pleasedly down the path toward the ocean where they will take baby to paddle.

A lot of joking from both Rebecca and Bjorn, who have been told that it's a secret, a game, maybe we'll win, and if so, they get a cut.

Our personal histories reveal that Rob (now named Sheridan) is a doctor while I am a social butterfly and charity volunteer eager to quit doing all that and be a mother.

We are rich, of course. Months of reviewing records for Manor admissions has supplied me with documents I can photograph. I'm counting on the Tirza operation being so borderline illegal that they don't check. I steal an Oyster Bay Cove, New York, address from our Manor files. But the phone number poses a big problem. No, we agree, we can't just invent some numbers. And we can't buy a new phone; why would Sheridan be buying a new cell phone all of a sudden? Finally we decide on Rob's cell phone, with the greeting changed to a hello from Sheridan.

We send all the material off and toast the event in wine and then celebrate the possible results by going to Rob's little apartment behind the hospital in Conestoga and staying up half the night and eventually falling soused into Rob's too-small bed. The bed smells pleasantly of dried grass. Not marijuana, just grass. Rob is baffled for an explanation but says he likes to sunbathe in the fields outside.

I've opened a new e-mail account for the Tirza correspondence. And quite fast, just four days later, we get a long communique requesting more. More, more. Perfecthome has given way to Perfect Solutions, the letterhead name offered in black and gold. Perfect Solutions would like more documents about us, further details: more on what kind of people we are, why we are special, and particularly, why we are financially special. Plus anything else we think of. And are we willing to travel? In order to learn further about this project?

Curiously, no mention is made of babies in this letter or anywhere else. Perfect Solutions could be selling art, land, stocks, race horses. Maybe it does.

We dispatch all of the requested material off to Tirza, or Perfect Solutions, or whoever is at the other end. We get fairly giddy writing the trash that goes with this submission. I'm feeling ebullient. "Rob, we're doing it. We really are." I squeeze myself against him in the intermissions between inventing artistic lies. We cobble up a new, heartrending letter detailing how hard we have tried to adopt a baby, how suited we are, emotionally, but especially financially, to support an exceptional baby. How happy we would be to travel anywhere and talk to anybody.

Having done this, Rob says, "Hey, let's go to San Francisco and eat a lot of crab."

We can't do that until tomorrow, which is Saturday. I've pledged myself to my dad for this evening. A three-person country-western band is coming to the Manor and we have to be there; Daddy is a committed country-western fan.

Rob arrives the next day for our date in his little Toyota and leans out the window, suggesting a variation. "Let's be wild. Bring some overnight stuff. Let's be ready for anything."

Rob has trouble with spontaneity. He always sounds as if he has practiced for it.

"Okay." I don't have trouble that way. In addition to which I've already thought of this possibility, and have canvased my dad, who says how wonderful for me, a trip to the seacoast, that's at Hurghada, is it? But he'll be busy here all weekend; he is feeling fine; there is a party.

"Great," I tell Rob. I don't add that I also like being wild.

And we are off to San Francisco, where we do not have crab, we have drinks. We settle in at one of the drinking sites high above the rest of the city, with a smashing view. We drink quite a bit and get silly, and then Rob, who isn't usually silly but seems to be encouraging the New Rob, says that the best crab is in Marshall, across the bridge and a little bit up the coast, where they catch the crabs right outside the restaurant.

So we head off across the bridge and up to Marshall, where Rob turns out to be right. There is plenty of crab, and also oysters. The crab place smells of crab, oyster, and sea salt; it has four rooms available for rent overnight for crab fanciers who decide they want an all-night experience. And that is what we decide.

We have a wonderful night, going downstairs frequently to get beer.

At one point in the evening we are sitting on the jetty with our feet in the water. Flip-flops and sneakers are stacked up behind us. A six-pack of beer, with two bottles missing, sits between us. In the air directly ahead is an almost full moon, hung over the water, illuminating brilliant glassy bay and three crab boats. One of these surely has caught no crab for ten years; it is decorated at the waterline with clusters of barnacles; its equipment elevator cants drunkenly. I drink beer from the bottle and slosh my feet back and forth. The shallow water is almost warm. I say something pious and drunkenly philosophic about the difficulty of believing, on such a pure and gorgeous and untrammeled night, in the

kind of sin we've been encountering with the Tirza exploration.

Rob grunts.

"I think Anneliese is Tirza," I say.

Rob drinks some beer. "I don't really know her, I've only
seen her from a distance; I guess she has to be smart or anyway a good conniver to do all that indigo stuff. But it's got
to be more people than Anneliese. There are men involved.
Everybody spoke about a guru. And a smooth male Tirza
operator. Another guy."

"Beau," I say. Then I feel dubious. That scar on the face?
Of course, it's easy to fake a scar.

"I dunno." Rob finishes his bottle and puts it carefully
back in the cardboard container. He isn't the sort to chuck
an empty into the bay. "Are you happy with thinking it's
Beau?"

"No. But villains can be complicated. And part of the
time sincere. Do you need an opener?"

He fusses with a new bottle. He says he declines to use
our opener, which plays "Take Me Out to the Ball Game"
when you push it down. He will not defile this innocent,
pristine setting with that vulgarity. After a short struggle
he gets the top off the beer with his thumbs. There is a re-
sulting cascade of beer.

I say that it must be Beau because there's nobody else.
And that I'm going upstairs to bed. I kiss Rob and the kiss
turns out to take a really long time. Kissing on the edge of a
jetty is fun if you enjoy harmless, run-of-the-mill danger. It
only seems that we are about to fall in. We teeter provoca-
tively, Rob still clutching his bottle. And if we did tumble,
the water is about three feet deep and the result would be
one of those cheap, cute movie scenes where everyone flails

around. "Good night, bro," I announce after quite a while, capturing a bottle for myself, along with my flip-flops and the offensive opener.

Even the guest rooms at Mike's Crabshak smell of crab, which is okay.

Before I finally snuggle down into my chaste, smelly bed—there are two of these; the other one is an unchaste, tangled mess, having been wrestled on earlier—I stick my head out the window and survey the sky. The moon is icily brilliant. Rob still dangles his feet over the jetty edge. He is working on a beer. And he is also talking on his cell phone. He is talking on his cell phone at 3:00 A.M.

People frequently ask the moon questions. Probably not very often in real life, but often in poems and songs. *Oh Moon,* I inquire, *who is he talking to?* The moon doesn't answer, but my inner voice does. *Cherie,* it says. I get that twist in the gut. Cherie. Then I decide, and quite fast, too, *Oh, well, the hell with it.* I must be almost honest in deciding this, because five minutes later I'm able, without looking out the window again, to climb into my chaste, smelly bed and fall right to sleep.

I wake up to a brilliant sun and a still-active crab smell.

The bed beside me is vacant.

Now I am really, really angry.

This fuels a lot of very fast action. I get myself dressed in record time, and am downstairs and out on the jetty, unwashed and untoothbrushed. My primary interest is whether or not Rob has left me his car. And he has not.

It is one thing to be deserted on your sort-of honeymoon. Deserted for last year's girlfriend. It is another thing to be

stranded in Marshall without a car. Of course, there is
Henry the cabdriver in Conestoga; Henry loves me and will
come to get me. My cell phone, like Rob's, will work out
here on the jetty; it has refused to do so inside. Maybe I have
Henry's number. And after Henry has delivered me, I have my
official gun, and I can go find Rob and shoot him.

I think about these possibilities and get the cell phone
out of my pocket. I am staring at it when it rings.

"This is going to be interesting, Rob," I say, pushing
buttons and not really looking.

But the person on the other end is not Rob. It's my father.

Daddy's new phone, of which he is very proud, has my
number preset, along with Rob's and Susie's. Otherwise my
dad's technological skill would not be up to his calling me.

"Hello, daughter," he says. "Where are you, daughter?
I've had an interesting talk with the young man. The one
who was your friend and my friend. The one who was in
Thebes."

"Rob," I say.

"He is somewhere and I do not think it is a good idea."

At first, of course, I think Daddy is confused and is remembering something that happened in the past.

Then it occurs to me, although this is very unlikely, that
he intuits Rob's romantic wanderings and disapproves.

"What makes you think that, Daddy?" I ask.

He says, no, no, it was a telephone call. This morning. A
call from Ed to Rob. "One that I made to him. This morning.

"And I think he is somewhere bad."

It takes me a minute to draw a deep breath and reset my
personal buttons. The furious-at-Rob ones. Then I have to

use another minute of telephone time to think. I have trouble doing that. Finally I tell my father that this may be very important.

"Oh, I think so," he says. "Yes, I called him. You see, there is this clever thing, perhaps you are familiar with it—I hit a certain place on my little phone and it calls him."

"Yes, yes," I say, "I know."

"And so I got him," Daddy says, "and it was very peculiar. He seemed to think I was you. He said, 'Hello, Carla.' I thought that was odd."

Suddenly there is a cold chill across this beautiful, sun-bathed day. An idea forces itself into my beer-clouded brain, past the shreds of anger that are still there about Rob. I'm imagining a situation in which Rob would pretend that an incoming call was from me.

"Try to tell me exactly, darling," I instruct my dad.

And of course he can't. But he does very well, for him.

"I am not so terribly good on memory. You know that. But lately I have been better. Almost good, sometimes. The thing was that in this call, when he thought I was you, he talked about being away for a little while. And then he said—and I do think I remember it, because it was so unusual and so incorrect—he said, 'Keep the home fires burning, like Ipuwer says about his brother.'

"And you, of course, remember what Ipuwer says about his brother."

My dad always compliments me by insisting that my Egyptian knowledge is greater than it is. Ipuwer wrote something called "The Admonitions," which is a very long and very depressing poem about how bad things are going to get in the world.

I have no idea what Ipuwer said about his brother. I'm amazed that Rob knew.

"Tell me," I instruct my dad.

He clucks. "Really, my dear, you should remember. That part of your knowledge is important. And you were very good at it once. What a pity. Well, what Ipuwer says is, *He who puts his brother in the ground is everywhere.*"

Daddy waits to hear if I'm impressed. I am. I say, "Oh, good God."

"It is a negative passage," my father instructs. "And does not go with keeping the home fires burning."

"Thank you so much for remembering, Daddy."

My father says of course he remembers it; he does not forget his Egyptian knowledge.

And I am thinking, *Rob, darling* (Rob has been promoted back into being *darling* again), this is absolutely awful; it was wonderfully clever of you to think of sending a warning that way; I am so worried about you, *puts his brother in the ground* is terrible, oh, Jesus, Jesus. But Rob, couldn't you have thought of a passage that told us what sort of danger you're in, and where it is you're in it, and what we can do to get you out?

First I try to call Cherie, which is a bust. Cherie is out chasing meth offenders.

And then I call Susie. I want to know whether she has heard from Rob and I don't want to ask her point blank, since I'm afraid my voice will be unsteady. So I ask, "How's Rob?" and she responds, "Fine, I guess; I haven't heard for a couple of days. Sweetie, how are you? I do truly miss you. You've been neglecting me."

I agree to come over this evening. After that I call Henry the cabdriver.

And then I sit down and brood.

I occupy a peeling metal chair on the jetty and stare out over the water and tell myself that this is what I get for taking Rob for granted. And for mentally sneering at him for being solid and sturdy and not impulsive, the way I am. Maybe he is trying to show me how impulsive he can be. Maybe he's on to something and is trying to save me from a horrible surprise.

He went off in response to an appeal. A phony story. Something to do with the Tirza scheme. Oh, my God, Carla, I tell myself, you are really stupid. Daphne La Salle warned that these are truly evil people. Resourceful and inventive. Smart. That was a really dumb idea of yours, cracking the Tirza code by guile and wile; all you had to do was bottle up your pride and ask Cherie for help and she would have put one of her new deputies on it and the whole thing would have been solved in the normal bureaucratic way. Probably pretty soon. In a while. But obviously not fast enough for you.

I send good thoughts to Rob along the ultrasonic airwaves. That's what Susie would do.

I am actually relieved two hours later when Henry the cabdriver arrives. Henry is not a good conversationalist, which is relaxing. "Well, babe," he greets me (he talks to everyone like that), "what happened; boyfriend off to fix a coupla flat tires?" I agree that something of the sort happened, and Henry tells me it's a bad road for tires, that road.

Henry gets me back to the Manor in time for dinner and I invade the dining room to chase down my dad and try to coax more information out of him. But he's not helpful. It's the end of the day. "I am tired," he says. "I haven't had dinner. No, I won't feel better after dinner, then I will be sleepy. But there was something important I had to tell you. Something I've been wanting to say. I will have thought of it by tomorrow. Give me a kiss, darling. How nice of you to ask.

"My dear, I do love you." And he beams at me.

So I climb into my little car and head off toward Stanton's Mill and Susie's house. That's the likeliest place for Rob to go. To his mother's.

Chapter 23

Susie greets me enthusiastically, of course. She always does.

I look at her sideways to figure out if she knows anything about Rob, and she appears to know nothing.

What is different in Susie's house is that Sunshine is there, jeeping around troubledly. She has her mother along, who just sits, looking puzzled. "Oh, wow," Sunshine says, "Carla. I was going to try to get you." And she drags me out to Daddy's porch, where she sits on his bed and clutches a pillow to her stomach.

"Listen?" she says.

I tell her that I already am.

"They got this meeting at the indigo place?" Apparently the temptation to finish a statement with a question mark hits Sunshine when she's feeling insecure.

"Well, they got this meeting. And I think you should be there.

"I mean," she continues after a minute, "it's important."
Yes. Normally I would have no question at all. A meeting at the indigo center. I need to know anything they might say.

And it's possible that something about Rob might come out . . . I decide not to have a stomachache now.

On the other hand, it's almost eight o'clock in the evening. And Anneliese is out there in the dark, along the path. With her psychoses and her gun.

I let that discourage me only for a minute. "Yes," I tell Sunshine. "Yes, I'm coming. Thanks for letting me know."

"I mean," she agrees, "my cousin Heather will be there. Her mother's gonna bring her and the baby. His name's Jeremy."

Sunshine's cousin Heather. The fourth indigo mother. "Yes," I tell her. "Absolutely." And I give her arm a squeeze.

Sunshine and her mama exit, and I start collecting my gear. I am locating a respectable flashlight in my backpack, trying unostentatiously to assemble my gun, which, yes, I have brought this time, although not stashed in my belt, where it ought to be. I am staring at my cell phone and wondering if I'll need it and why Rob hasn't found a way to call me on it, when, right on cue, the little thing beeps.

"Hello, hello," I say, falling all over myself. And it isn't Rob. The voice is my father's.

"Hello, dear daughter. I knew you would be impressed. That this was important, just the way I've been thinking, and that you would want to know. And I really need your advice. So I am getting in touch with you. Right away."

"Oh," I say. "Wonderful. Yes?" It's about time. I was starting to feel that I would explode unless I got some news of Rob.

"It's about that thing that I knew," Daddy says. "I talked to you about it. Something that would hurt somebody's feelings."

I say, "Oh." At first I'm lost. Then I almost recall. Something he was talking about. A while ago. "Daddy. It's not about Rob, then?"

"Rob, my dear? No. I think not.

"But I need to talk to you," he adds. "Important, perhaps? Possibly important?"

I have to think for a minute. "Maybe you can write it down . . ." I grind to a halt, recognizing the impossibility of this. "Maybe get Mrs. La Salle to help you? And tomorrow I'll be there and I will—"

"Oh, no," says my dad's voice, sounding awfully strong, I suddenly realize, to be part of a cell phone call from the Manor to Stanton's Mill (reception at both places is awful). "Oh, no, darling. I am *here*. With you. Almost at Susie's. I'm, right now at this moment, outside your door. As soon as my friend Henry finds the right turnoff."

Oh, shit, I think. And Henry, damn your old well-intentioned eyes. There seems to be nothing else to say, so I repeat this meaningless, if silent, remark to myself and repress the desire to lie on the floor and kick. Rob is missing, Anneliese is crazy and at large and armed with a gun, the Tirza crowd are having a meeting, which I emphatically have to go to, and my father has projected himself into the middle of it.

Susie's screen door rattles, a voice outside calls "Whoo-ee," and it is Henry, my pal the cabdriver, this time with Daddy in tow. Susie, of course, does not have a front door bell; no one in Stanton's Mill lives like a normal person.

Susie is delighted; my dad is delighted. She calls his

name, and embraces him, and tells him it has been a long time and she doesn't understand why he has been neglecting her. Henry makes cheerful noises and says that I owe him thirty dollars.

It would be the most upbeat *home again* scene you ever imagined, thoroughly suitable for family evening TV consumption, except for the lurking background of chaos.

Susie wants to feed and refresh Henry, but I manage to get him out of there with only one cup of Long Jan tea. I'm able to do this only by sitting with him and talking about my father, and how he is better from that gunshot wound, and what a great old gent he is, and how Henry really understands him, and how Henry would drive him free if that was necessary, but you don't ever get rich that way, do you? And thanks, and hey, anytime. He really likes my dad. He gets his thirty dollars and a commendation, by which time I have clenched the fingers of one hand hard enough to drive my fingernails into my palm in four neat semicircles.

Freed of Henry, I kiss my dad again. "I have to go now; it's really urgent, but tomorrow we'll have a wonderful talk; it was so good of you . . ."

I deliver a spiel about what a good visit we'll have.

He doesn't agree. He needs to talk to me right now. This is important. We need to discuss. It will take some time.

Finally I just kiss him very enthusiastically and say, see you tomorrow; there will be all the time in the world. "Won't that be great?" And after a final loud kiss, I am out the door.

I have never treated my father that way before this.

Well, there is always a first time.

I have even managed to bring my flashlight and gun along with me.

So I am off, stumbling along the path to Scope's house. Anneliese's house. A likely place for her to go back to.

The path is dark and lumpy; shadows try to tackle my feet; the flashlight is better than nothing but still not good. Scope's is supposed to be next door, but in Stanton's Mill that's a relative concept. It's dark and really hard to see and there are a lot of bushes.

I am feeling guilty about my father. What was I supposed to do? And why did he have to get so enterprising now, all of a sudden?

I try not to think about Anneliese, creeping around with her gun. There seem to be occasional rustles and shifts in the terrain behind me. I decide not to listen to them.

And finally I'm pointed down to Scope's by lights. I round the corner of a bush and there is a little burst of illumination ahead, and then another bush and there is more light, which is reddish. And finally lots of light as if Scope's little dwelling is giving off a red or purple glow. I stagger down toward it.

Guess what, the INDIGO SPIRITUAL sign is lighted and flickering.

It imparts a strange color to the front porch but makes it easier to see the steps. And to see the rest of my environment. And my environment includes another human being. Who is very close, right behind me in that little corner of space you can almost see with the edge of your eye. Who reaches out to touch me on the arm.

"My dear," says my father's voice, "are you all right?"

I say, "Daddy." I suppose I sound both irritated and relieved.

"I followed you," he says. "I was worried about you. Your whole posture indicated confusion."

"Father," I say, attempting finally for a Sunday school firmness, "I am fine, and I really appreciate your concern and I do love you, and now it is time for you to sit down right here on the steps, sit and not make any noise; you absolutely must wait here while I go inside for a while."

He says mildly that oh, no, he doesn't think so.

I reach down to check on my gun. My father says, "Good heavens, darling Carla, what are you doing?"

I remind myself that I have to be careful with these grandiose gestures around him, "Nothing, nothing, it's only because I'm a sheriff, did you know that? A sheriff is supposed to have a gun."

He is immediately interested; yes, he has heard of that. He wants to look at the gun. We have a brief scuffle in the semidark on Anneliese's front steps before I can jam the gun back into my belt.

"I am coming with you," my dad says. "I think it is necessary."

When I don't answer, he says, "If we argue here on these steps, we will end up making a lot of noise."

I think that is a threat.

Alzheimer's patients can often outmaneuver you, and one of my books calls these moves *instinctive cunning*, but in this case I prefer to describe it as brains.

He reaches out and pulls the screen door toward us. The gizmo on that door still rings a bell.

The entryway is very dark. It is purple and hung with velvet and overwhelmed by the big picture of the guru.

And Anneliese's consultation room, directly ahead, is even darker. The purple here has accumulated since the last time I visited; there is more purple paint; there are new and obstreperous velvet hangings; there are rows of little

Christmas-tree-type lights with purple coatings. A second guru picture has been added, the same size as the other one but shot against a space-age city background; it splays out, framed in crunchy silk, all purple.

This guru appears to be a different one, but I don't have time to contemplate. There's no sign of the bamboo curtain that Anneliese disappeared behind last time I was here. I guess it's been taken down.

The room is so dark that it's hard to be sure, but maybe there's a row of chairs lined up for a meeting, and some people sitting on the chairs. With a person in a peculiar long white raincoat ensconced up front behind a table. After a minute I think this looks like somebody I know.

That is, somebody I've seen before.

The person is standing commandingly. And is wearing this white raincoat-type garment; the person is halfway in drag to perform as Anneliese's guru. The guru in the picture. But still this person seems to be someone I've seen before, several times. And talked to. And never thought of, at all, in this role.

The person, in spite of all the differences, seems to be Scope.

Which is impossible. Scope appearing ready to chair a meeting. Scope doesn't chair meetings. He's not equipped even to attend one. What Scope is good at is sitting back and looking like a refugee from the depressed areas of Appalachia.

The figure that may be Scope says, "Well, Carla." And it is Scope; I have to understand that. Scope. As weird and out of his setting as a talking dinosaur.

A new Scope who has acquired a new demeanor, measured and stately. And a new, different voice. A much deeper one. "For certain," he intones, almost booming, "no one invited you. But you are here." He gestures. "And you have brought your little Alzheimered parent, and you might as well come in and sit down."

I don't want to come in and I emphatically don't want to sit down in front of this new person that Scope has metamorphosed into.

He bulks too large and tall. He is leaning at me.

And I certainly don't want to drag my dad into the situation, but that's an academic question now. Daddy is right on my heels, breathing hard. He murmurs, "Oh, this is interesting."

I could kill him.

I can more or less see now; my eyes have adjusted.

Well, I have my gun. It is tucked into my belt, in the back.

There really isn't time to pause and hover.

This is the enemy's stronghold. Artificially darkened and empurpled and full of phony stage props and dominated by a threatening man who has always pretended to be somebody else. And is acting a role. And I don't know what the role is.

Inviting me in is probably exactly what happened to Rob. He was invited in, over the phone. And he hasn't been heard from since.

I find a chair and more or less quietly subside on it. My father follows agilely behind. This parent of mine is as much trouble as an indigo baby.

By now my eyes are working and I can examine the rest of the room. There are maybe twenty people here. Most of them look familiar, co-op types, people that I've seen up on the Rock. And in the row ahead some people that I

know: Sunshine for one, and then her mum. After that someone else I know. At first I can't identify her, and then I can.
It's Molly Littlefeather. Talkative Molly. And then a fourth
person whom I think I don't know. But since she is seated
with Sunshine and her mom and is holding hands with the
mom, I presume she's Sunshine's cousin Heather. So we have
the Sunshine family. It's a group that has some issues in
common.

Definitely.

They are all indigo relatives.

I feel like the guy in *The Wicker Man* when he realizes he
is surrounded by initiates. They press closer and closer.
They're friendly. He knows them all. And then they sacrifice
him. They burn him alive.

I shake this off and tell myself to quit putting Carla in
the middle of the drama. Maybe I'm just an onlooker.

Scope says, "Welcome to indigo consciousness, Carla.
You've been suspecting outrageous things, haven't you?"

Yes, indeed.

I want to add, "Scope, if you could sound like this all
along, why did you put on that stoned-and-stupid act?" But
I restrict myself to staring up at him passively.

"Well, here we are, Carla. Free and open, as you see. Just
a few indigo aficionados, getting together in a forum. And
glad to have you here, even if you don't trust us.

"We were anticipating some other visitors today," Scope
continues. He has an almost operatic voice. Its resonance
and timbre set up echoes; the purple Christmas lights
quiver each time he speaks. "Some invited guests, Carla," he
intones. "You were not invited. But you barge your way in,
that's pretty daring of you, don't you think? You never
know what will happen when you do things like that, do

you? But we are very glad to have you. And maybe our invited guests will also get here; our backwoods community is hard to find. They are visitors interested in some of the mysterious powers of indigo, friends who want to see what indigo adherents are like."

Scope pauses here.

He gives us time to think about all this. Enough time for me to do more catching up. New inquirers. Oh, yes, my God. Like new customers at Tirza, like me and Rob, alias Rebecca and Sheridan. The rich prospective parents. I start imagining the communiqué that waits for us buried in my e-mail somewhere, very diplomatic and low-impact and sent over the Internet on a beautiful replicated letterhead. "Be our guests in the sweet little hamlet of Stanton's Mill, where one of our babies comes from."

That's pretty much what they would have said, and is that what Rob's phone call was about?

Where is Rob now? Stanton's Mill is replete with places to hide a prisoner. Or a body.

Stop that, Carla. Rob is resourceful.

Scope is intoning again. "But our meeting isn't just for some visitors to the wonderful indigo experience. It's for us, especially for us, the parents of indigo. The ones who've felt it all. Anneliese, the seeress of our understanding, can't be with us today . . ."

No, I think, I bet she can't; I flash on Anneliese exiting backward through Susie's French window, clutching her gun.

"But I am here," Scope continues. "And of course you know me. Yes, I'm the guru. Or the wise one. I've appeared before you, on this very platform. Maybe a little exaggerated, that appearance, a little stage-managed, and most of you didn't know who I was in daily life. A deception, maybe. But how good for our feelings. And feelings are the key, aren't they?"

So Scope is the guru. That is Scope in the pictures. I almost recognized him, even earlier. Stand Scope up in a long white robe, put a lot of makeup on his face, big dark haunted circles around his eyes . . . Except that Scope, the one I knew, was presenting his Stupid Andy personality and I wasn't willing to stretch my imagination enough.

An imposing guru, he might be capable of almost anything. Has he just, for instance, recently doped Anneliese to send her out into the underbrush unhinged? She's always seemed somewhat strange. But not nuts.

Scope has changed the subject. He's saying that he's going to show us some pictures. "You're the relatives of our beautiful babies. You fine relatives have sent your babies off, but just for the time being. After a while they're going to come back to you. You know that; it's been pledged. Meanwhile your babies are having magnificent lives with folk who understand how much the word *indigo* means. It means special. Extra special. These are people who were willing to do incredible things to have your beautiful babies, even for a little while. They are showering them with love and attention and every advantage. Your children get the very best, because they are the best."

I drift off for a moment of wondering what the financial split is between Tirza and these parents. Who gets how much money?

Most of the former hippies in Stanton's Mill came here because they were poor and the community was cheap. After a while they got tired of being poor. Anybody gets tired of that. How much money would be enough to tempt you to give up your baby?

The Tirza organizers are getting a million per baby, more or less. But twenty-five thousand, a minor percentage of that million, would seem like a lot to most folk in Stanton's Mill.

Scope has darkened the room and is making motions with a handheld machine. A whitened screen has appeared.

Darkening the room makes me sit up straight. I finger my gun.

I've been around Stanton's Mill and on this case for a month, and still nobody tells me anything.

"So, Molly, my dear," says Scope. And he presents some views of a fat blond baby in the arms of a skinny blond lady, emphatically not Molly Littlefeather, probably not a daughter; this new, thin, fashionable lady wears spike-heeled boots, skinny pants, a psychedelically printed top. We see the baby being cuddled by a washed-out blond gentleman. There are quietly ostentatious settings: a yacht, then the paneled stateroom of the yacht, then the backside of the baby, photographed from floor level, and crawling purposefully along the teak of an expansive modern house. Scope doesn't say, "You see, Molly, you could never have imagined giving your poor little scrap any of this; she was going to have to sleep in the pottery room." But he implies it. And Molly, sitting in front of me, reacts. Her shoulders shake convulsively. "What a wonderful ambience for this beautiful, exceptional child," Scope enthuses.

Other babies are presented. Tirza doesn't favor blondes only; Heather's little sprout has dark eyes and abundant dark curls and is apparently in some Neverland on the Emerald Coast, whatever that is. The Emerald Coast has white sand and green water and aggressive modern architecture. Scope doesn't specify a global position.

Scope's patter is compelling. He flashes a sequence of pictures, of radiant children surrounded by purple auras, then portraits of Leonardo da Vinci, Jesus, and . . . Yes. I am amazed, and briefly amused. And after that upset. There is a slide of Marilyn Monroe. It reminds me to be frightened.

For some reason the photo of Marilyn, lying back, her mouth open orgiastically, so innocent and so suicidal, scares me plenty.

I want to call out, "Take that down, you sadist."

Scope has saved the best for the last. "Now, a lot of people are wondering about this particular beautiful baby. Penelope, the child of the community's own dear daughter Tamina, who fell so tragically, but left behind her the lovely indigo baby, her legacy to the world . . ."

And he flashes a view that has a blue or purple overlay but may be that of a stately English house complete with lawn, long entry drive, multiple windows, turrets. "Here is where Tamina's lovely little Penelope is living now," Scope says. "In this estate on Easthampton, the home of a brilliant entrepreneur, at the top of the Fortune 500, where Penelope will get everything she deserves, all the beauty and luxury that her mother never imagined when she teetered uncertainly on the edge of our own meeting place, holding out a hand for someone to keep her from jumping—because she knew, dear indigo friends, that life is hard, and it was hard for a mere wisp—a fifteen-year-old who had a baby. And so she went over, not knowing that all was available to her indigo child, if only the indigo were recognized.

"And it will be recognized, dear friends. We know that. It's planned; it's in the cards. The qualities of every single indigo baby have eventually been recognized, if only the world waits long enough. Think of Jesus. And Moses and

Galileo and Dante and that poor man who didn't recognize his own true value, Vincent van Gogh. And how the world salutes him now. Dear indigo parents, the world will salute you that way, too."

It takes Scope five more minutes to wind up his spiel and suggest that everybody repair to Molly Littlefeather's to celebrate.

"And I will wait here for a while with Carla. Because Carla has very generously come to our meeting and now I want to talk to her.

"And Carla, I am watching your father; I'm really interested in him. And Carla, I have a friend of yours here. I'm sure you're curious about him. So, Carla . . .

"I know that you'll want to stay here and talk to me.

"I can't imagine that you wouldn't want to stay."

I remain glued to my chair while the rest of the indigo crowd files out.

They don't seem excited and verbose the way they might after an uplifting meeting. They seem awfully thoughtful.

Sunshine gives me a straightforward stare as she leaves. I hope that stare means, *I understand the kind of fix you might be in. I'll call Cherie.*

Maybe it just means, *Hey, interesting meeting, what?*

Scope allows time for the door at the end of the room to slam shut. And then he says, "Okay, Carla, on your feet. I want to talk to you."

✝ Chapter 24

"Oh, you son of a bitch, you evil son of a bitch."

That isn't me talking. The voice at first appears to come from the wall of the purple room. Then it comes from under one of the wall draperies. And then the drapery parts to reveal a figure, and the figure is that of Anneliese.

She enters from the side. Apparently there is one of those floor-to-ceiling windows in this house, too, behind some of the purple hangings. She comes into the room fast, and since it is still dark, she's hard to see, but as far as I can tell, she looks like Medusa, the one that if you really stared at her, you would turn to stone. Her face is awry, her hair is in her eyes, her black shift half off her shoulder. It's cold to be out there dressed like that. And of course, she has her gun.

She gestures with it. She seems to want to include me and my dad in her gesture, but finally concentrates on Scope. "I'm going to kill you, you bastard. Get ready. Take a deep breath. Listen, bastard, I just loused up whatever big plans you've got. I did it just now; I did it real good. Whatever way you've got planned to take over my work and my ideas and wreck them and wreck all the rest of my whole life the way you've been doing and tell the insurance people to come kill me, I've loused it up. You did that, you and that bastard son of a bitch with the chopped-up face that you brought in to do the dirty work for you. But I've stopped you.

"I don't know what you got planned now, but you won't get to do it. I fixed it up for you, chum. Scope, I opened that door. You should learn never, not ever, to tell Anneliese not to do something. *Under no condition*, was what you said. *Under no condition*, well, big deal and fancy language, under no condition, Anneliese, are you to open that door; well, bastard you don't tell Anneliese not to. I am indigo, did you know; I guess you never believed in that, did you?

"Anyway, I opened your goddamn door and the guy didn't look too great but I let him out and what do you think about that? And he was off and I got this indigo instinct that that's gonna be bad news for you and your scarface friend, but the real bad news is right now."

I am trying to think what Anneliese is saying. Is she saying that Rob was here and she let him free, is that what she means with the stuff about a door and she let someone out; I find myself hoping that . . . oh, God, Rob, she said something else awful and . . . I will not think about that now; there was an evil statement that I'll come back to later: she said somebody didn't look too good but she let him out. That's Rob, I think. I'm on my way; I'm coming; I'll do something. Don't be too badly beat up.

Anneliese waves her gun. "Say whatever prayers or evil spells you got in your evil craw. Do it fast, because here it comes."

I've been prepared for her to engage in a lot more long discussion. The stuff so far has been revelatory. Disconcerting. I want to know about Rob. Where he is.

Instead she acts decisively. The only thing wrong with her decisive action is that it doesn't work. Scope is unaffected. She shoots and it makes a lot of noise and he stands massively beside his table, staring at Anneliese. Then he pulls out a gun of his own and without making a speech of any kind shoots her. Effectively.

He walks over to examine; he stands above her where she is spread out like a traditional sacrificial victim. He seems interested, but not overwhelmed. He looks like somebody who is admiring his artistry.

After that he turns around and levels the gun on the audience.

No. Correction. My dad and I are the audience; the gun is turned on us. "All right, Carla. You're on." He looks at me briefly. "I've got your father in my sights, Carla. Come along."

It's up to me now. This feels like Showdown at the O.K. Corral. He plans to take us somewhere and I don't plan to go; I have only a few seconds; I reach back and wrestle my gun from the back of my belt and aim. I remember all the right things: arm at the side, steady the gun with your opposite hand, aim carefully, sight with precision.

And I must have done all of that okay, because Scope is knocked backward. He has to hold on to the table in front of him; he clutches at his shoulder. A red stain starts to show under his clutching hand. He says something, one of those exclamations indicated by dashes and elisions—"Oh . . . oh, God . . ."

I sight again. I think that this is not a very good gun that Cherie gave me. There are guns that you simply point and squeeze and the piece keeps right on shooting until all your bullets are gone. I go through my whole aiming procedure once more, thinking with some empty part of my brain that I haven't ever shot at a living creature before. Only a target. I get all the motions started.

But I don't get a chance to shoot. Something happens on the other side of the room. A noise, a kind of scuffle, the sound of feet. My arm jumps and the gun is knocked out of my hand. I look down at a limp, white, empty hand hanging on the end of my shaking arm like an empty rubber glove. I'm probably hurt. I can't tell. Right now I can't move my fingers; the gun has fallen onto a chair and then onto the floor and lies vibrating at my feet.

At the same time the ceiling lights come on full, slinging all the purple and silver and tat into color, and a voice to my left, where the noise has been, says, "So, Carla, yes that gun is a relic of the past now, a disabled gun, quit staring at your hands, put them down by your side. Nice to see you again, Carla." And someone that I think I don't know walks up the aisle.

When he reaches the front and turns around, I see the scar on his face.

"Carla, do you recognize me?"

Scope is bent over the table making noises. I watch him. Part of me thinks, yes, I did that. My arm hurts. Maybe this guy broke my wrist. I'm not going to answer.

This man who is standing in the front of the room as if he's framing himself is tall, well dressed in a respectable business suit. In costume to be the Second Man. And he has the scar, from the bottom of his right eye to the left side of his mouth. Of course I don't recognize him. Why should I?

"Think," this person says. "I'm interested. You were just a child, but you ought to have residual memory . . . Scope, for God's sake, cut it out." Scope is making gargling sounds, as if he's going to throw up.

"You make a mess," the person says to Scope. "As usual. One that needs cleaning up. Every time you do something, it's the same. A mess that means I have to come and try . . . God," he says with a slight change of tone, "I hate messes. In the navy we knew what to do with messes. We took action, we took it right away, didn't let things accumulate . . .

"Shut up, Scope.

"And here, in this deal, I didn't let the mess accumulate. But, buddy"—here the man pokes Scope, who makes another strangled noise—"you got me into a couple of fixes where the neat answer wouldn't work. Like letting that little teenage bitch find out too much and you didn't know what she'd found out and you didn't understand that even if she was just fifteen, she was out to reform the world and tell everybody everything she knew. She thought that would help her kid; she thought it was holy, she said a lot of sickening pious cant about her duty to herself and to her child.

"So pushing her off that cliff was my idea but I had to come up with it fast, at the last minute; fifteen minutes further along and she would have broadcast to the whole world. Your fault, Scope, you let her find out and then you didn't stop her. After that, we had her feeble little boyfriend and I had to slit his throat. The Commandos teach you that very thoroughly; you really know how to do it and make a decent job of it.

"A quick solution.

"Almost a neat one, if you can choose the place to perform.

"Scope, will you shut up? Maybe she broke your collarbone. Bite down. Chew on your tongue. Give yourself something else to . . .

"Oh, for God's sake, *shut up.*

"Well, back to basics here.

"Carla, I kept hearing about you and now I get to meet you. Again. But I think you should remember me from before. What a shame. True, you were just a little kid, but still . . . And our association now won't last very long. I learned that lesson back in the Commandos. Action. Now. Don't let it pile up. I'm talking too much to you, but I'm interested."

He stops; he seems to be watching my father. "*He* knows who I am. Don't you, Ed?"

My dad doesn't answer.

"So what good will it do you?" the man asks my dad.

"It'll do some good," Daddy answers.

"Ed, absolutely none. You can do nothing about it. You've addled your wits. Lost your marbles. It doesn't make any difference what you know. You can't tell anyone."

"News gets around," my father says mildly. "That's the most amazing thing, Squeegee." He smiles his sweet smile. "You're Squeegee. I knew; I recognized you; I saw you on the Rock and wondered if I should tell, but it would have hurt dear Susie so much . . . probably a lot of people know. As it says in the *Book of the Dead*, *The children of the impotent revolt shall never rise up again. The children of the impotent revolt*—

My dad doesn't get to finish his quotation. There's an

interruption, but I'm not sure whether it's of noise, or light, or pressure.

Actually what I remember is kind of pressure. As if the sides of the room are forced out. Over a heavy wind noise and a voice yelling, "Carla! Ed! Lie down on the floor!"

And in a sudden burst of pain and breathlessness, we're surrounded by a brilliant white and blue light that comes and goes and seems to revolve. And after that, compression and pressure in my ears and against my throat. I reach out to grab my dad and both of us go down. I feel his bony little frame next to mine. I think, well, at least I've got him. I think we are sliding between two chairs. I hurt, my wrist is numb, my chest full of fire; something terrible happened back there. I have gone deaf. And almost blind.

Maybe my father's voice intrudes into the echoing: "I spoke to Beau."

Now why would he say that?

I go down into a dark space.

⌐ Chapter 25

"Fireworks?" I say. "You mean all that was from fireworks? I'm burned, I've gone deaf, my poor dad is totally traumatized; you mean Rob did that, why in hell did he——"

"You aren't hurt and you've got one minor burn on one hand and your father is downstairs eating ice cream," Dr. Tallulah says. "You're just slightly shaken up and plenty upset. That was resourceful of Rob. And Beau."

I think, *Rob and Beau*. So Rob went to Beau. Rob went to Beau and told his story and called Cherie and . . . my head is still ringing; I'm having trouble making a meaningful story of all this.

Then I think: fireworks. Beau had a stack of them in the store. Oh. Yes, okay. I sort of get the picture: the two of them sneaking in the dark to the indigo hangout with their bundle of fireworks and some matches and finding that floor-to-ceiling window in the back and lighting the fireworks and . . . "It's ridiculous," I tell Tallulah. "Childish. A ten-year-old boy's stunt. For God's sake. Fireworks."

I picture the two men, clustered by that back window with their bundle of blow-up stuff and their matches. I can almost hear them giggling. But then I remember that Rob had been . . . oh, hell. *The guy didn't look too great,* Anneliese said, or something like that.

"I guess it was creative," I admit reluctantly.

Tallulah tells me severely that it saved my life. That was a serious man, that Squires, he knew what he wanted and didn't delay about getting it; what he wanted was every-body else dead and him safely outta there. "He was trained to kill people," she says.

I have to think to remember that *that man Squires* is Squeegee. Yes, I guess he was serious.

"And Cherie had two deputies and some guns," Tallulah continues, "but she was twenty miles away."

Tallulah is about to give me a *cut it out and quit complaining and think about how lucky you are* lecture, but she's stopped by the arrival of Rob, who is not, like me, a patient. He wears his white coat and is a doctor.

He gives me a kiss and says, "Boy, what an ordeal."

He won't talk about himself, except to say, "Well, sure I recognized him. He was my stepfather, remember?

"I was just a little kid, but I always thought he was weird.

"He didn't recognize me, but I recognized him. And I wanted to entrap him. I had all kinds of plans. That was my mistake."

He waits for a minute and says, "Carla, that fireworks thing could have been a big tragedy. A stunt. Lately I've had trouble with that, trying to be more daring.

"I got carried away. Maybe showing off, for myself and for Beau. The minute we chucked them through the window, I thought, Jesus, what in hell have I done?"

"Rob," I tell him. "It worked. It was okay; it really worked. Cherie came in and nailed everybody and there was really nothing more to do. Come on, sit on the edge of this bed."

But Tallulah objects that I'm not going to spend the night here. There is nothing the matter with me and they need the bed for other patients who are really sick.

Rob and I are allowed to kiss for a minute and then I have to get up and get dressed.

It is two weeks later and we are going on a picnic.

"How fine it is to be back here again," my father says. "I think I missed those cushions." He is referring to the Near Eastern pillows with bits of mirror sewed on them that Susie puts on Daddy's bed.

He and I are staying, once again, in Susie's cottage.

Susie is worried about the cottage. "I don't know whether I'll get to have it anymore," she says. "Possibly dear Squeegee will want it back. Now that he is not dead."

I point out that dear Squeegee will be in San Quentin and probably on Death Row; he'll be away for a long time. "And Susie," I instruct, "you must stop calling him dear Squeegee. He is an evil man. You know that as well as I do. A professional murderer. He murdered Tamina and Arby and he planned to do away with me."

Susie sighs. "That wasn't the real Squeegee. The real one was back in the past with me.

"He was such a handsome man. And in his will he thought of me."

You mean he used you as a way to disappear, I think, but don't say. I still am not used to a Susie whose conventional side can fall in love with a hunk of heavy-duty destructive macho. "He belonged to the Green Berets," I tell her severely. "Both the army ones and the commercial ones.

"He was a trained murderer. He was really good at slitting throats.

"And," I add, "don't ask Rob what Squeegee did to him. When he had Rob in that underground cupboard."

Susie cannot bear to listen to this and has to walk out of the house onto the front porch. When she comes back in, she says, "That is all over with now. I am so grateful. That it is over. It reflects badly on human beings. I prefer to believe that people are intrinsically good. In fact, I know that they are.

"Now," she adds, "I am going to start packing our lunch."

Susie will be making sandwiches for our picnic at the Rock. The purpose of the picnic is to celebrate what Happy Dawn calls a Commitment Ceremony and Beau calls a Nonsense between the two of them. But Beau agrees that, yes, they need to commemorate the fact that they have more or less been together for eighteen years, that they had a daughter together and now have a granddaughter.

It isn't the best day, weatherwise, for a Commitment Ceremony, since it rained last night and looks as if it will try again today. "Oh, that is just our usual fresh weather," Susie says. "I am doing egg salad and olive-pimento and ham-and-cheese, and now, what else can I make?"

My father suggests pine nut couscous with lamb and Susie says, "Oh, dear Edward, how inspiring. This will take a little time, but I'm sure I can do it."

I survey my dad. He looks fine. Apparently he has no bad aftereffects from our encounter with Squeegee and our fireworks liberation. He is dim about exactly what happened there and refers to it as a bombing, which I guess is pretty much correct.

He is better. After two weeks I also am better; Rob is perfectly okay. Squeegee apparently knew some complicated forms of water torture, which don't leave traces. When I ask Rob about psychological effects, he shrugs his shoulders.

Anneliese and Scope are in the hospital at Innocente Prison. Both of them are reported to be pretty sick, but Anneliese more so.

I still have trouble understanding the fact that I aimed at and shot Scope. But of course I meant to. And I would feel even more peculiar if, in such a crisis, I had aimed at him and missed.

Rob has spent the night at the hospital. He arrives now and asks how my night was and I ask about his. We are still being tender with each other, the way you are after a crisis. He kisses me and I kiss back; we are tentative; that also goes with our special kind of self-awareness.

He and I, Susie and my dad, walk over to the Rock carrying three picnic baskets. I have had to stop Susie from embarking on matzo ball soup and tiramisu and other complicated dishes. "But this is a celebration," she protests. "Of course, everyone knew about dear Beau and dear Happy, but still it is special. There should be *unusual* . . ."

The Rock seems to have blossomed blue overnight. I suspect Sunshine of doing some decorating; the surface is strewn with garlands of juniper and electric blue morning glory. Happy Dawn wears a long blue semitransparent garment and a blue ostrich plume.

I sit down with Beau on one side and Rob on the other. Beau and Rob are still inclined to remember their Boys' Night Out by poking each other in the ribs and saying things about matches. Today Beau seems to be celebrating with a bright blue shirt. I say, "Quit showing off."

"You're worried about me, Snoop Lady. Or at least wondering seriously. I can see . . . You project all those questions, *Beau, have you thought this through? Do you know what you're doing?* So, okay, Inquiring One, quit worrying; it'll be okay. This thing with me and Happy. I've thought about it and decided."

I say, "Yes, but . . ." What I mean is, *Yes, BUT she is very simple and you are very complicated.* I look at Happy Dawn. She is pretty and she's now drug free. She had a remarkable daughter; she was okay on raising her. And Beau is, for the first time, publicly claiming Tamina as his.

"You used to know Anneliese, didn't you?" I ask.

"I used to know a whole lot of people."

"Was she different then?"

"Who can say? She was quick, which I guess she still is. And smart, which she maybe isn't anymore. And neurotic and ambitious and younger. And devious, but not yet criminal. If you're asking did she come here because of me, yes, I guess she did. But I didn't ask her. I hadn't kept in touch with her; I didn't like her. She tracked me down, maybe mainly from boredom. Do you think boredom is the eighth deadly sin, Carla?"

"What's going to happen to that grandchild of yours?"

Beau holds up his hand to make me shut up. A lot of people have assembled with baskets and bags and plastic containers; the air is redolent with the pleasant smells of egg salad and dill pickle, and Happy is standing. Thank God she doesn't stand near the edge. She chooses the left side of the Rock, where it digs into the hill. The wind blows her chiffon dress and she fights with her tossing ostrich feather for a minute. Then she takes it off. She tips her head back.

Clearly she's about to make a speech.

"She is very beautiful," my father's clear voice cuts across the silence. "Like that statue of Hathor. The one in Thebes. An inhabitant of the deep skies, the hieroglyph indicates. Of the deep blue skies. Very suitable."

"Hey, all I want to say," Happy starts out. She has to yell, but she makes herself heard, which I wouldn't have expected. "Beau would be a lot better at this than I am, so all I want to say is . . . Well. Today, we think about Tammy, who tried to do something brave right here in this place. And Beau and me . . . Beau and I, that is . . ."

She glances sideways at Beau to see if he approves of the grammatical correction. Beau is okay about this. He doesn't react like a schoolteacher; he doesn't smile approvingly or do any of that *you are a good little girl* stuff.

"Because of Tammy, he and I are getting together. And taking the kid back with us. Because maybe Penelope's in a real rich place right now; I mean those people have lots and lots of money and we're poor. But we're her real relatives and what kind of parents would those people be if they're willing to buy a baby illegally?"

I think, hey, that applies to Heather's baby and Molly's grandchild, too. I wonder what those mamas are going to do.

Cherie is a lawyer. Probably she'd be happy to help them get their babies back.

Happy doesn't go on to say, *And we're both still almost young, nearly the age of parents instead of grandparents and we're going to give this baby a lot of love.* Maybe I'm imagining it, but I think I read that in her attitude and in Beau's.

Beau really loved Tamina a lot.

I look at the other people who have assembled, Sunshine especially. I hope she's going to be okay. Growing up in Stanton's Mill doesn't prepare you for a whole lot out in the world. Molly L/K is also here and I look at her and think that I didn't understand her and still don't. She's camped next to Sunshine and I don't like that; I want Sun to have better friends than Molly. Maybe Sun can be friends with the new deputy with the glasses.

Here I swat myself over the hand—just mentally, but hard—and resolve to stay out of it.

Beau has moved to stand beside Happy, and my father sits down beside me; Rob is on the other side. Daddy takes my hand. He intertwines our fingers. "This is a pleasant place for her spirit to come back to. There is a fresh atmosphere and the sound of busy people and a view. I do not think the spirit will mind that the end was so sudden."

He squeezes my fingers. "My memory is not very good, daughter; have you noticed it? You might not have, because I am able to obfuscate. That's the word, am I right? But sometimes, like now, everything is clear and I remember, just the way I'm remembering that little Ta-Ent.

"She was very inquiring, which is always a joy. She ended too fast, but one still remembers her."

I turn to look at him. This is the first time he has spoken so specifically about Tamina's end.

Rob says quietly, "It's good to think that, Ed."

At first I agree 100 percent, and get the warm feeling that comes with someone saying it exactly right.

After that I get a surge of pain.

I grab Rob's hand.

Yes, it helps to think that Tamina lives on in the consciousness of the people who knew her. It helps sometimes.

The rest of the time you want to fight the fact that she went down so early with so much to do.

"Hathor is in the bright tall sky," my father says.

Rob squeezes my hand hard, and that works for a minute.